THE
HABITANT

P. L. WEAVER

Keith,
Librarians forever!
P. L. Weaver

PWM
publishing

PWM Publishing
1333 Red Cedar
Ardmore, OK 73401
First Paperback edition: November 2015

P. L. Weaver, 1952-
The Habitant: a novel/ by P. L. Weaver – 1st ed.
p. cm.
1. Ghosts – Fiction. 2. Universities –Fiction 3. Oklahoma –
Fiction. 4. Electromagnetism—Fiction 5. Angels -- Fiction

For Kenny,
my personal shaman.

Contents

Chapter 1 7

Chapter 2 23

Chapter 3 34

Chapter 4 49

Chapter 5 69

Chapter 6 90

Chapter 7 99

Chapter 8 115

Chapter 9 132

Chapter 10 144

Chapter 11 164

Chapter 12 192

Chapter 13 209

Chapter 14 234

Copyright Permissions 240

Acknowledgements 242

About the Author..................................243

Chapter 1

"I am standing upon the seashore. A ship at my side spreads her white sails to the morning breeze and starts for the blue ocean. She is an object of beauty and strength. I stand and watch her until at length she hangs like a speck of white cloud just where the sea and sky come to mingle with each other. Then, someone at my side says; "There, she is gone!"

"Gone where?" Gone from my sight. That is all. She is just as large in mast and hull and spar as she was when she left my side and she is just as able to bear her load of living freight to her destined port. Her diminished size is in me, not in her. And just at the moment when someone at my side says, "There, she is gone!" There are other eyes watching her coming, and other voices ready to take up the glad shout; "Here she comes!" And that is dying."

--Luther F. Beecher, *What is Dying?*

Bernadette got up as the lanky young woman entered the library door. She was stiff, really stiff, from sitting so long and needed to get in out of the cold. She followed the young woman, her curiosity piqued by the intensity she had sensed in the young woman when she looked upward, sighed and pushed open the door. Bernie hurried in just before the door closed. She had a thing about conserving energy and always tried to squeeze in doors just before they swung shut. It was a game, and Bernie almost always made it without having to even lean in. It was her contribution to the energy crisis. She conserved hers and used everybody else's. Getting rides from others was another of her contributions to global climate change. Weren't there signs in the student union about ride sharing? Bernie was just doing her part to limit her carbon footprint.

Although Bernie had intended to follow her door opener, she suffered from a very short attention span and her nose led her another direction. As the warm air from the building enveloped her, she could feel her stiffness abate, and the smell of coffee drew her to the right corridor as the young woman walked on. The right corridor held the library school offices, which were thinly populated this time of the day, and Bernie had regularly helped herself to a cup from the unattended coffee pot, usually when the school's secretary slipped back into the bathroom that was tucked inside the turret next to the conference room. She pretended to read the bulletin board in the hallway while waiting for the secretary to leave.

This time the secretary came out the door with her purse and coat. It looked like a good opening, and Bernie sidled in as she glanced over both shoulders. Hoorah, there were cookies too! She was inordinately fond of sugar cookies with icing and sprinkles, the more colorful the icing, the better. Holiday cookies, Halloween more specifically, were her favorites, but St. Patrick's Day was dutifully appreciated because if you can't have orange, then green will do. These cookies were heart-shaped, so she would have to settle for red frosting, but the sprinkles had been generously applied so they would do.

Bernie inhaled deeply, savoring the steam from the coffee pot as she furtively glanced over both shoulders. She imagined the sugar crystals catching in the corners of her mouth and unconsciously licked her lips. She had felt a bit puckish earlier, but the warmth and smells of the office always cheered her up. She was a regular at this coffee pot, but she was pretty sure no one had figured that out.

More than once, Bernie had used the turret bathroom as a hiding place, locking the door and counting on the politeness of strangers to seek out another lavatory when they tried the door of this single-holer. She was patient and loved the little room with the old-fashioned tile floors, little six-sided tiles and dated paper towel dispensers. She could sit on the toilet and look out the narrow window at the gothic-styled walls of the old building for hours, feeling cozy. It was one of her homes away from home. She'd spent many nights cozily tucked away there, out of sight of the security guards on their closing rounds. She'd spent zillions of hours reading there and in other nooks and crannies that let her go undetected. She'd been on campus for a long time, and as she had aged, she thought she was now mistaken as a local professor, rather than a student. Ha! The more people see you somewhere, the more they assume that's where you belong.

Today she left still licking her lips and made her way up the staircase, as she made up her mind to make the library her home, *not* away from home, for the next few weeks. She had a sense of ownership about the library. Her easy familiarity with the building and years of sleepovers, as she affectionately called her overnight stays in the building, made the decision an easy one. After all, she would be contributing to the living-small movement, she had read about. Why pay rent or utilities when the building was virtually empty most all night long and the security guards easily eluded? Bernadette often pleased herself with her cunning rationale.

Years of living on campus, sidestepping custodians and campus police, had almost made her adventures seem stale. She knew where the refrigerators were and which was likely to contain a forgotten lunch or leftover pizza from a staff birthday party. She slipped easily in and out of locker rooms with shower facilities. She sometimes marveled at how people rarely noticed her, and those who bothered to take a second look generally dismissed her like she was wallpaper! She couldn't help but laugh to herself as she passed several students on the staircase, absorbed by their cell phones. Cell phones were such a boon to her campus lifestyle. Once they had become popular, fewer people looked up to watch where they were going, much less look at her.

She was getting sleepy, what with the warm building and all the carbs. She headed for the decks as she recalled the old elevator, when she reached the landing. That was the place for a good nap. Napping was one of her favorite things to do in all the buildings on campus, but the library was the best of all of them. It was always quiet and peaceful. She never used the comfortable sofas, although many college students could be found napping on them, especially during finals week. It was her policy to be a bit more reclusive. And it was a good policy. She had lived on campus for many years going unnoticed, and it wouldn't do to become recognized in the library as a regular napper with a favorite sofa. That could make people curious. No, she rather preferred an out of the way study room or some secret corner that afforded more privacy. She'd spent years watching the guards on their rounds and identifying nooks and crannies that could be used to her advantage. She'd begun her lifestyle before the video cameras and motion detectors were installed, and she had very carefully mapped them all in her mind after she witnessed some students on a prank, detected by the system and rounded up by the campus police about 3 a.m.

That occasion had made her a little sensitive, and she had avoided the library for some time. But eventually her constant "wallpaper" presence had given her a special present. Ignored as she wandered the book stacks, Bernie had one day witnessed an elderly faculty member leave his faculty study and hide the key to the study in a Latin text by Euripides on the shelf. Classics were waning in the curriculum, so it was a book that would have grown dusty without its key cache. Not likely that the key would be found by accident, an assumption on which the professor relied. It was Bernie's go-to bedroom, with an old sofa that had been pulled into the study in the 1980s when furniture was being replaced. There was even a throw on the sofa that Bernie used to avoid detection by the custodians who irregularly checked the trash can in the study about 3 a.m. Bernie simply slept on the floor under the couch, using the throw as a drape to hide her presence. She entered the study after the last round of the security guards before the motion detectors were engaged and stayed until the library opened the next morning. Cozy, yup.

She never went to the study during library hours. Today her strategy was to use another space only she knew about. The old elevator presented her a space rarely seen by anyone other than physical plant workers, those individuals servicing the massive air conditioning units and elevator motors that were housed in the attic. Yes, few people knew the library had an attic, but Bernie knew. It wasn't easy to get to, because it was securely locked and restricted to authorized personnel. Bernie just bypassed all the doors and entered through the service hatch of the old east elevator in the decks. It was so clever, she always felt a thrill when she stepped on the elevator and the door closed. She had a tool she had devised to unscrew and lift the service hatch, giggling when she imagined the elevator opening at the next floor – empty. She was still there, just a few feet displaced. Bernie rode the elevator all day, asleep on the roof. At the top of the elevator shaft, the large wheels pulling the steel cables left plenty of clearance when the elevator arrived at the top deck. The whir of the wheels always made her feel part of the building machinery, as the small vibration relaxed her like a massage pillow.

   The text Sarah got from her mother made her anxious. She was in the middle of Physics class and saw her phone light up. She had silenced it before class, because Professor Simmons, an enthusiastic lecturer who sometimes donned fuzzy wigs to make a point, required some attention and demanded courtesy. She held it low and silently typed, "In class, call u soon." But she found it hard to listen to the lecture in the meantime, even though Professor Simmons was pretty animated. Her mother's text had been cryptically urgent. "Call plz need u." It reminded her of when her father died.
   Sarah's dad had died of lymphoma. At first he responded to chemo, but later his slow decline had caused her mother to activate her career when Sarah was just eleven. He'd died when she was seventeen. The call then had been lifeless, used up. Tired.
   As she tried to concentrate, she appreciated the distraction provided by the effort Professor Simmons put into his lectures. It was enough to make her show up, rather than just watching the videos he was willing to share. He wanted his students to learn, so didn't dole out his lectures to only the early risers. His ego was willing to suffer a half-empty classroom, just as long as the students got it. Interestingly, the more alternatives Simmons provided, the more students seemed to want to be there. Simmons took questions, always responded like a man in love with his job and, frankly, his lectures were fun. Going to the

lectures was like attending a concert compared to watching a video. It was worth getting up at 9 a.m. on a Friday morning – at least most of the time.

Sarah hurried out of class and hit the button to dial her mother as soon as she cleared the doorway. Heading down the stairs at the back of the Physics Building, she stopped in the stairwell. "Mom. What's up?" she said hesitantly, trying to keep the worry out of her voice.

"I was laid off this morning. Chesapeake is downsizing," her voice broke, and Sarah knew she was sobbing silently. Sarah was stunned but found her voice quickly.

"I'm sorry, mom. But you are really good at what you do and I know that you will be able to get another job soon. How many people were let go?" Sarah tried to divert her mother and give herself some time to think of more upbeat and constructive replies. She wanted to convey positive thoughts. Some of the most treasured moments with her mother were moments in which she felt she had made a difference as a cheerleader for her mom, particularly after her dad died. It had been hard, really hard, and her mother often fell into a depression and spent some nights drinking margaritas with friends or sometimes by herself. It had been two years, and those times when her mother seemed to fall back into a sad place were less frequent, but they still happened. When Sarah felt sad, she frequently thought of her dad, who was good at jokes and always seemed to divert her attention and get her laughing. She wished she could think of something like that to help her mother, but all she could muster was a question, as her mind started to think that this could be the end of her college career ….

"They laid off over 600 people," she replied. "Everyone in our division was laid off; that division doesn't exist anymore."

"Maybe this is the time to go back and finish your degree? You have always talked about wanting to do that and now you could do it and concentrate on it," Sarah stated with more optimism than she felt. She wasn't sure that her mother had enough money to pay for her own schooling plus Sarah's and her sister's.

"It's true, most of the people they laid off didn't have degrees. But I don't think I could swing that and pay for your tuition and housing and your sister's. There isn't that much left of your father's life insurance. I should be eligible for unemployment. I don't know how long we might have to live off that money before I can get reemployed ... Sarah, you may have to delay your education or ...." she trailed off.

Sarah thought quickly. "Mom, we have already paid this semester's tuition and dorm costs. What if I can get a job to help with the living expenses and save for tuition next fall? Lots of kids here have student loans, too." She didn't mention that some grad students she had overheard joked about working for drug cartels to pay off their loans when they graduated, although the thought intruded.

"Besides, it might be cool to have the three of us be college students." She said it with an upbeat lift in her voice that was a bit forced, but anything to keep her mother from getting negative.

"Well," her mother slowly exhaled, "That might work. I don't think they would have laid me off if I had finished my degree. I'd have more job security if I could get that done. I wish I had started it a few years ago, but with your dad being sick and starting to work again and everything, I just couldn't swing it. Do you really think you could get a job to help?"

"Sure! If nothing else, I could work at McDonald's like you did," Sarah smiled, feeling like things were turning around.

"Hmm, you know, when I was in school, I worked lots of fast food jobs, but the best job I ever had was working in the library. You don't get tips or anything, but they are usually good about working around your school schedule and it's on campus. Oh, why didn't I finish when I had the chance," she moaned as her thought process derailed.

But, like all single mothers, her mind started to wrestle with the finances. Sarah could almost hear the wheels grinding. "Since you don't have a car, it would be easy to get there. Why don't you get online and see how students can apply for jobs on campus? I'm going to go by Rose State College tomorrow and see exactly what it would take to get a degree here in the city. The tuition there is cheaper than at OU. I want Abby to finish as soon as she can, but maybe a few loans and part-time jobs will work."

"Great, mom! I'll get online when I get back to my room. Maybe we'll all be coeds – Abby, you and me," she said, hoping her mom's optimism would be stirred by the idea of college and a new beginning. In the meantime, Sarah could feel her forehead wrinkle in consternation. She didn't have any idea how hard it would be to get a job on campus, but she wasn't going to let that stop her. The more her mom talked about the lay off and how a degree could have made a difference, the more sure she was that she needed to stay in college, regardless. Fear spurred her past her anxiety. She exchanged texts with Abby as she walked back, quickly explaining and asking Abby to call her mom and keep her tracking on the idea.

Sarah walked to the dorms quickly. When she got to her room, she pulled up the computer screen to complete the application. In the middle of typing, her eyes filled and tears rolled down her cheeks. She missed her dad. She felt overwhelmed and scared. It was a while before she stopped crying. Her roommate was out, as usual, so she gave herself up to some sobs and tears. Funny, she thought, how grief can just grab you like a big wave, rolling you in the surf until you are gasping for air. Inhaling and sobbing once more, regrets surfaced in her mind like so much flotsam. She had said things as a hormone-ridden, resentful teenager. The counselor she saw after her dad's passing had said it was normal to "distance" yourself from someone who is dying. It was a method of self-protection. But the dark memories floated around her, and she wished things had been different. Her dad's long, slow decline had been hard. There were good times, but somehow she more often remembered the regrets. Grief plagued her the last two years in high school and did so still. It colored the scenery of her life with a wash of gray, like a watercolor painting of rain.

Later she found herself staring at the screen, then roused when her phone dinged with a text message from her mom. She texted back that she had found some jobs. The application form was simple but focused her attention, and she could feel herself calm down as she made the effort to "work the problem." It was a phrase that always calmed her – one of her dad's favorites, "work the problem, don't worry the problem." She finished up and felt better. She yearned to lose herself gaming. The real world hadn't been much fun today. But she knew it was a bad idea. She would end up exhausted in classes without her homework done. She texted Abby but didn't get an answer. A walk was what she needed. She checked her face in the mirror to make sure her eyes weren't too swollen. She grabbed her jacket and headed down the stairs, walking fast with her head down, breathing deeply. She crossed the grass and felt a whack to the back of her head. Sarah turned and said, "Ouch!"

An awkward nerd ran up to retrieve the Frisbee. The tall geek said, "Sorry, huh, hope you aren't hurt. Looks like this Frisbee wants you. Interested in tossing it around with us? I'm Adam." The young man ran on before she had a chance to respond. He turned his head slightly, raised his eyebrows quizzically and smiled encouragingly. "You don't want to disappoint Mr. Frisbee." He held up the red disc and twirled it on his finger. "This thing has a mind of its own. Sometimes I think it's channeling a Frisbee golfer from the past," he grinned.

The remark caught her attention. Her dad had been into Frisbee golf when he had been in college and spent hours with Sarah at the park, tossing a Frisbee and helping her with her technique. It was their time together, walking to the park and tossing the Frisbee. He had coached Abby in volleyball but had gotten sick enough that coaching hadn't been in the cards when she followed her sister. Frisbee in the park on "good" days had been a time she cherished.

Normally, she would say no thanks, burrow inside herself, and trudge on. But somehow the sight of the Frisbee twirling on Adam's finger reminded her of the good times in the last few years of her dad's life. That recollection helped buoy her from the dark thoughts she'd had earlier.

"Sure. I guess he knows me. But since you don't, I'm Sarah," she said, nodding at the Frisbee and putting out her hand to shake.

He grinned and handed the Frisbee over, saying, "We're just tossing it around, so aim it toward anyone. Remember, though, it's got a soul, so it may exhibit a bit of 'free will.'"

"Understood," said Sarah, pleased with the idea that the Frisbee was imbued with an attitude. She leaned over, pulled back and let it fly, aiming at the most distant player. It sailed high and floated down into the hands of another geeky guy. He didn't even have to take a step.

Adam turned to her and said, "Awesome. Guess the Frisbee knew something! This could be the beginning of a beautiful friendship." Sarah looked over at Adam – he seemed a bit corny but rather nice. He reminded her of her dad. He didn't look like him. Adam was tall and lanky, while her dad had been much shorter and balding. But that was the kind of thing her dad might say. She caught the Frisbee and aimed it toward Adam. Again it sailed cleanly, and he caught it without moving. As she felt her Frisbee talents reemerge, she began to relax and hope crept into her consciousness. Who knew, maybe Adam was channeling her dad, and her dad "arranged" the Frisbee's flight? Perhaps it was silly, but she liked the thought because it brought her dad back into her life; she hugged the feeling of being watched over. They played for about an hour and stopped when a couple of the other players said they needed to get to class.

"So, Sarah, do you live in the towers?" Adam said with a tilt of his head toward the dormitory high rise.

"Yeah, I live in Tarman Tower. Do you guys often play Frisbee here? I haven't played in a while, but this was really fun," she said.

"If you give me your number, I'll text you the next time we play," Adam replied. "Would you like to go get a cup of hot chocolate?"

"Sure. I used to play a lot with my dad, and I didn't realize how much I missed it," Sarah observed. They exchanged numbers and walked over to the cafeteria for the chocolate.

"My dad was really good at Frisbee. He even helped plan and install a Frisbee golf course at our neighborhood park," Sarah said, surprising herself. Although she frequently thought of her dad, she rarely brought him up in conversations, fearing that she would tear up.

"There's a couple of Frisbee golf courses in Norman parks. I think they've been here since hippie days," Adam replied. "My friends and I have tried out the one in Reeves Park. It's not bad. I started playing with my uncle back when I was a kid. It must have been something guys your dad and my uncle's age did before online gaming."

"Yeah, it's hard to imagine what it was like for them in college before the Internet really took off. Does your uncle still play?"

Adam looked down momentarily, swallowed and said, "My uncle died in a car accident a couple of years ago." He looked abashed, and Sarah sympathized immediately, knowing how she felt when the subject of her dad came up.

"Maybe he's *somewhere* playing Frisbee with my dad. My dad died of cancer almost two years ago," she said in an attempt to find something that might comfort. It made her feel better just saying it, because she could picture her dad standing in the sun, smiling about an accurate throw.

Adam looked curious and ruefully sympathetic, "Do you really think that's possible? That people who never knew one another when they were alive could meet and do things they enjoyed when they were alive – elsewhere? Do you believe in heaven? I'd like to, because I miss my uncle. He helped me a lot when I got into arguments with my dad. I'd bike over to his house and talk to him when I was mad. He'd always pull out the Frisbee, and we'd stand in his yard and toss it. We'd usually end up on the porch talking, and I'd always feel better after, even if we talked about movies or games or something totally unrelated. He was younger than my dad, and he was easy to talk to."

"I don't know about heaven, but sometimes I feel like my dad might be hanging around looking out for me. If that can really happen, outside my mind, then I bet your uncle's hanging around you, too," she surmised. "Or … maybe our memories generate some kind of quantum level energy field and that's what makes me feel my dad might be there …," she trailed off for the moment, hesitating because she thought she might sound a little wacko. Adam didn't seem to think so, though, because he responded,

"You know, matter behaves a lot different on the quantum level. Are you a Physics major?" Adam changed the subject quickly, blinking, and she recognized the desire to move away from memories when recollections were painful.

"Engineering. How about you?"

"I'm in Meteorology. I decided weather was pretty important after my uncle died in an ice storm. You can make a difference telling people about weather, helping them get out of the way," Adam said with some intensity. "Why Engineering?"

"I'm good with numbers, and working problems was a way to take my mind off things after my dad died. I had Physics my senior year in high school, and the only time I didn't feel bad was when I was focused on solving problems in that class, the harder the better," she said.

They both sipped their chocolate and sat quietly. Sarah had often felt isolated from others by her dad's death. Sometimes she felt like a wounded animal trying to hide in a den and lick its wounds. This was one of the few times sharing with someone besides her mom and sister felt comforting. She wondered how Adam felt. Did he prefer to lick his wounds privately? She sipped the warm chocolate and pondered a setting in which her dad and Adam's uncle were playing Frisbee. Well, if there is a heaven, she wondered what the Frisbee golf courses look like?

"I've got to get over to the Meteorology Building to work on a forecasting assignment, but I'll call you next time we play, if you want?"

"That would be nice," she said smiling. "Maybe we'll generate some quantum fields?"

Adam smiled, "If you can generate a quantum field, maybe you can control it."

Sarah went back to the dorm room with a very different mindset. She was going to go by the library tomorrow and ask someone at the front desk about a job. Maybe she could get some pointers from one of the student workers on how to stand out from the crowd of applicants. The Frisbee game had energized her, and she nursed the feeling that her dad was looking out for her, helping in some ethereal way. She wasn't going to talk to anyone about that feeling, because she figured it sounded a bit wacked out. But, still, the feeling persisted and gave her courage.

The next day, Sarah walked into the library looking at the statuary, angels, decorative faces and gargoyles adorning the Cherokee gothic towers on each side of the heavy wooden doors. Silently, she asked for their help as she stopped to note their expressions. It was a bit crazy, but somehow she thought it might help. Today she was talking to gargoyles and yesterday she was speculating on quantum energies. Was it crazy? She stood momentarily as her eyes swept upward, moving past the statue of Bizzell toward a series of faces adorning the edifice above the door and focused on the center face, which seemed the most serene. She closed her eyes, whispered, "Please," and stepped toward the door before anyone noticed her pleading with statuary. Sometimes ... oh well, she couldn't help it.

The library was old enough that it was a mazelike affair with three additions. The first was 1930s, the second addition was very 1950s, and the last addition seemed to have been built, well, sometime in the last several decades. All of the additions were connected, and, once inside, you walked across years of campus history and architectural trends as you sauntered further inward. There were faces along the top ridge of the original building, all of which were turbaned. She remembered something about Cherokee gothic being a combination of old world styling and Native American concepts. Sequoyah, the originator of Cherokee script, was the face of some of the turbaned heads or so she thought she remembered from a freshman campus tour. There were also gargoyles tucked into the corners of the turrets and, in more recent years, sculptures of noteworthy donors were tucked into crèches. It made for a character-rich building façade and added to her feeling that there was someone to "talk" to as she took a deep breath and pulled the heavy wooden door open. A small gust of wind swirled some leaves in the atrium, and Sarah felt pushed inside.

As she worked her way through the three additions to the circulation desk, which was located in the newest addition, she walked up to a petite young woman dressed in a sari at the granite-topped desk and queried about jobs in the library.

"You have to apply online. They go through all the applicants, and then they call you," she said automatically, like she'd been asked many times before.

Sarah smiled and said, "Why do you think they hired you?"

The young woman had warm brown eyes and a sympathetic manner. She appraised Sarah for a second and seemed to conclude that she was all right, because she said, "It has a lot to do with your schedule. If you are available for the shifts they need to fill, then they pull your application from the stack." She reached into a bin of recycled papers and added, "Why don't you write your name and class schedule on this piece of paper, and I'll take it to the circulation supervisor."

"Thanks!" Sarah said as she scribbled her class schedule on the paper and handed it to the young woman.

To Sarah's surprise, she said, "Wait here. Luke, the supervisor, is in the back. I'll pass this to him. You never know, he might come talk to you. He hates going through the pile of applications that we get. Maybe you can convince him to put your application on top." Sarah stood at the desk, nervously shifting her backpack to her other shoulder. She smoothed her hair and hoped she looked OK. She was dressed much like the other students she saw in the back sorting books, so she stood up straight, something her mother always harped on, as she noticed a really strong, athletic-looking, 30ish something man emerge from the back with the student who took her schedule.

"Hi, I'm Luke Fisher," he said as he held his hand out.

Sarah took his hand firmly and gave it an assertive shake. Luke said, "Nice handshake!"

It was automatic, after her dad spent an afternoon at the park with her and "taught" her how to shake hands. He always said that how you shake hands could make a big difference in your life, and the last couple of years he seemed to want to give her life pointers when they were together. "My dad was big on handshakes," she said.

Luke compared her schedule to a shift list and said, "Hmm, I see that you have Monday, Wednesday and Friday afternoons free. Most students want to sleep in and pick afternoon classes and that makes it hard to cover the afternoon shifts. Normally, we have already hired everyone we need, but I just had a student quit unexpectedly. Have you put in an application online?"

"Yes, I did that yesterday afternoon," Sarah said. She tried to think of something to say, but could only try to look cheerful. Luke seemed to appreciate that, because he asked her to go past the security gate and come in to the office area through the side door.

"I'll take a few minutes right now to talk to you about the job and then pull up your application online, if you have time?" he queried.

"Absolutely," Sarah eagerly responded as she turned toward the gate and entered the office area. She followed Luke back to his desk. He had a chair next to the desk and pointed to that. She sat down but leaned forward and tried to look serious and eager at the same time. Since she was both, it wasn't hard, and she made a better impression than she realized.

Luke turned to his computer and pulled up the human resources screen, searching for her last name, the computer screen reflecting on his dark skin and brown eyes. Her application appeared. He said, "Yes," under his breath, looking at the application. After viewing it for a minute or two, he swiveled toward her and asked her why she was applying for a job in the library.

Sarah hesitated for a moment and then decided to just tell him about her mother's lay off, and her serious need to get a job. She also mentioned that her mother had worked at the library when she was in college. Luke listened patiently. When she finished, he gave her a description of the job, what was expected of student workers, how shifts were covered. He talked for about ten minutes. As he spoke, she was surprised he would go into

21

such detail and started to think she must have a good chance at the job, because his phrasing seemed to suggest that he had made a decision. He wound down and concluded, "If I check out your references and everything is OK, when would you be able to start?"

"I could start tomorrow," Sarah replied.

"Good. I'll text you this afternoon if everything checks out," he said matter-of-factly. "Is this your correct number and can I text you?"

"Great! Thank you! Yes, that's my number and texting is fine." Sarah replied as she reached to shake his hand. She floated out of the office. As she passed the desk, she smiled at the student worker and whispered, "Thanks!"

The young woman introduced herself, "I'm Lubna, and I hope it works out for you."

"I'm Sarah, and I really appreciate the help. I think he is considering me. I really need the job," Sarah replied, as a student walked up to the desk and needed help. Lubna smiled at her and turned toward the student.

Sarah walked slowly toward the Physics Building. Her Physics discussion session met in about 30 minutes, so she decided to text her mom and Abby to say that she *might* have a job in the library. After two classes, in which she barely paid attention, Sarah checked her phone and found a message, *your first shift starts tomorrow at noon. Plz arrive at 11:30. Luke Fisher.*

Chapter 2

"Now, I realize that not infrequently books speak of books; it is as if they spoke among themselves. In light of this reflection, the library seemed all the more disturbing to me. It was then a place of long, centuries-old murmuring, an imperceptible dialogue between one parchment and another, a living thing, a receptacle of powers not to be ruled by a human mind, a treasure of secrets emanated by many minds, surviving the death of those who had produced them or had been their conveyors."

--Umberto Eco, *The Name of the Rose*

Sarah stood at the front desk feeling the awkwardness of any new worker in a new job. She had worked a couple of short shifts and felt she had the basics. But, she hadn't actually helped anyone yet without the supervisor backing her up. Sarah stood there pulling books out of the deposit and opening them, looking to replace date due slips before she put them on the cart. Sarah was still really pumped about the job. She recalled her conversation with her mother when she called to tell her mom she got the job. Her mother had "done the dance." She could hear her celebratory hooting and knew that her mother was dancing around the room like a fancy dancer at a powwow. It was their standard celebration reaction. After the hooting, her mother quieted down and eagerly told her about a conference she'd had with a counselor at the college. Sarah could hear the excitement in her mother's voice as she explained that she would try a couple of online courses and then make a decision about fully enrolling in the summer. Abby would graduate next year in nursing. She wanted to be a PA, but could work for a few years before she returned for the extra schooling or take out loans to get it done quicker. It might all work.

As Sarah was preoccupied with her thoughts and the book cart, the wily student supervisor, Michelyn, who had been orienting Sarah, calmly eased behind the decorator panel when an odd middle-aged woman approached, leaving Sarah alone to help this particular patron.

Dr. Patty Nakamura was a library veteran. She usually entered the front door dressed in full battle gear – her version of it. She carried an umbrella, wore white gloves and a layer of pale makeup, paler even than her sun-starved Eurasian complexion. The umbrella protected from the sun or rain. Although her clothing wasn't particularly unusual, except for the white gloves, her hair was tightly arranged in a bun on the top of her head. Her eyes were heavily lined, suggesting a 1960s model wearing a miniskirt with holes cut out of the midriff. Patty's hair was arranged so tightly that it seemed to stretch the skin on her face and act as a helmet. She never let a stray hair fall, except on bad days. On good days, it was an effective battle flag. If her hair could be controlled in the gusty Oklahoma wind, then maybe she could hold onto something else – like her sanity.

Today she had circled the display cases by the circulation desk. It was a favorite spot. Patty regularly pinned some unsuspecting stranger to an eccentric verbal wall. They generally stepped off the elevator; she made some observation about the display and then verbally impaled anyone polite enough to respond. The more polite, the longer she had them in her verbal web. Patty stood momentarily perplexed by the hasty departure of an elevator rider. Eventually her eyes panned the desk and her feet followed.

As she walked up to the desk, Sarah was pulling used date due slips from a couple of books, licking the glue on a new slip and pasting it in the books. She did it unconsciously, forgetting to reach for the sponge-topped water bottle.

"I'm taking a short break, be back in a minute," grinned Michelyn.

Sarah innocently looked up and said to Patty, "May I help you?" Sarah tore another date due slip from the next book.

Patty smiled. From that point on, Sarah's face transitioned from a pleasant query to a strained mask of confusion.

"Do you know what you are doing?" Patty stated.

Sarah shrugged quizzically, "I'm checking in books?"

"Spreading AIDS!" Patty stated, pressing her lips together and raising her eyebrows as her internal alarm spread. "There was a Pakistani student here yesterday, and I am sure she is a terrorist, maybe a Muslim. She was licking the books, too! I need to see a supervisor, the Dean of Libraries, someone who understands the danger."

Sarah stood by, stunned, as she was new and hadn't seen Patty in action. "Huh?" was all she could think to say. Since she had only started working the day before, she stood with her mouth open, unwilling to comment further. She needed the job and didn't want to start some kind of argument about viruses and discrimination against people who were sick. However, she could feel herself getting flustered. Silently she wondered if you could spread AIDS this way – and then dismissed that thought as crazy. Sarah knew that lots of people believed the implausible, though, because in Oklahoma there were a lot of people who claimed that the Earth was created in 7,000 years – forget the dinosaurs, forget geology.

As Sarah stood by, dumbfounded, Michelyn sat behind the decorator panel shaking with mirth. As the experienced worker, she knew Patty well, which was why she had vacated the service desk quickly, but she liked Sarah, so far, and couldn't actually leave her totally undefended when the desk supervisor was in the back office.

Patty said, "My mother knows more details. The conspiracy is spreading … it's bio-warfare. It could be Ebola!" Patty stopped, a look of suspicion crossing her irrational face. "What's your religious preference?" she countered, squinting suspiciously.

Sarah paused; like a lot of college students, Sarah's religious preference swung wildly from agnostic to Christian to Buddhist or nihilist – depending on the number of lectures she attended in her philosophy class. "That's kind of hard to answer," she said, struggling to refocus and assuming Patty was seriously inquiring. "I'm reading Nietzsche and am undergoing some real changes in my personal value system. Have you read Nietzsche?"

Patty rarely got questions, as most people were eager to end conversations with her. Unwittingly, Sarah had stopped her in her tracks. Sarah unconsciously stacked two books together as Patty eyed her suspiciously.

"That's bad," she said, staring at the two books. Then, almost robot-like, she closed her eyes and cryptically said, "Books speak to other books." Her eyebrows shot up, and she turned abruptly toward the book stacks and hurried away. The secretaries in the Dean's office would probably be seeing her on the second floor soon.

Michelyn emerged surprised from behind the panel where she had waited to rescue Sarah with a spray can of Lysol, the usual condiment used to sooth Patty's OCD. Sarah looked around at Michelyn and said, "What was that?"

"That," Michelyn giggled, "was Patty. She's one of our regulars."

"Regular isn't a word I would use," Sarah noted dryly.

Michelyn, choking on her giggles, replied, "Regular doesn't describe her personality, just her frequency."

"What's so funny?" Luke, the desk supervisor, emerged from the back office coming up behind them. The shift of workers was supposed to change in the next few minutes, and he had come up to talk to Sarah about how to complete her time sheet.

Michelyn turned and drolly stated, "Patty." Further explanation was unnecessary.

Luke simply said, "Word."

Luke, Sarah had observed after just one orientation for new employees, seemed like he was trying hard to be culturally current. He was really rooted in the institution and had lots of football memorabilia on his desk. So she wasn't surprised at his reply, just felt it was a bit unhelpful.

Still flustered, she was surprised at her own response when she stated with some emotion, "It is really unfair how AIDS victims can be treated. It sucks. It isn't even based on science."

Michelyn, who had been warming to Sarah, paused with a curious look on her face. Michelyn turned to Luke and said,

"Patty saw Sarah lick a date due slip … I think she headed upstairs to the Dean's office."

Luke responded animatedly, "That's a reason, a reason to update to new technology. These date due slips are so lame. We need a new printer. Are you good with computers?" he turned to Sarah and asked. "I would have to justify the cost of the printer cartridges, but if I had someone who could handle printer problems, then I could argue for the upgrade, even though there are about 40 cases of date due slips in the attic …."

Before Sarah could respond, Luke continued, "Patty's a wacko. The secretaries in the Dean's office can be counted on for sympathy because they see her weekly, but the Dean never sees Patty. Nobody gets past the secretaries."

"Sarah," he paused and sighed, "use the sponge bottles, it will make your life easier. You aren't the first person to be 'Pattied.'" Lubna was her target last week, and Patty was convinced Lubna was a terrorist. Lubna is about 5'2", a highly motivated pre-med student and, well, not a likely candidate for martyrdom," Luke mused.

Sarah stood still, anticipating a more in-depth explanation and rattled by Patty's abrupt, volatile appearance. She just didn't expect that. Sarah assumed, like most people, that libraries were quiet, calm places of rationality. Trying to keep the rattled, irritated sound out of her voice, she queried, "Patty … is there a procedure I should follow?"

Luke refocused from slips to the situation at hand. He turned to Sarah and noted a rapid influx of people through the front door – classes were changing. "Sarah, we have some customers who you will get to know on sight. They are unusual, to say the least, and they are like ugly wallpaper, a constant background of annoyance, in an otherwise sensible landscape," Luke said with some pride at his metaphorical description. Luke, a former football player who had played second string but lost out to knee injuries, had been taking classes for more than a decade. He was a perpetual student and many of those were literature classes. Looking at his muscled physique, you would never believe he had a literary bent.

Sarah lifted an eyebrow and replied, "You mean this is *normal?*" But she knew the answer. Anyone who had experienced one semester in a college dorm developed a new wisdom about the variety of humanity. Odd obsessions with reality television shows, Minecraft or just extreme sports mania ensured her coed dormitory was populated with a television-worthy assortment of *real* people "So I don't need to call security or anything? Patty isn't likely to explode or self-immolate?"

Michelyn chimed in, "Who knows? So far, she seems harmless. I haven't seen any armaments, and she'd have trouble holding an Uzi *and* her umbrella." After the recent movie theatre massacre, it was more troubling than funny as Sarah tried to assimilate Michelyn's comment. Just then a student came up to the front desk with some books that needed to be checked out. "I forgot my ID, can I check these books out without it?"

"Do you have a driver's license with you? I have to have some kind of photo ID," Michelyn replied as she moved toward the desk. Normalcy was returning, and Luke herded Sarah to the back office to watch her sign out as her shift ended and give her some instructions.

Sarah took another look at the two books as she placed them on the cart to follow Luke to the back office. The titles were *A Predictable Tragedy* by Compagnon and *Silent Spring* by Rachel Carson. She'd read Rachel Carson's book in high school English as her teacher had been a strident environmentalist. If these two books "spoke among themselves," then she could see how Patty might be a bit disturbed … it made her think there was more thought behind her strange comments. This was typical. Sarah usually figured things out or thought of a witty repartee about five minutes after most conversations ended.

Sarah headed downstairs after her shift to get a coffee. It could become an expensive habit, but she rationalized it by convincing herself it was a good way to start studying. She would have to economize and keep herself to just a couple a week. But, Physics took a lot of study time and a considerable quantity of caffeine. Classes were changing and the coffee shop was busy. She found an empty table and unloaded her backpack while she waited for her espresso. In the meantime, Sarah looked around the shop at various coffee enthusiasts. She thought she recognized a table of two librarians talking. For some reason, she hadn't realized that a fair number of people worked in a library this size until she started her job. There are a lot of shifts if you are open 18 hours a day.

Her first day on campus, when she walked in the South Entrance of the library, she felt herself drawn to the building with its gargoyles, angels and gothic towers. Apparently so were the pigeons, because the physical plant workers on campus had canopied the front cupola over the doors with yards of chicken wire and spikes to deter the pigeons from roosting at the entrance and pooping on innocents below. It worked most of the time, but a few ballet-inclined pigeons could still be seen perched awkwardly on the wire spikes or fluttering as they tenderly lowered themselves to the battlement. She guessed they were great-grandchildren of pigeons that had roosted in the same place in earlier decades. That was the thing about the library, you couldn't help but feel that you walked the same steps that had been walked when students were talking about the Vietnam War or, for that matter, World War II. She had stopped once when she was new to read a plaque on the wall dedicated to students who had lost their lives in that war. For some reason, she guessed it was her new sensitivity to mortality, she thought more now than she ever had of people who died before they had lived a full life.

The espresso was warm and stimulating, so she pulled out her books and started working the chapter problems. Soon a couple of hours had passed. Once she got going on Physics, it really focused her thinking. It wasn't something you could scan and memorize. You had to be able to work through the problems to pass any of the tests. She got up with a sore butt and stretched. She headed for the dorm and Adam. She had told him she would go with him to the cafeteria for dinner.

As she walked back to the dorm, she examined her feelings. She couldn't help smiling when she pictured Adam. There was something about his love of twizzlers and bad kung fu films. Since the day he whacked her with a Frisbee, they had spent an evening together in his dorm room, kung fu gaming. The crazier the kung fu, the more enthused he was – sometimes somersaulting on the bed after she'd removed his character's head with a kick. Early on, she'd made a comment about the impossible trajectory of some of the moves and quoted a Physics formula, and he had responded with unintelligible commentary in fake Mandarin while miming silly kung fu poses standing on his roommate's mattress and jumping up and down. He made her laugh even though he was a nerd. It was easy to laugh with him because he had a deep laugh that rumbled like distant thunder in a summer storm.

Adam was waiting for her at the cafeteria entrance, and she felt the warmth of her own smile as she responded to his. Adam asked her about work at the library, and she told him the story of Patty. He looked surprised but made an odd connection. "Hmm, that sounds like something I read in a novel last summer." Adam was a pretty eclectic reader, which surprised her. "The book was about a bunch of murders in a monastery. It was all tied to the monastery library. I don't remember exactly, but I think the author implied that books talk to each other in a library and share secrets. For some reason, I get that feeling at the campus library, probably because of the gargoyles and faces on the old entrance. It adds a sense of creepy antiquity. The old decks and the dark corners of the old addition kind of set a mood, too. How about stir fry?"

"Sure," said Sarah, as they walked over to the stir fry section of the cafeteria. Sarah watched the server flip the vegetables and pork she had selected and couldn't get Adam's comments out of her mind – especially since she had made that odd connection with the two books she had in her hands when Patty made her parting comments.

Honestly, Sarah's thinking process had been changing. Between her mother's layoff and finding out the problems of a lot of dorm mates, she was more introspective. She had read some books in high school that had made her think, like, *To Kill a Mockingbird*, but she had spent a lot more time gaming than reading and, quite frankly, was beginning to feel that she had been a pretty superficial person, wrapped up with her own problems and her dad's illness. For some reason, that was beginning to rattle her. Maybe …maybe she didn't like knowing that she had been that self-absorbed. She hadn't been a cheerleader or anything popular, which she had always thought of as a kind of self-absorption. But maybe she had just been getting by in the sensitivity department. As she stabbed at her stir fry, she looked up and caught Adam looking at her.

They headed out to take a long walk on the south end of campus. Once you passed married student housing, the buildings thinned out, and a park and the various sports fields gave you plenty of open space to walk. Adam had gotten her walking after dinner. He said he had to walk every day because it was something he did with his dad – a habit. Adam mused that his dad was probably trying to keep him from becoming a gaming couch potato, but he appreciated his dad for it, and Sarah thought again about her dad's efforts to get her to the park and play Frisbee.

It was a beautiful evening, really warm for late January. A light jacket was all that was needed. Oklahoma was like that. In the middle of winter, you could get several days in a row where the temperatures were almost balmy in the high 60s and kind of spring-like. Of course, you could get a bad ice storm the next week, but the warm days were great.

A full moon was rising, and they had walked almost all the way to the highway when Adam turned toward the golf course. As they rounded the eighth hole silently walking the golf cart path, a furry streak ran out from the underbrush pursued by another, a coyote. It was fast, but the bunny changed direction and it was a mistake. They heard the cry, almost like a human baby, and the coyote trotted off with the rabbit in its mouth. Adam had frozen when the drama began. He turned, and she was crying. She said, "Why is life so short and sad?"

Adam reached out and pulled her close and hugged her. For a moment, it made her cry harder. Then she felt a total relaxation with Adam. She had felt awkward with other guys. Not that she had much experience, because she had been pretty tall early in junior high and never seemed to spark any interest from

31

guys. She had friends, nerds who played videos with her, but being with Adam was like eating a hot caramel sundae, comforting and tantalizing at the same time. The moonlight made it seem primeval. He looked down into her face, and she was surprised that more primitive interests seemed to be overcoming her awkwardness. They kissed. It lasted for a few minutes and diverted her completely from her thoughts about the bunny.

She stopped and made an observation to interrupt the moment, her standard response when she felt unsure where things were going, "This is like a movie, like *Romeo and Juliet*. Life and death and passion, wasn't that what *Romeo and Juliet* was all about?"

"Interesting thought," Adam said. "I hope you don't expect me to swallow any poisons?"

Sarah blushed and said, "I didn't mean that we were lovers, I just meant it seemed like a play, like Shakespeare."

"Well, I'm glad it wasn't *Macbeth* you thought of," Adam quipped. "Maybe lovers isn't a bad idea?" He tipped his head and raised his eyebrow like he had when he first proposed she join the Frisbee game.

She breathed deeply and began walking. "Maybe …."

It was a long walk back, but they were both immersed in their own thoughts. After a few minutes, Sarah said, "My mom thought she was a hippie – second generation. She had my sister after smoking dope at a party and relaxing her guard," she mused. "She dropped out of college and married my dad, but when he died … she really struggled as a single mother. She always talks about how she had wanted to be a geologist but had to drop out of school. She wants something different for me. She says if women are only going to make 80 percent of what men make, then they'd better start on a higher pay scale." Adam glanced sideways but kept walking. Frankly, it was getting cold, and Sarah could feel herself picking up the pace as they crossed the street and headed for the complex of dormitories. She told him Physics called when she reached the dorm, and he hesitantly said, "See you this weekend for Frisbee golf?"

"Yeah," she said. She hesitated and quickly pecked him on the cheek, then turned and ran up the stairs. She felt awkward again and overanalyzed the peck on his cheek. It seemed goofy when she got to her room. Why had she done that? Maybe she should have just kissed him again? Maybe he didn't like it, but he seemed to be interested. Her insecurities occupied her thoughts for the next few hours, interrupting her studies.

She silently wished that she had gotten more of this behind her in high school. It seemed like she was so immature compared to other girls in the dorm who talked about romantic, even sexual encounters. She always listened intently but never offered a story of her own. She didn't really have any experience to share. Her roommate, Jennifer, who had a steady boyfriend, was out of the room overnight a lot. They hadn't really gotten close. Jennifer and she rarely were in the room at the same time since Jennifer had gotten hot and heavy with Zach. They'd had some nice conversations, but Jennifer was more social and had rushed a sorority. She would be moving into the sorority house next year, and that was where her social life was focused. Sarah regularly texted her sister Abby, but Abby was living with her mom while attending nursing school in Oklahoma City. Abby wanted to become a physician's assistant. The distance sometimes made it hard to really communicate her feelings.

Sarah looked out the dorm window and became more aware again of the night, the moon and reality. Who knew that profound moral questions were going to dominate the second half of her freshman year? Lovers or not? She was attracted to the thought but anxious. Fear and longing both together confused her. She preferred something simple, black and white, like a Physics problem. The thought stunned her. Physics was always a pain, or so she thought. Now it looked like morality, relationships and strange encounters in the library with prophetic crazy people were going to dominate her college life and be more difficult than a test on vectors. Where's a vector equation when you need a clean, uncomplicated formula for a problem? She was going to take her mind off things by trying to write that essay in philosophy. The night seemed right for circular arguments and situational ethics.

Chapter 3

It was cold and dark, and Sarah hurried in the library door, not pausing to look at the gargoyled entrance, but feeling welcomed by the longstanding faces overhead. Some of the faces smiled and some frowned. She felt a kind of kinship to the stone characters, and now she was beginning to consider them family. Her thoughts were occupied by Adam, but she couldn't yet muster the courage to text Abby about it. She was pulled, but still anxious when she thought about the 'maybe' she had left him with. At least the gargoyles didn't require any negotiation. They were a welcome constant of quiet, but steady friends. Anxiety certainly figured into her thoughts about Adam, along with some very real hormonal feelings.

Her work schedule included one late night shift and tonight was that night. She started at eight and left at closing. After she hung her coat and signed in, she went to the front desk and was told by the student supervisor to sort books. That could get interesting. Since the day she had encountered Patty, Sarah had talked with Michelyn about the two books, *Silent Spring* and *A Predictable Tragedy*. Now everybody in the sort room had begun a game. They called it Patty's Prophecy. You looked for two or three books on the sort cart and tried to find titles that suggested something. You got two points if the combination was related to current news. It had a kind of poker-like scoring, because each combination that included an additional book, relevant to the theme, got scored higher. The limit was six books, and if the titles all related in some prophetic way, then it was like getting a straight. You were limited to the books on any one cart from a single book drop so that you couldn't organize the cart with more interesting titles. Sometimes it got out of hand, and debates about the quality of the combination could keep workers so engaged that patrons sometimes had to ring the service bell to call them out of the sort room.

She was alone in the room glancing at the titles while she sorted them by call number. There was a sheet on the desk where students sat and talked when it was quiet and the sorting was caught up. The sheet listed some of the "best" of the winners, and Sarah wanted to get on that sheet. Michelyn had talked about declaring a winner at some point. It was the kind of game that helped you get to know the rest of the crew and helped you make friends.

As she sorted tonight, it was slim pickings on her first cart. Some grad student in mathematics must have finished a thesis because the cart was full of mathematics texts on fractals. She wasn't real clear about fractals. Sarah was good in math, but this stuff was pretty advanced. As she gave up the game and began to shelve the books, a student security guard, Stanley Youngwolfe, stopped and stood there. He seemed to be looking past her but was stopped right in front of her as she turned to pick up more books.

Stanley was a graduate student in art and had worked in the library for some time. She thought he was a bit odd. Most Native Americans were understated about being Natives. So many Oklahomans had some Cherokee or Chickasaw or some other tribal heritage that Sarah rarely thought much about it. But Stanley was different, he had red hair and maybe that's why he made a point of always wearing braids, moccasins and turquoise bolos to remind people he was Native, even though you couldn't tell by looking at him. He also had several tats on his arms that were actually better than a lot of tattoos that she had seen. They were pretty artistic and had some designs suggestive of Native American art. He was an art major and seemed to need to wear his art. Maybe that explained the exaggerated clothing. She had noticed that many of the students coming out of the Fine Arts Building almost looked like sculptures. Gravity-defying haircuts, thrift shop clothes, body paint and tats were all used generously, and she sometimes wished she had the abandon to try something dramatic herself. Mostly she just settled for t-shirts and jeans, staying under the radar, as she had done for years in high school when she'd just spent time cooking for her dad or helping him with personal hygiene when he became too weak to get out of bed.

Sarah knew she had some Cherokee blood, but it was only mentioned in passing by her mother, when she told Sarah that they weren't on the rolls so she wouldn't qualify for any scholarships. Most Natives she knew just dressed in t-shirts and jeans like she did. The ones into it attended pow wows and such, and a couple of guys she knew from high school wore braids. But, for the most part, they just hung like everybody else. Stanley reminded her of an old Hollywood version of an Indian, circa 1950s Lone Ranger. Momentarily she thought of Johnny Depp. She smiled and said, "Hi."

"I see you are working with fractals. That's intense," he said.

"I guess. I am really not fractally aware," Sarah hesitated.

"Artists, good artists that is, have to know about fractals. All of nature is in fractal patterns. Did you know that they did a mathematical analysis of Jackson Pollock's work and his splatter technique wasn't random but was really painted in fractals? Fractals are the only mathematical way to represent natural, amorphous things. I am really into painting unstructured forms."

"Cool. I didn't know that. Sometimes I think that mathematics seems awfully distant from real life. I have to take a lot of math as an engineering major, and I don't usually think of it relating to nature. Sometimes I just get swamped with formulas and problems." Sarah thought for a moment and wondered – if you are painting something, doesn't it by definition have to have form?

"Engineering, huh," Stanley said. "I guess that means you only believe what you see – what could be measured scientifically?"

"I don't know. I'm not sure about that," Sarah said, questioning herself. She momentarily thought about philosophy and figured that was probably not very measurable. Her professor, though, was trying because he regularly asked for volunteers on some of his research projects, and she assumed he was measuring students' responses to situational ethics questions. At this point, she couldn't think how to move the conversation forward and just turned to grab another book. The book she picked up was *On the Nature of Things* by Lucretius. The title struck her, since it seemed to address their conversation, and she looked at Stanley for a moment and held up that book and a fractal title. "Maybe they are trying to get in on the conversation," she jested.

Stanley looked at her curiously, "Did you know that artists try to represent things that don't exist for everyone?"

"Really?"

"Yeah, like ghosts," he said, while intensely looking for her response. This was the kind of situation in which Sarah felt stumped. She was sure that when she got off work and was lying in bed later that she would figure out an appropriate reply. She wasn't sure if he was serious or yanking her chain or weirder than she had first surmised.

"Oh," was all she could muster. But it was just encouragement enough for Stanley.

"I've seen ghosts in the old decks. I think I am more sensitive to seeing them, because my grandfather was a shaman." He began to tell her about closing down the library on holiday short hours and walking around with just the safety lights on, checking for lingerers and seeing apparitions.

"They're amorphous, you know, so painting them requires fractals," he stated. Sarah couldn't help thinking about her Uncle

John. He always made her laugh talking about a show on television she thought was called *Looking for Bigfoot*. He regularly broke out in mimicry of the "reality" show participants who claimed to hear Sasquatch sounds as they walked through the woods or attributed conditions to the presence of a totally unseen and never-caught-on-camera Sasquatch. Her uncle could get her laughing really hard by responding to some common everyday sound by turning to her suddenly and saying, "It must be Sasquatch."

Her thoughts made it really hard to keep a straight face while Stanley's conversation went on. She could barely keep herself from suggesting it might be Sasquatch. But she sensed Stanley would be deeply offended so she kept her eyes on the books she was sorting while taking a listening stance. She hoped concentrating on the books would keep her merriment to a minimum, while she occasionally responded with "hmm" or "interesting." Her noncommittal stance was apparently encouraging because Stanley talked for some time about ghosts and auras and fractals in an oddly dramatic way, somewhat suggestive of his Hollywood-like outfit – over-the-top with lots of eyebrow lifting and pregnant pauses, none of which she cared to fill in. The more he talked, the more odd it got, like getting lost on Dupont Circle.

"Do you think you'd want to stay after closing and walk the library with me?" he said as he studied her.

"Oh, I have a quiz tomorrow, and I need to hit the books tonight after I get off," she countered quickly. "Sounds like you have the makings of a *Ghost Hunters* episode, though."

"I thought of that and suggested it to Luke, but he said it wouldn't be approved by the Dean's office. Too bad. I think they pay for episodes, and we might make some real money. Then again, ghosts are sensitive. I don't think they would appear in front of a camera crew."

"I'm not surprised. I didn't really see anything on the couple of reality shows I watched," Sarah replied drolly, with a hesitant smile that seemed to confuse Stanley. Sarah looked over at the desk and made an excuse about needing to help up front, ending the conversation which had begun to take on a parallel universe quality. She in one and he in another. Stanley left to do his rounds.

Sarah stepped up front to handle a customer while Lubna emptied the book bin. She liked Lubna. Lubna had been the student worker who had taken her schedule to Luke, and she was grateful because she was sure that had gotten her the job. Lubna was scrappy and really down to earth. Pakistani, Lubna had grown up in Lawton, Oklahoma, as a military brat. It was always surprising to hear her Oklahoma accent. You expected her to sound like any other international student or a character on the Simpsons. Lubna sometimes wore saris and shawls, and other days, blue jeans and sweatshirts. She seemed to transition between Lawton and Lahore without missing a beat.

"Have you ever talked with Stanley?" Sarah asked Lubna.

"Uh, I've *listened* to Stanley," Lubna smiled. "It's hard to get a word in the conversation. I'd say he's a monologue shaman; he mystically manages to do all the talking and no listening." Sarah laughed. It was comforting to know that she wasn't the only person who found Stanley unusual, or, as her mom might say, a beer short of a six pack. Lubna added, "I once had a conversation, I should say monologue, with him because I wore a sari. He spent half an hour talking to me about tribal clothing and the importance of channeling your ancestors. Funny, I actually thought it was pretty interesting, but I couldn't tell him because he never gave me a chance to talk. Mercifully, the security supervisor came looking for him. I had a friend once who got pretty depressed and she seemed to develop that same talking diarrhea. She got off the antidepressant she was taking and finally returned to normal. Maybe it's drug related in Stanley."

"I don't know, given his clothes and mannerisms, I think it is more Stanley-related. He does have an interesting perspective, though. Speaking of drug-related behavior, have you ever encountered that middle-aged Japanese woman with the umbrella? I think her name is Patty?" Sarah asked.

"Oh, yeah. Everybody knows Patty. According to Patty, I'm a bio-terrorist," Lubna observed dryly. "Too bad Patty lacks a clear understanding of germ theory. But then if she did, it wouldn't be nearly as much fun to see what she is going to do next," Lubna grinned.

"Don't you find it a little disturbing? She kind of unnerved me when she said I was spreading AIDS. It makes me want to hide when I see her coming," Sarah admitted. "I don't know what to say, and I'm not sure just how excited she's going to get. Do you think she could be dangerous?"

Lubna shrugged, "You're not the first person to run from Patty. I think they ought to keep a scorecard in the back office and give student workers points for Patty encounters. But, without her, we'd never have Patty's Prophecy." Lubna paused and looked at Sarah, "I don't think you need to worry. Luke seems to be able to calm Patty pretty well, and there's always the Lysol can in the back. I used that one night when she got pretty agitated. I just started spraying and waving the can in the air and wiping with paper towels, and that seemed to really make her feel better. Just remember it if you ever get anxious. It's our secret weapon."

Sarah nodded and turned to pull books from the drop. She thought for a minute about her own anxiety about AIDS and sex. She also realized that she found the antiseptic wipes at the grocery store comforting and usually used one to wipe the basket handle. She turned to Lubna and said, "Maybe it would be a good idea to get some of those bottles of hand sanitizer and put them on the counter? Then when Patty comes to the desk, we could make a big show of washing our hands with it?"

"Brilliant!" Lubna said. "Wish I had thought of that. It's quicker than the Lysol trick, and you can get pretty elaborate about sanitizing. A real show of hand wringing might make Patty happy. You go girl! I'll bring a couple of bottles myself to contribute to the effort. Of course, we can't do something this special for all our favorite customers, but I consider Patty our oracle," Lubna smiled. "Did you see the newest Prophecy winner? It's really good. Mac scored it. He said it was perfect for the Sochi Olympics, Putin and anti-gayism in Russia ... *The Thurber Carnival*, *Invisible Man*, and *Men as Women, Women as Men*."

Sarah had to acknowledge that Mac's combination rang true. The clock turned nine, and it seemed like a witching hour because the library began to fill with students. Night classes were over, and lots of people on campus for the evening stopped at the library for coffee and to work on papers. Night students usually worked full-time, and they were desperately short of time or just plain desperate. They always seemed confused, rushed and tired. It made her think of her mom, who had decided to go back to school at night if she could get a day job. Sarah helped several night students with class reserves as the night progressed and sent some over to the graduate student at the reference desk, with questions she couldn't answer.

It slowed again, and she managed to read some of her Philosophy text the next few hours. She looked up at the clock about midnight and saw Adam loping toward the entrance. He had this awkward loping walk that made him look gangly. She found herself trying to catch his attention, "Hey Adam, in a hurry?" He looked over and seemed surprised. He walked over to the desk.

"I didn't know you worked tonight. You didn't mention it on our walk, Juliet." Sarah blushed as he said it and felt herself getting flustered. She was determined to get past the awkward feelings.

"Very funny. I'm just working and hoping, and hoping and working," she sung. She was thinking of the song but suddenly blushed when she realized that next line was "that you care."

"That's an old one," Adam observed, but he seemed to miss the connection that had caused Sarah to blush. "Do you know Stanley Youngwolfe? He works here, too."

"Yeah, we've met," Sarah said cautiously. "How do you know him?"

"We met last semester in a transcendental meditation class that I took over at the student union one weekend. It was something I saw on a sign on the bulletin boards. Stanley was in it, and we worked together in a group. At first I thought he was a bit peculiar, but I really liked him by the time the weekend was

42

over. He has some unusual talents – metaphysically speaking. In fact, I am looking for him because he told me that he expected to have a sighting and that I could walk with him."

"He sights ghosts," Adam said. "I'm not saying that I expect to see anything, but I like to keep an open mind about what other people see. People have different talents. If one person can throw a Frisbee farther than another, I figure some people may be able to see things that I can't. That seemed to happen in our class when Stanley took his turn in the group, so I think he has something I don't have. "

"Really, REALLY?" Sarah couldn't keep the sarcasm out of her voice. "I bet you watch *Ghost Hunters.*"

Adam shrugged. "That's just commercial crap. I'm not into it. I am open to the adventure in being somewhere and doing something I have never done before. It doesn't have to make sense. I'm suspending disbelief. Besides, it's not hard to believe that something could happen in here. This building has seen a lot of souls."

Sarah paused, "I get that feeling, especially when I come in the south entrance. I think the gargoyles get me thinking, and then the turrets are pretty suggestive of other times. I guess I feel like the gargoyles are friends or familiars or something."

"Now you are opening up to seeing the possibilities," Adam smiled. "The adventure begins. Why don't you stay with us and walk the building when Stanley closes up?"

"Stanley asked me if I wanted to, but I told him I had a test to study for. I wasn't sure it was a good idea. I don't want to lose my job, and I'm not sure that closing with the guard would be OK."

Lubna walked over to where they were standing. "I'm the official front desk closer. That means I have to wait here until the guard completes his building tour and confirms everyone is out. I think Sarah is right. She is supposed to close with me, which means she has to stay with me at the front desk until Stanley completes his round. Sorry to be prissy, but I like my job, too. I don't think it is a problem for you to walk with Stanley, though. You're just talking to him as he closes. Frankly, it isn't a bad idea to have someone else there, given Stanley's *abilities*. Could add an air of authenticity to his observations. I'll radio him to come down and meet you here."

Adam smiled, "Thanks. I tried catching him but was giving up when Sarah stopped me. It's a big building."

Stanley showed up a few moments later. "I was just downstairs by the elevator," he said, as he walked toward Adam. "Good thing you came tonight. I've been having lots of vibes, probably because of the cold front and change in barometric pressure. I think they will really be active."

Adam accepted Youngwolfe's explanation like he had just said the basketball team won last night with an affirmative nod. Stanley looked from Sarah to Adam and said, "Are you interested in going on the last round?"

"That's why I'm here," Adam stated.

Sarah looked at Lubna, who stepped up to the desk and did her student supervisor thing. "Sarah can't go on the round, Stanley; she's scheduled at the desk with me. But if you see something interesting, just narrate the experience on the radio or use your phone to get a video. We'll watch the front doors in case some spirit gets interested in leaving the building."

"Oh, that won't happen. Spirits are pretty place-bound," he stated matter-of-factly. "I like your idea about the video, though. I don't usually carry both the radio and the phone to keep the EMFs down to a dull roar around me. I am sure they affect spirits. In fact," he pointed to a necklace hung on a black twine and said, "this Q-Link reduces the effect of EMFs on me, so I think it makes me more receptive." He turned to Adam, and before he said anything further, Adam responded.

"I've got my phone. If you don't think it will create a negative field, then I can be the videographer. I've made some of my own movies at weather events so I think I can catch the action," Adam said, his meteorology major peeking through.

Stanley replied, "Cool. Let's do it," turning on his heel and heading toward the staircase. Adam smiled at Sarah, raised his eyebrows cocking his head to one side in his characteristic invitation pose, and loped behind Stanley disappearing in the stairwell.

Lubna asked, "Do you know Adam very well?"

"We've played some Frisbee and games together," Sarah answered, and then added quickly, "I'm surprised he hangs with Stanley because I wouldn't have figured that. I like him," she said, surprising herself. I guess there's more to Adam than I thought," she mused.

"Yeah, he's compelling, in a nerdy, Ichabod Crane kind of way. He has that tall, lanky look of the actor in the Sleepy Hollow series. Not as good looking as the actor, but he does have appeal. I can see where you are coming from," Lubna nodded her approval. "Of course, he might just look better tonight as a foil to Stanley …," Lubna observed dryly.

Sarah giggled. "No, he actually seems more appealing without Stanley."

It was Lubna's turn to guffaw. "You have to hand it to Stanley, he draws them in like a moth to a flame. Adam isn't the first guy I've seen looking to do a closing round with Stanley. I think it has to do with seeking behavior. Have you ever read any books by Temple Grandin?"

Sarah replied, "Is she the autistic animal person they made a TV movie about?"

"Yeah, she thinks animals are happiest when they are looking for things or seeking. You know, like a dog smelling every tree and chasing every rabbit on a walk. I think that applies to a lot of people. Everyone likes adventure now and then. Stanley offers a relatively safe geek adventure. No worries about breaking a leg snowboarding but still a thrill when you are walking in the dark with the emergency lights in this building. Give them a couple of flashlights, and it's almost like they are in that old TV series *X Files*," Lubna observed, as she moved toward a student with a handful of books who approached the counter.

Sarah examined her thoughts and realized that Lubna was probably right. Adam's parting glance made him look like a little boy off to do a prank on Halloween night with a friend. She remembered doing some similar things on Halloween with Abby

45

when they were younger. Scratching on window screens and running away – feeling the thrill of adrenalin. She'd text Abby after tonight and tell her how all this went down. It made the last half hour go really quickly, and as the last of the students left the building, she and Lubna waited for Adam and Stanley to show up. As Sarah watched the lobby, the second floor lights went off. She looked over at Lubna when she heard footsteps running from the back of the first floor.

Just then a disheveled couple ran out of the back and headed for the door. The guy's shirt was open and flapping as they hardly slowed for the security gate and breathlessly began laughing as they cleared the double doors. Sarah and Lubna turned toward each other, and Lubna laughed, "I wonder if they are running from a spirit or from spirited lovemaking?"

Sarah responded, "Does that happen often?"

"I've heard that the guards sometimes encounter students in the dead end corners of the decks. I guess some people find it thrilling to have sex where they run the risk of being discovered. I'm wondering if Adam caught that on his phone? I guess he'll have the makings of a different kind of film," Lubna stated with a big smile.

They waited ten more minutes until Stanley and a grinning Adam sauntered toward the desk. Stanley left Adam standing in the lobby by the desk and made his way to the back office. He had motion detectors to enable and video cameras to reset.

Sarah queried Adam, "So did you see any ghosts or should I say naked ghosts?"

Adam's grin changed, and he said, "How did you know we found something *different* from a spirit?"

"A guy and a girl ran out a few minutes ago, and it looked like they had been, well, let's just say they looked like they had been in a scene from *Romeo and Juliet*," Sarah smiled.

"Yeah, Stanley wasn't happy. He said those kinds of pursuits sidetrack the spirits. I guess the spirits haven't totally given up on the earthy side of things even though they are incorporeal," he grinned. Sarah felt herself leaning into the counter, unconsciously responding to Adam's suggestion.

"Earthy is a good description," Lubna chimed in. "They looked like they were rolling around on the ground."

Sarah and Adam both laughed. Stanley came from the back office and pushed the button on the alarm system. Lubna and Sarah picked up their things, and everyone headed for the door to get out before the 60 seconds elapsed on the alarm system exit timer. Lubna and Stanley turned toward the parking lot.

It was cold again, and the wind had picked up. "I can drop you at the dorms if you want a ride," Lubna offered, as she zipped up her parka and turned her back to the wind.

"I think I'll walk. The wind's out of the north so it will be easy getting back to the dorms." She looked at Adam, and he quickly turned and said, "I'll walk with Sarah. She'll need some ballast," he quipped, as a particularly strong gust whipped around the building. "Thanks, Stanley. I'd like to come back and try again."

"Sure, man. Anytime. You know where I am. Just call me," Stanley said, as he turned and took off toward the parking lot at a run. He didn't have a heavy jacket, so he was motivated to get to his car by the gust of cold.

As Sarah walked toward the dorms, she pulled up her hood and felt almost warm. The wind at her back was blocked by her jacket, and it felt like a friend pushing her along; she almost felt she could lean against it when another sustained gust came through. Adam pulled on his knit cap and turned to her and said, "Hmm, cozy. I'm wondering why a ride didn't sound good?"

She looked up at the stars that were crisp and sparkling, and simply pointed upward with her finger. "That, and I guess I was hoping for the company," she answered with a smile. She thought of the spirit adventure and couldn't shake the feeling about her dad. This time, it felt like he was in the wind, gently shoving her along.

Adam leaned back into the wind and slowed while he looked up, "I see your point and given that 'Juliet is the sun,' I can see why you appreciate the other heavenly bodies."

Sarah blushed deeply and to shake the embarrassment she joked, "That's a pretty Shakespearean reference. Do you use that on all the girls you know? They must all be English majors."

"Actually, I've never used that line before. I don't even know where it came from. When I think of you, I think of starry skies and Romeo and Juliet. I know why, but I don't know why Stanley thinks you have some kind of unusual quality, too. He told me he thought he saw a spirit guide at your shoulder this evening when he was talking to you about fractals. That's one reason he thought tonight might be a "good" night. But ..."

"But what?" Sarah replied, intrigued by the spirit guide and wondering if it was just coincidence that she had been thinking of her dad pushing her along when Adam mentioned it.

"But he thought it was ruined by me because I had "earthy" interests in you, and that caused us to find the couple in the decks. He thinks our thoughts can disrupt or sustain a spirit contact. I guess I'm disruptive, at least when you are around," Adam admitted grinning. "I don't know why, but I don't seem particularly shy around you. That's not something I would usually say to a girl. Apparently I'm full of unusual thoughts around you. Normally, I'm not this cool, sexy guy. I'm normally a geek with a Frisbee," he laughed.

"Funny, I'm pretty shy, too. I wonder if Stanley is "gifted" in some way? It's interesting he mentioned a spirit guide. When you asked me to play Frisbee that day, I was thinking about my dad. When you said the Frisbee was channeling a Frisbee golfer, I said yes because my dad played Frisbee golf," she said.

They both walked further, saying nothing. Sarah worried that Adam thought she might be wacky, but when she looked at him, he stopped and looked skyward. "Who knows? There's a lot in the universe or the universes. I wonder if it has something to do with parallel universes? Maybe we never die, maybe we transmute or continue to exist in another way that's just out of reach of our physical senses? Or maybe your dad just likes me," he grinned as he tilted his head in that suggestive way that seemed to invite you to join in with him on some kind of adventure.

"Or maybe Stanley is a bottle short of a six pack, and I just miss my dad," Sarah panned.

"My money is on Stanley as an extracorporeal sensitive and on multiverses. It may not be as pragmatic, but I like the possibilities," Adam expanded. "If you're going sailing off the edge of the world, it helps to believe in the captain. Besides, thinking Stanley is a crackpot is just too easy. I don't like to make assumptions about people who have an imagination that is beyond my grasp. Some of the best books I've read, the best ideas, the best Ted Talks come from somewhere I've never been in my mind. So I'm suspending disbelief," Adam said, with almost a challenge in his voice.

"If my dad is out there, then I'm with you, captain," Sarah said, looking up as a cloud closed in over Orion. She turned to Adam, feeling the wind hit the side of her face making her eyes water, or maybe it wasn't the wind but the thought that her dad was still at her side, hanging around, pushing her from behind.

"I've got class at eight tomorrow. It must be about one. I'll never stay awake in Calculus with the heaters on in the basement if I don't get some sleep," she shivered.

Adam stepped in close and said, "How about a kiss for the captain?"

"Aye, aye," she said as she reached up and gave him a lingering kiss that came easy. "Did we really just say all that mariner lingo? We must definitely be channeling somebody," she giggled as she ran towards the dorm doors.

"Argh, me matey. Batten down the hatches," Adam quipped, as he hunched over into the wind to cross the field toward his dorm. He texted her for 20 minutes after that, using pirate speech and talking about sailing the multiverses. It was pretty geeky but imaginative. What was it the counselor said? You protect yourself from losing someone important to you by distancing yourself. Maybe she'd been distancing herself from experiences and from people. She nodded off with her phone in her hand, wondering what her spirit guide looked like to Stanley? For a moment, her mind conjured up a Sasquatch hovering over her shoulder, and she drifted away smiling to herself.

Chapter 4

"Those who are pure in heart and single in purpose are able to understand the most supreme way."

--Buddha

Sarah woke up remembering parts of a dream. She hadn't recalled doing that in forever, it seemed. On the edge of her consciousness, she could just grasp the dream. Her dad was there. There was a Frisbee, and something about a Calculus test and her wearing her pajamas to class. That thought sat her up quickly. She searched for her phone under the covers, checked her calendar to see if she really did have an exam this morning and with a pang of anxiety and a loud groan realized she saw "calculus quiz" listed. Why hadn't she checked that last night when she used it as an excuse with Stanley?

When she groaned, she was surprised to see Jennifer pull the covers over her head and roll over in the next bed. She panicked and ran toward the bathroom, mentally calculating that she had time for a shower, a banana and about 15 minutes to review formulas at the back of the chapter before she ran to class. Tripping over Jennifer's clothes – the girl had a bad habit of dropping her clothes as she climbed into bed – Sarah stumbled into the bathroom, turned on the shower and peed while the warm water made its way to the third floor. Jennifer must have almost been sleepwalking when she came home so late last night, and Sarah wondered why she was in the room? She'd been gone overnight most nights in the last couple of weeks, rarely separating herself from her new boyfriend. Why would she straggle back so late?

That intense devotion to Zach was something that niggled at Sarah. As she showered, she thought about Zach and Jennifer, and then mentally compared Zach to Adam. What bothered Sarah about Zach wasn't his behavior, but Jennifer's. When they were together, it seemed like her voice got babyish around Zach and she acted different. Their relationship was a little unsettling. When Jennifer was in the room, most of her talk focused on what Zach liked and what Zach did. It seemed like Jennifer forgot about Jennifer. She had stopped talking about her own schoolwork and her goal to become a television anchorwoman. Jennifer now was always talking about Zach. It creeped Sarah out and made her wonder if she changed her behavior like that around Adam. She hurried to brush her teeth, grabbed a banana from the small refrigerator and a granola bar, pulled on her jacket and raced out of the room down the stairs.

As she rounded the corner, she was dazzled by the white light in the first floor lounge windows. It had snowed, and everything was covered with about two inches of powdery sparkle. It was a dry snow. Not any good for snowballs, but it reminded her of the fake snow sometimes attached to Christmas decorations, the kind that reflected an almost rainbow sparkle. She flipped up her hood to cover her wet hair and breathed in the crisp, clean scent of cold snow. The wind had died down. The cold front that had pushed them to the dorms last night had passed through, dumping the snow and leaving the scent of Colorado mountains in the air.

She munched the banana and tried to recall calculus problems as she walked along the sidewalk past the buildings on the South Oval headed toward the basement of Felgar Hall. She found herself enjoying the crisp air but dreading the dry overheated room that always made her yawn when she came in from the cold. As her cheeks warmed in the classroom, she could feel herself get drowsy and was glad that her hair was still wet. She was hoping it would keep her more alert. The quiz was just five percent of her grade, but she wanted to bank all the good grades she could get early in the semester. The instructor had told the class that anyone who was satisfied with their grade before finals, could skip the final.

She emerged from class feeling pretty good about the quiz. Luckily, she'd done the homework before her work shift last night and didn't seem to have a problem recalling how to work the problems. She figured that she'd dodged that bullet. As she walked over to Dale Hall for her Philosophy class, she thought about Jennifer again, a nagging feeling that she couldn't quite classify. She walked slowly and stopped on the South Oval to watch some birds look for food in a flower bed. Sarah loved the snow but always worried about the birds getting enough to eat on a bad winter day. She felt around in her pocket for some crumbs from the breakfast bar she'd scarfed down with the banana and tossed a couple, happy to provide some help. She stood still and waited for the birds to hop over and grab the morsels, noting their delicate footprints in the white powder. She was captivated by their hopping and the fluffed up feathers. It was like dancing puffballs in a sparkling field of white.

Philosophy class was intriguing, as usual. Her professor was always posing situational ethics scenarios. What would you do if … kinds of questions. What would you do if some stranger knocked on your door and asked you to hide them? What would you do if you lived in 1930s Germany and someone knocked on your door and asked you to hide them and you had a family with two young children? He could really get you thinking. As she walked back from class, she thought again about Jennifer. Who are you as a person? How do you really know who you are, until you are faced with something significant or, as her mom might say, until push comes to shove?

Her thoughts came back to Jennifer. It seemed like Jennifer was so solid, really goal-oriented when they met on move-in day. Now, she seemed sidetracked. Besotted, that was the word. Almost like she was drugged by love and just not thinking. Was that the way it was supposed to be? Was that normal? Did she feel that way about Adam? Adam made her smile, but so did Abby. They had fun together, and she enjoyed thinking about kissing Adam. But she didn't want to talk to him in baby talk, and she was still focused on getting her degree. Watching her dad die had made her determined to have her own career, clear that you couldn't count on someone else – anybody could die, anytime. Being dependent on someone else, like her mother had been for several years, was NEVER going to be all right with Sarah. You can't count on people. It isn't that her dad wasn't trustworthy, it was just that even he couldn't change cancer. She knew he had wanted to live, and they were all buoyed when he did so well the first two years, but, when he relapsed, it didn't matter what he wanted, he died anyway.

Sarah could feel herself digging in, telling herself not to count on Adam or anybody. It was how she made it in high school, and it worked for her then. She was afraid to relax. She didn't want to be dependent, she could go it alone. We were all alone anyway. Wasn't that on the old *Star Trek* episode she remembered vividly? Spock inhabits the mind of another alien and that alien, used to a communal mentality, bemoans how alone humans are? She remembered mind games she played as her dad faded, driving on the highway imagining what it would be like when he was gone, telling herself that she could deal with it.

Sarah caught herself in the anxiety-induced mental rant. OK, maybe she was overreacting, maybe Adam and she could be friends, maybe Jennifer wasn't really a Zach groupie. She climbed the stairs of the dorm and opened the door to her dorm room. Jennifer was lying amidst twisted bedclothes. She'd been crying. Her mascara was smeared down her cheeks and she lay there. Sarah lifted her eyebrows and tentatively walked toward Jennifer. "OK?"

A sobbed emerged and Jennifer groaned "I guess I look like such an idiot mess. I can't believe I fell so hard for that self-obsessed groupie magnet! He dumped me. He said I was too clingy and that he was moving on. I thought he loved me. When I told him I loved him, he just looked like he wanted out of the room – wanted to be anywhere but there with me. Am I so awful? What's wrong with me?"

"Why do you think there is something wrong with you, just because Zach isn't interested? You are still the person you always were, and you have a lot going for you. Don't measure yourself against someone who isn't even in the picture anymore. Let it go. Figure you learned something and had a good time," Sarah encouraged. "Zach isn't the measuring stick for all things. He's just a college student like the rest of us."

Jennifer sat up and wiped under her eyes, getting at some of the mascara. Her eyes were puffy and her hair disarrayed, but she plumped the pillow and sat up and looked woefully at Sarah. "But I feel used. I feel like he just put up with me because he wanted easy sex, and when I started to expect something, he bailed. Why?"

Sarah shrugged, "Maybe that's true. If it is, you are better off without him. "

A stifled sob escaped Jennifer, and she quietly said, "I'm in love. I have never felt like this about any of the other boys I dated in high school. There was always something that bored or irritated me about them. Zach is different. He has direction and seems so sure of himself, so clear about what he wants to do and how he is going to get there. It made him seem so assured and strong."

"Funny, when I first met you, that's what I thought about you. There's a girl who knows what she wants and how she is going to get it. It was only after you started dating Zach that I noticed you seemed to let your own goals get sidetracked. You seemed to, well, lose yourself. Put yourself in the backseat."

Jennifer sat in bed and stared at herself in the mirrored closet door. "Somehow I just feel like I put myself out there and got kicked in the gut. I'm mad and sad at the same time. It felt so good to cuddle and feel cared for. Now I feel mad when I think that I was the only one involved. It feels like he was just going through the motions and I was a stupid groupie." Jennifer let out a "Fuck this," that turned into a sob and threw her pillow at the mirror.

Sarah thought before answering, "I remember when you first started dating. I thought I saw Zach look at you with some real love-puppy eyes. He had me believing. Later, though, you looked that way and he seemed less interested. Maybe it was just that he's just interested in the chase? Where did you think the relationship would end up?"

Jennifer's face took on a sheepish quality, "I was pretty deluded. I actually stopped by a bridal shop when I went home two weekends ago and just looked around. When I think of that, I really cringe and then find myself wanting to throw things at Zach. I'm so embarrassed." More tears rolled down her cheeks.

"What classes do you have today? I had a quiz this morning. Maybe trying to focus on some homework would help you put Zach on the back burner? I kinda think that mooning over him wouldn't help. I think it would send exactly the wrong message, even if you thought you might get back together."

"Ugh," Jennifer said, "I've got a big group project in Communications this semester. My group hasn't even met yet to decide on a topic. I guess I could send out an email to the group and try to get a meeting set up. I'd rather just stay here under the covers."

"If you do, you'll miss the snow. It's so sparkly. It makes the whole campus look like a Christmas card. Why don't you see if your group will meet at the library coffee shop this afternoon? A hot chocolate will sound good to everybody, and you might get them to agree to meet. At least getting that project off the ground will give you one less thing to feel bad about. Besides, you can walk to the library with me. I have an afternoon shift today," Sarah added, hoping that it would be a diversion for Jennifer. She grabbed her feet under the covers and started pulling her off the bed.

"OK, OK, I get it," Jennifer rallied and began to move under her own steam.

As the bathroom door closed, Sarah sat back on her bed and felt her own anxiety rise. She thought about Adam and told herself to back down. She was determined not to end up like Jennifer. It was a good lesson. Jennifer was vibrant and beautiful, and somehow Zach still lost interest. She quietly texted her sister, explaining the situation and using several exclamation points as she inserted herself into the scenario and told her sister that she wouldn't be pulled into anything similar. Abby always helped. They texted for at least half an hour because it was the first time Sarah had mentioned Adam, and Abby was eager to hear more details, while Sarah was determined to build an armor of indifference. She texted Abby, emphasizing Adam's geeky qualities and minimizing his character. It was a diatribe on why she shouldn't like him. Abby replied with common sense commentary about guys being just people. Sarah maintained her rant, though, and kept her back up in defense of Jennifer and down with guys, a position she developed as worry and anxiety overtook her. So when a text from Adam popped up about a Frisbee game in the snow, Sarah made an excuse, telling herself she needed to stay focused on school and work – thank you very much.

Snow angels, they just had to. Sarah dragged Jennifer over to the open grass area of the South Oval and told her to make one. Jennifer had used the hot chocolate ploy and got her group to meet at the library that afternoon, so she and Sarah walked from the dorms together. Snow balls were flying, launched by a variety of class goers, but the snow was too powdery so most balls dissipated into a puff of white as they landed – if they landed. It was like a Harry Potter movie, with sparkling light coming out of kids' hands like spells coming from a wand. Sarah sprinkled an oatmeal bar on the head of her angel. She'd pocketed the intended bird meal when they set out. She wanted to feed the birds again. This time, she and Jennifer stood quietly and the delicate opportunists landed quickly on the angel's head making a footprint halo. Jennifer quietly pulled out her phone, took a picture and mailed it to Sarah with "Thanks."

Shelving books was one aspect of Sarah's job that was mundane, but which she appreciated because she found it peaceful. Everyone had shifts staffing the circulation desk and shifts shelving books. This afternoon Sarah was given the keys to the elevator in the old library decks and was expected to roll a couple of loaded book carts upstairs and get the items reshelved by the end of her two hour shift. She grabbed a cart and headed out, rolling it in front of her. Pushing the cart through the library and negotiating multiple elevators was like solving a puzzle.

The old stacks didn't actually line up with the newer addition floors and you needed to use two different elevator systems to get the cart to the level where the books resided. The first set of elevators was in the 1958 addition, and the heavy book cart caused the elevator itself to drop about half an inch in an unsettling way. Misaligned when it arrived meant there was a gap between the floor and the elevator. It took some muscle to manhandle the loaded cart over the elevator threshold. After she negotiated that, she had to use a ramp to move the cart into the glass decks. With their low ceilings and old suspended glass-tiled floors, the decks were the source of most "ghost" stories. They also contained an ancient, decrepit elevator that really felt crypt-like. There was always the smell of machine oil and usually a small puddle of grease dripping on the linoleum.

Sarah turned the key that enabled the button that would take her to the basement level of the decks. As the door began to close, it dawned on her that when it did, she would be in the dark. The light wasn't working. The dark didn't really bother her, but she hoped she had pushed the right button to get her to the basement. She waited to feel the elevator bump as it launched itself downward, but there was no bump. She stood patiently in the dark. Still nothing.

"Shit," she whispered, as she realized she stood in complete darkness and hadn't remembered which button on the panel opened the doors. She waited another minute and then stabbed at the panel again, hoping her memory of the panel configuration was correct. A small tickle of anxiety crept up the back of her neck as she failed to get a response. Total quiet descended as her brain began to think about how an elevator worked and why it would not respond when she had clearly called it earlier. She didn't have elevator anxiety about crashing downward. Years ago, her dad had clearly explained safety brakes when they had been briefly stuck in an elevator at the hospital. There had been company that day, and the lights were working. But this was a really, really old elevator, about a hundred years old, and she could imagine roaches using the wiring as a highway and eventually causing a short. Besides, it was unnerving trying to analyze the problem without being able to see.

Her predisposition to look at physics and math challenges analytically kicked in, and she traced her steps mentally. The key. She didn't need the key to call the elevator but had inserted and turned it to select a destination. Maybe the key mechanism was the problem. She felt for the panel, found the key and turned it back and forth. She pushed a button and waited. Nothing. She repeated the sequence, pushing different buttons in combination with the key in different positions.

Again, nothing. She jumped up and down, hoping to slightly reposition the elevator, and then systematically began turning the key in combination with different button selections. Nada. A quiet resolution formed in her mind to never put her cell phone in her locker when she worked again. She had on stretch pants that day and was without a pocket, so she had stuffed it into her locker with her backpack. Silently chiding herself, she began to wonder how long it might take before someone found her accidentally?

She reasoned that if someone else called the elevator with the outside buttons, it would probably solve the problem and open the doors. But there weren't many people in the decks on a busy day, and this wasn't a busy day. Strangely, as she worked the problem and eliminated possibilities, she was less anxious. That's why she loved binary analysis, moving from one idea to the next and individually eliminating possibilities, yes, yes, no, yes, fit into her comfort zone. Relaxed her. Social possibilities, to kiss or not to kiss, that made her anxious. Thinking about kissing naturally brought up images of Adam, and the darkness caused her to pause and savor the daydream, leaning against the book cart as she had leaned against Adam when they had kissed the other night. It was a pleasant recollection and diverted her momentarily from the problem-solving sequence she had undertaken. Had she tried every button with every combination of key turns?

It was beginning to run together. She told herself that if it was an electrical short, then more jiggling and button pushing might still work if a breaker hadn't been tripped. Luckily, she didn't need to go to the bathroom. So she stood quietly and engaged in an extension of her previous daydream, smiling to herself and imagining a more involved exchange with Adam. A feeling of languid pleasure overtook her. After a few Walter Mitty minutes, she forced herself back to the present reality. After all, she was working and she was expected to get two carts of books shelved by the end of the shift.

After trying about 30 combinations of key and button sequences a second time, Sarah tried to open the doors manually, wedging her fingertips in the crack and pulling. She couldn't force it open, but she could create a small crack that let in a sliver of light and confirmed that the elevator sat on the same level and had stubbornly stayed where it was. She began to sweat with the effort of trying to force the doors. She paused and breathed deeply. Footsteps, a shuffling, soft-footed sort, seemed to be coming toward the door.

"Hello, hello. HEELLLOOO," Sarah said, raising her voice a little after each utterance and placing her mouth over the crack in the door. She saw a shadow walk past and shouted, "I'm in the elevator!" The steps stopped, turned and shuffled back. As a shadow reappeared, Sarah's eyes focused on a figure that stopped in front of the doors and leaned in toward the crack. Relief flooded Sarah as she explained through the crack, "The elevator is stuck, could you please push the button?" I think it might open the doors?"

Quietly, the doors slid open and her rescuer came into full focus. "Thank you so much … Dr. Nakamura. I've been stuck in there for about ten minutes. I was beginning to worry," Sarah flushed as she spoke, remembering her last conversation with Patty Nakamura. "I really appreciate your help."

"That's dangerous. It should be reported," Patty stated in a much calmer manner than when she had the strange exchange with Sarah at the circulation desk. Except for the white gloves, Patty actually seemed rather normal.

"I agree. I think I will park the cart to hold the door open and go downstairs and report it. Thanks again for your help. Being caught in the dark was kind of frustrating, and it's always a little eerie in the decks. I really, really do appreciate it," Sarah said, feelings of gratitude causing her to reassess her previous feelings about the odd woman she had thought of as a little scary.

"Elevators are a daily miracle of overcoming the gravity well – for a few feet anyway. We all probably take that miracle for granted," Patty said. "I find the decks a bit eerie myself. In point of fact, I have felt lately like I'm being observed or followed on this level. Do you think someone could have tampered with the elevator?"

Sarah's feelings about Patty's conspiracy-ridden conversational style resurfaced, and she recalled Lubna's comment about Patty being an oracle. "I think it's just old age. This elevator is original to the building. It is only reasonable to expect it to need repairs," Sarah said, trying to sound calming and pragmatic. "I'd better get downstairs and report it right away."

"Yes, reporting it is important. I think you should report a stalker as well. I have that feeling. Someone always seems to be behind me or ahead of me, or below me, particularly on this level."

"Have you seen someone following you? Could you describe the person?"

Patty whispered, "I've never seen him, only heard him.…"

Sarah's skepticism was piqued, and she replied, "If you've never seen him, how do you know it's a him?"

"I just feel it. I have to go," and as abruptly as their previous conversation had ended, Patty turned and walked quickly away, moving like a character in a movie who has heard footsteps in the fog, with a backward look over her shoulder and a quickening of her pace.

Sarah skipped down the stairs, surprised that her short captivity had made her appreciate the feeling of freedom. She thought about Patty and crazy. These days, most people thought about mental health and equated it in America with guns, dead people and political grandstanding. But she didn't feel Patty had a massacre in her. It made her think about one of her favorite movies, *As Good As It Gets*. The main character had really bad OCD and didn't play well with others, although he was basically a kind and generous person underneath his quirks. Maybe Patty just didn't play well with others because she was always seeing a conspiracy in everything? As she arrived at the department, she looked for Luke, who wasn't at his desk, and then ran into Stanley.

"Hi, Stanley. As the security guard, should I report an elevator problem to you?"

"Yeah, I can radio some physical plant personnel to come. Is someone stuck? They will show up pretty quickly if we tell them someone is trapped," he explained.

"Well, someone was trapped. Me. But I got out with some help. I think there may be an electrical problem in the button panel, and it's complicated because the light in the elevator is out, too. So when you get stuck, you are in total darkness. It's the west elevator in the decks," replied Sarah.

"We've been having problems with that elevator. Do you mind coming back with me and showing me how you got trapped – what you did? It helps if I can provide details to the serviceman, especially since he came and *fixed* it just last week. Or at least he said it was fixed," Stanley said.

"No problem, I have to go back and get my cart. I left it parked halfway in the elevator to keep it from being used. I have to get those books shelved, and I don't want to get back in the elevator to move the cart to the basement without someone on the outside who can let me out if the thing messes up again," she stated.

As they left the back office and made their way through the building, Stanley asked, "How long were you there in the dark, and who helped you get out?"

"I was trapped about ten minutes, I think. I kept trying combinations on the button panel and jiggling the key. Eventually I pulled the door apart just a crack, but it was enough to catch Patty Nakamura's attention when I yelled as she passed by. She was able to get the doors to open by pushing the call button on the outside," Sarah replied.

"Rescued by the Oracle, that's auspicious," Stanley said. "Guess you and Patty Nakamura are entangled."

"What do you mean?"

"Just that you intersect in time and space, and that it may not be the first time, because there seems to be some spiritual gravitation," Stanley explained. "How was it being trapped in the elevator? Did you feel panicky? I ask because there was a guy last week who got trapped and when he was rescued, it looked like he had been, well, rattled," Stanley said, shifting to the present problem. "He managed to push the doors open a little like you, but the carriage was stuck between floors, and it took more than an hour for the serviceman to get here. Maybe he just had to go to the bathroom because he took off like a rabbit."

Sarah paused, "I had a moment of anxiety, particularly because it's a total blackout in there. But I kinda got caught up in trying to analyze what was wrong with the thing. I started trying to find combinations of button sequences and key positions that might wake it up. And nature wasn't calling me, so I could relax and focus on the problem."

"Did any of the sequences have any effect at all? I am sure the service guy will ask me," Stanley said.

"Nada. Until I cracked the doors and caught Patty's attention when she walked by, nothing happened." They had traversed the building and arrived at the elevator and the cart. Stanley stepped into the elevator and turned the key. He seemed to look around the doorway with some intensity and, as his eyes moved upward looking through the gap between the ceiling and the elevator door, his attention was riveted momentarily. The sound of steps moved off hurriedly as it was clear someone had been on the level above and had walked away rather quickly.

"I'm going to radio in the problem now and go get the out-of-order signs. We'll just key the elevator to off and leave it here," he said. "How did you get the Oracle's attention when you were trapped?"

"I just yelled through the door when I heard footsteps. She was calmer than usual but still dreaming up conspiracies. She actually claimed that she thought she was being followed. I am supposed to get this and another cart shelved. Is there another way to get the cart to the basement of the decks without using this elevator? So far, I haven't shelved a single book."

Stanley thought for a moment and replied, "Yeah, you can take it down the '58 addition elevators to that basement and then roll it around to the ramp that takes you through the fire doors to the library school. Do you happen to remember what the Oracle was wearing?"

"A dark skirt and sweater. Of course, she had on her gloves." Sarah said, as she gave the cart a push and left Stanley talking to the physical plant dispatcher. She was getting used to Stanley, but his nickname for Patty Nakamura imbued Patty with a seriousness that made Sarah imagine Patty might be a magnet for other souls in the decks. Questioning herself about whether spirits made sounds and whether Patty's stalker existed, she caught herself thinking, it could be Sasquatch and chuckled. Spirits, vague shuffling in the upper decks, and the isolation of the old basement kept her musing on such thoughts until she finished. As she pushed the second empty cart though the old doorway, she was startled by a man turning the corner abruptly, causing Sarah to say, "Sorry, I didn't see you!"

The man looked like a graduate student who had been in school awhile, because he was about 30 years old, with black-rimmed glasses. He grunted, kept his eyes averted and hardly slowed as he darted past the cart hurrying down the hall. Sarah turned her head to look at his back and shrugged. If he had responded in anyway, she wouldn't have bothered to turn and watch him. She observed that his pants were hitched up pretty high, and he bounced a bit on his toes. As he hurried away, she wondered why she noticed when men wore their pants too high or too low?

She had once been on a subway in Chicago visiting an aunt when she and her mother exchanged raised eyebrows and suppressed chuckles as three young men entered the car. One stood out, because his low-slung pants seemed to defy gravity and his penguin walk, necessitated by the crotch of the pants around his knees, made him stumble as he and his friends exited at the next stop. Several subway riders giggled as the door closed. Was it fashion or obsession? Who knew? It didn't seem the same as when Stanley wore unusual combinations of thrift store clothing. As she saw him more often and the variety of outfits he wore, she had come to think of it as art – wearable art.

As Sarah emptied her locker and pulled out her phone when her shift ended, she saw Jennifer's text and the photo. It was touching. Maybe they'd have more time to be friends now that Jennifer was un-Zached. As she grabbed her backpack, she noticed Stanley in the sort room. Still feeling the effects of the decks, Sarah remembered Adam's comment about Stanley's spirit vision and Stanley's comment about spiritual gravitation. She couldn't leave without asking, "So, Stanley, Adam said that you noticed a spirit over my shoulder the other night. Care to elaborate? Was it another kind of spiritual gravitation?"

Stanley grinned, "Everybody wants to know, but I don't give out details."

"Yeah, I guess it's like *Ghost Busters*, things are always off-camera," She wasn't completely successful at keeping the sarcasm out of her voice. It surprised her, because it sounded kind of edgy.

Stanley stood quietly for a moment, took a deep breath, and said, "I've made the mistake in the past of sharing visions, and it hasn't gone too well. It's better if the receiver sees for him or herself." Stanley actually looked a bit pained, like he'd seen her reaction before. "My purpose is to make the situation open for alignment but not to direct or interpret. It's too easy for me to put my own spin on things, unconsciously. It isn't ethical."

"I'm sorry, I didn't mean to sound like that. It's just that I was hoping it might be my dad," Sarah trailed off – stunning herself with the admission. It was an unconscious slip. She thought often of her dad but normally didn't talk much about him.

"That's what I thought. People usually are the most intense if it is someone they need to see. That's also when it is most likely to be misinterpreted or balled up by someone in the middle," he answered. "The more emotionally laden, the more fuck-up potential. I'm not a medium or a wizard or anything like that. I'm a descendant of generations of shamans. It's sacred to me and powerful ... but it is there for you if you choose to look. I'm like an outdated GPS. I point you in a general direction, get you close, but you have to find the way yourself. It's your journey."

Intrigued, Sarah asked, "How long does it take, usually?"

"Hours, maybe days, maybe years, maybe a lifetime, who knows?" Pausing, Stanley took another slow breath. "Remember, what I saw on your shoulder was *my* vision. It could be related to you, but it may just be a projection of something I wanted to see or someone who wanted to be seen by me that really has nothing to do with you. Or maybe I thought I saw something because I wanted to get to know you better? Sometimes it takes me awhile to figure out what or why I see things. It's my journey. We might travel together for a while … or not. I'm not immune to spinning things my way for my own reasons, but I know it isn't right, so I try to stay present but not add my interpretation."

"I hadn't really thought about how somebody might spin a vision. Frankly, I hadn't really thought about visions. I just was thinking about my dad and something I said to him that I wanted to talk about. Something I'd rather not have said. I guess something I'd like to take back," Sarah replied, looking down at the carpet. She could feel her lower lip begin to tremble slightly and pinched her lips together to get a grip. She felt a bit silly and was surprised that she was so emotional in front of Stanley, a guy she labeled goofy a few days ago. Now he seemed a lot different. He took his role as security guard seriously. He wasn't always absorbed with the metaphysical. He was someone she felt she needed to know better.

Stanley looked up at the clock and said, "I need to start my round. It seems to me you have a journey to take. Just keep taking steps and you know where I am when you need some direction. You're pretty analytical and apparently not easily rattled. I think you'll get there."

Sarah looked up and smiled crookedly, still pressing her lips together to hold off her emotion, "Thanks." She watched Stanley walk away and appraised him again. He had on his usual arty garb, a Hawaiianesque shirt of electric polyester, blue jeans and moccasins. His wrist tattoos gave the illusion of a long sleeved shirt. She just realized that she never heard Stanley when he walked. The moccasins never made a sound, even when he walked across the tiled atrium. It reminded her of *The Last of the*

Mohicans. She heard a locker door shut and turned to see Lubna, sheepishly realizing that she might have overhead their discussion on visions.

"Hi Sarah. I see you are finding Stanley more enigmatic than odd? I've had some more talks with him myself about tribal dress, and I mean talks this time, not monologues. I'm beginning to think there's more to Stanley than meets the eye, and that's saying something, considering he usually catches your eye," she grinned. "I'm beginning to like the shirts. Yesterday he had a really interesting bowling shirt on, embroidered with the name Lefty. I asked him if he was left-handed. He said no, but that sometimes he channeled left-handed spirits and that the shirt made it easier."

"Whoa. That's … disconcerting but definitely intriguing. I'm going to the coffee shop to get my Physics caffeine hit. Wanna come?"

"Sure." As they stood in the order line for coffee, Lubna asked Sarah, "Do you mind my asking what's your religion?"

"No, but I am not sure I can give you a clear answer. My mom took us to church when we were kids, but I lost interest when the Sunday school teacher couldn't explain how dinosaurs fit in. My dad was part Native American and he never went. My mom's interest in church was pretty anemic. She never seemed to need or want organized religion, although I think she took us to the local Christian church when we were kids because she was raised that way. I asked her once, and she said she thought the Russian Orthodox priests that my grandmother idolized were not women-friendly and felt her mother was used by the small town priest in Pennsylvania. She told me that her father wasn't allowed to be buried in the church cemetery because he didn't attend, and I think that pretty much settled her opinion on Christian tolerance.

My mom has never been much of a joiner and my dad was even less involved. He once told me that churches were the poor man's social club. I thought it was his idea, but I later read that it's something Mark Twain said. After that, I could picture my dad reading the quote in the paper and shaking his head. I think it summed up his opinion on religion in general. I guess this is a long way of saying I'm a kind of open, unaffiliated sort of agnostic/atheist undecided? I guess you could say, or Stanley would say, I'm still on that journey," she quipped. "How about you? I figured you were Hindu."

"Buddhist, actually," Lubna replied, "but culturally Hindu-influenced.

"What's it like to be raised Buddhist?"

"Hmm … that's hard to explain because I don't know what it's like to be raised Buddhist. I chose to be Buddhist, when I was about 12," Lubna commented.

Sarah changed tacks and said, "How does it feel being Buddhist in the middle of the Bible Belt? "

"It might be a bit like being a Native American shaman in the Bible Belt," Lubna remarked. "Actually, that's not really a bad description. There aren't really many Buddhists left in Pakistan; they were encouraged to leave centuries ago much like the Native Americans were encouraged to be gone. Perhaps that's why my family is in Lawton and not Lahore."

"I've seen the Dalai Lama interviewed on TV. I thought your dad was in the military? It seems like Buddhists are pacifists. How does that work?"

"Actually, my father is Hindu and I was raised Hindu, even though my mother inserted a lot of Buddhist commentary into our daily lives. She is comfortable with Hinduism but has a subversive Buddhist bent. I picked up on that and made a decision to become Buddhist. My dad shakes his head and clucks about it, but he's more flexible than he wants you to think he is."

"So what does a Buddhist think of visions and shamans and spirits?"

"I don't know about all Buddhists, but this one doesn't have a problem with it. Frankly, I'm starting to think Stanley is kind of cute. When you read some about Buddha, and try to put yourself in his time and place, you begin to realize that he might have been considered pretty wacked out by people back then. Sure, these days his words seem profound, but he left life in a palace, lived in a cave, sat under a tree for years and didn't eat much. I expect he looked … unkempt? Anyway, his *journey* was out of the ordinary," Lubna explained. "I'm not saying that Stanley is a prophet, but he doesn't seem interested in *profiting* from his shamanism. Is that a word, shamanism?"

Sarah shrugged, "Yeah, I was impressed with his ethics about it, and I guess it's a word if we agree that it is. That makes us two humans communicating a concept. I had an English teacher in high school who spent several weeks talking about Shakespeare and how he created words that didn't exist. Let's just figure you are channeling Shakespeare."

"Just call me bard then or maybe bardie?"

"That's sounds scarily close to Barbie," Sarah said as she looked at Lubna. There was something composed and peaceful about Lubna. Her warm brown skin and eyes, her smooth black hair, the way she sat straight up but with an air of relaxation. Diminutive, she still seemed to own her own space. Sarah wished she felt peaceful, but her anxiety about her dad crept in, making her ask, "Do you actually think Stanley saw a spirit over my shoulder?"

"I don't know, but I wouldn't rule it out. What was it Adam said about some people throwing a Frisbee better than others? I suspect he saw something, but was it more than a shadow? Well, like Stanley said, be careful of spin. Speaking of Adam, how is that going?"

Sarah smiled. "He's looking pretty cute too. But I'm not going there," Sarah stiffened and launched into a description of Jennifer's experience – how she thought it could get messy and how she felt anxious about school and how Jennifer seemed to bury herself under Zach's personality. It was an anxiety rant that went on for some time. Finally, Sarah saw Lubna grinning and stopped, "What?"

"Me thinks she doth protest too much," Lubna quoted.

Sarah blushed, "OK, *bardie,* I get it."

"Well, an attraction can be fun. It's not necessarily a lifetime commitment. Adam seems like someone who could be a friend and a lover. I was wondering if you and Adam might like to go out with Stanley and me?"

"Are you and Stanley …?" Sarah's eyes opened wide involuntarily.

"Not yet, but I'm thinking that some time spent with Stanley could be intriguing. What if we ask them to go bowling with us?"

Sarah's eyebrows lifted, "You are full of surprises. I never figured you for a bowler. I'm sure not. But I'm up for it."

"I'm a military brat. I've spent some serious time in bowling alleys," Lubna replied. "I've got to get to class, but I'll see you on our shift tomorrow and let you know if Stanley is willing. If he is, I figure you can ask Adam. I'm betting he'll come. How about Friday night?" Lubna got up and gathered her stuff.

"Sure. Just let me know," Sarah responded with only a slight hesitation. She could feel a small kernel of excitement well up when she thought of Adam. Somehow Lubna had made her anxiety seem unnecessary and renewed her interest in seeing Adam. She recalled their last kiss and thought another one might not be a bad thing. They exchanged numbers, and Lubna told her to expect a confirming text as she left.

Sarah opened her Physics text and started reading while sipping the last of her double espresso. Thoughts of Adam interrupted her study time with surprising regularity, and she knew that she'd have to spend some additional hours on the same chapter before the quiz. Thoughts of Adam were much nicer than thoughts of vectors. It reminded her that she would have to ask Adam if he was available. That seemed like it would be easier in a text so she pulled out her phone again and texted Adam about Friday night, explaining that Lubna was checking with Stanley. She paused only a second before hitting the send button. She didn't have to wait long for a response. It looked like they were going bowling at the end of the week.

Chapter 5

"Without the presupposition of established culture, it would not be possible to step out of the confines of convention."

--Martin Seel, *Aesthetics of Appearing: Cultural Memory in the Present*

The characters on the building's edifice were shadowed by the floodlights along the front of the library as Sarah entered. She'd made a point of coming and going from the old entrance so she could greet them every time she started a work shift. It was a bit of superstition, like a baseball player wearing the same shirt and spitting in the same spot to keep a streak going. Sarah figured the shift would go better if she mentally high-fived the faces as she walked in. After all, she'd gotten the job when she needed it, after looking up and hoping they would help. Now, she counted on them helping her to keep this streak going and her anxieties in check. Habits, like studying after her afternoon shifts in the coffee shop, calmed her and gave her a sense of order. Even regularly talking to gargoyles in her mind was comforting. She had a few favorite t-shirts too.

The sort room was full as Sarah walked by on her way to the locker room. After the first six weeks of school, some papers were due and book pickup reflected a heavy night of last minute paper writing. Sarah walked up to the desk and noticed Lubna helping a professor turn in some reserve material. Lubna wore braids and a garnet-colored sari with the scarf wrapped around her torso. It made her look a little native, like Stanley, and very

Pakistani at the same time. Sarah was used to seeing Lubna with a single braid down her back, but two braids was something she hadn't noticed her wearing before. She had actually wrapped the braids with a leather thong, and Sarah was reminded of a bronze statue outside the library of a Native American woman wrapped in a shawl holding a book. The statue was made by a famous Native American artist. The hairstyle flattered Lubna's face and made her look even younger. Sarah started to empty the book drop, and Lubna looked over and greeted her.

"I like the braids," Sarah said. "They look ... well ... tribal."

"That's the point. Stanley and I are comparing native costume and wearable art. Lubna held out her hand and showed a henna tattoo that looked something like what she had seen on Stanley. "Stanley drew this, and I drew one that is traditional on him. Her eyes crinkled and a smile flashed as she turned to ask the next patron what she needed.

Sarah grinned and stepped up to empty the stuffed book cart. It was loaded, and her mind began trying to string together titles that were promising for Patty's Prophecy. As the patron left, Sarah looked over at Lubna and said, "Looks like it took quite a bit of time to draw that tattoo. I guess you were holding hands for a while." Sarah wanted to see how Lubna would describe her creative liaison with Stanley. She was looking for juicy details and Lubna sensed it.

Lubna tipped her head and arranged her arms in the air, holding both hands with her middle finger and thumb touching. She looked like a Bollywood dancer as she shifted her shoulders up and down and then twirled once, fluttering the shawl. "A blending of cultures, tribal and exotic at the same time, old world and new world."

Sarah quipped, "Did you say tribal and erotic?"

Lubna laughed lightly, like a flute, "That, too."

Sarah giggled and thought for a moment about Lubna's relaxed, welcoming attitude about Stanley and what might turn into an erotic exchange. She yearned for a similar feeling. Sarah was drawn to Adam and felt comfortable with him at times but couldn't shake her anxieties about where it might lead. Lubna seemed to delight in the cultural differences between her and Stanley, and in the potential of something more. Lubna, Sarah realized, wasn't scared. Sarah couldn't imagine Lubna talking baby talk to Stanley like Jennifer had done with Zach.

Lubna appeared to have a strong inner core. Maybe it was that growing up as a military brat gave her confidence because she'd had to adapt to so many new situations. Or maybe it was being Buddhist? Or maybe it was just Lubna? She had clearly set her own course. Choosing to be a Buddhist in a Hindu family in a country of Christians was gutsy, and becoming a doctor was not an easy goal to achieve either. Besides, she was funny, and Sarah sensed that Lubna was caring. As she looked back on her emotional exchange with Stanley, overheard by Lubna, she realized Lubna had probably started a conversation just to be sure Sarah was OK. It added to her appreciation of the library job. She was making friends that she truly valued, who seemed to really care about her.

"So did you check with Adam? Does he want to come bowling?"

"He said yes. He's going to stop by sometime this evening and talk about it. I think he was going to try to meet Stanley again tonight and go on another quest," Sarah surmised.

"Ah, an *X Files* moment! I just radioed Stanley and asked him to go up to the decks. A student stopped here a few minutes ago and said he thought he heard someone screaming for help. It may mean that someone up there already had a 'sighting,'" Lubna replied.

"I wonder if it may just mean someone is stuck in the elevator again? Patty Nakamura helped me get out of the deck elevator the other day, and I was stuck for about ten minutes. I'll bet Stanley is checking that elevator right now. He called to have it serviced, but maybe there's a *ghost in that machine*." Sarah said.

"If there is, it might be a real *X Files* experience tonight for Adam, there's a full moon." Lubna answered.

"What do you mean? You aren't a believer in werewolves, are you?"

73

"I've worked the desk for three years now. You develop a healthy respect for circadian rhythms and other cyclical phenomena when you regularly have weird experiences on nights with full moons. It's just understood that if anything unusual happens, it's most likely to happen on a night with a full moon," explained Lubna.

"So what kind of phenomena?"

"For example, I had a young woman come up to the desk during finals week and start to say something. She passed out cold, and her head hit the tile floor and it sounded like someone dropped a bowling ball. It was probably a case of low blood sugar or something, but that was a full-moon night. Another full-moon night, two freshmen came in the front door running with sanitary napkins taped to their arms and sanitary napkin boxes on their heads. They ran through the building and ended up breaking some lights in the decks because the boxes hit the lights as they ran. It was a sorority/fraternity prank, but it was also a full-moon night. No surprise," panned Lubna.

"Hmmm, was the girl OK?"

"I think so, we called an ambulance. She seemed to be reviving as they wheeled her out. It's not the only ambulance call I've made, and they have all been on a full-moon night. I find the statistics pretty convincing, and circadian rhythms are an area of study I want to look at when I am in medical school," Lubna asserted.

"I'm convinced. I guess I need to align my calendar and work schedule with a moon phase calendar – just to be prepared," Sarah said.

"Not a bad idea," Lubna answered as she picked up the radio. "What's up, Stanley?"

Sarah stepped forward and asked an approaching student if they needed help. The student was looking for reserve materials, and it took Sarah's attention to help the student find the needed materials and go pull them from the shelves. Most of the time, she could show them how to get the items off the campus net, but professors still left a few books at the library behind the main desk. When she finished helping the student, Sarah turned to see

Lubna walk over to the handicapped counter and lean over to talk with Stanley. He was wearing a gray shalwar kameez, and Sarah could see his right hand was covered with an elaborate henna tattoo. Sarah thought it was subdued compared to Stanley's regular attire of colorful thrift shop wear, but maybe it was because his other tattoos were covered by the long sleeves. He'd combined it with a turquoise squash blossom. Sarah had to admit the two cultures made an eye-catching combination. Stanley had clubbed his hair, rather than wearing braids. Right now, he had a serious look on his face. He stood next to a young woman who'd been crying and seemed shaken.

Lubna turned and walked over to Sarah. "Can you stay up here at the desk? I'm going to the back office to help Stanley. The campus police are on their way. When they get here, will you show them to the back office?"

"Sure," Sarah replied. She felt her forehead wrinkle with concern as she watched Stanley escort the young woman to the office door. A campus cop arrived a few minutes later, and Sarah held down the desk for an hour by herself. She was still there when Adam came through the front door and smiled.

"Hi, Juliet. The moon is really beautiful tonight. Perfect for a balcony scene," Adam said as his eyes sparkled. "Have you seen Stanley?"

"Yeah, but he's involved right now with the campus police. I think you may need to find a spot to relax or study, and I can tell Stanley where you are when he gets done," Sarah replied.

Adam self-edited, "Anything wrong? Duh, I guess the police wouldn't be here otherwise. Let me rephrase that. Is it serious?"

"I don't know the details, but they've been talking to the campus police for a while. I haven't seen a SWAT team, so I guess it may not require reinforcements. But there's a young woman who looked pretty upset," she said worriedly. "Lubna is in the back with them. I think she is a calming influence."

"My ears are burning," said Lubna as she walked up behind them.

"Is everything OK? I hope no one got hurt or anything," Sarah said.

"I think it is all going to be OK. Nothing physical. The young woman was just freaked out. It seems that she got caught in an elevator on the decks. It must have been the one that you got caught in. She was stuck for a few minutes. Stanley was on his rounds and heard her screaming; luckily, when he pushed the outside elevator button, the doors opened," Lubna said. As she finished, Stanley, the student and the campus policeman left the back office. She paused for a minute until Stanley came back to the desk and greeted Adam.

"Hey, Sarah, looks like your calm attitude isn't universal. That girl got caught in the same elevator you were in. Luckily, she had her cell phone and called the campus police who contacted me, and I was able to get her out before they arrived," Stanley said. "Too bad it was after she started to freak out."

"I can see how being in the dark could scare someone," Sarah replied.

"Well, that's just it; she had her phone and turned on the phone's light. She called right away, but then when she was just standing there waiting for someone to get there and let her out, she started hearing some scratching noise that seemed to come from the elevator shaft above her. Or that's what she said. She called to them, it or *whatever*. But the scratching stopped. Then it started again and included some tapping. That started to bother her, and she tried to get a response again. The tapping stopped, but no reply. That's when she began to freak. At first she thought it might be a repairman, but then when no one replied, she said she felt watched. Then the tapping started again in a pattern of some sort. She said she dialed again and started yelling at the ceiling, telling whoever or whatever that she was on the phone to the campus police. That's when I arrived and got the doors open. She didn't start crying until after I got her out. I guess it was the adrenalin."

Adam asked, "What do you think it was? Do you think it might have been one of your spirits or something more tangible?"

"The security guard in me thinks this seems like a prank, maybe a fraternity thing. The shaman in me kind of agrees with the guard. But I could be wrong. I did hear someone walking away in a hurry above us when the girl started crying. Could have been just someone curious about the noise we were making who took off. Or it could have been the prankster," Stanley said. "It was something solid because I saw a shadow though that glass flooring. You know how that is, the lighting shines down and you can see something kind of vague. She was still in the middle of telling me the story so I really only put it together a few minutes later. The campus cops are going to do a couple of rounds through the building tonight. I think that will run off any pranksters. I've turned off the elevator," Stanley replied. He turned to Lubna. "I'm going to step up my rounds, too. Be sure you keep the radio close by. I may ask you to watch the exit if I see anybody that I want to track."

"I guess this isn't the night to go on closing rounds with you," Adam said.

"Actually, if you're interested, I'd like to have you. It wouldn't be a night of spiritual pursuits. I'd probably ask you to check some bathrooms with me or stand in a stairwell as I sweep a floor. Sometimes pranksters try to hide in the building as we close. We've got quite a few motion detectors and cameras that would detect them and alert the police once the alarms are engaged. But they don't know that. If I miss someone, then that just means they'll trip the alarms after we leave, and I'll be talking to the security supervisor tomorrow explaining how I failed to get everyone out of the building. She'll get the call from campus cops after I close and will probably be asleep when that call comes. I would rather she not get that call," Stanley explained.

"Sure. I was hoping to walk back to the dorms with Sarah, so I was planning on hanging out studying for the next couple of hours anyway," Adam said, as he raised an eyebrow and looked at Sarah expectantly. Sarah nodded and smiled. She felt her heart skip a beat and then mentally chastised herself for being too eager.

Some students walked toward the desk, and Sarah and Lubna turned to help. Adam and Stanley headed down the stairwell. The next few hours were uneventful except for a call from Stanley to look for a guy "with his pants hiked up to his chest and glasses."

Lubna told her, and Sarah felt a momentary hair-raising at the back of her neck. It sounded like the guy who had breezed past her in the basement the day she had been trapped on the elevator. A few minutes later, that guy walked past them in the same hurried manner he'd had in the basement. He had a backpack and a zipped jacket, so you couldn't see his pants. But Sarah had seen him before and figured he was probably still wearing his pants the same way. "Lubna, did you see the guy who just left? I think he wears his pants up pretty high. I saw him in the basement the other day," Sarah explained.

"I didn't notice, but he'll be on the security camera," Lubna said as she glanced at the clock. "It's 12:14. I'll tell Stanley to pan through the recording to this time and see if it's the guy he wanted us to look for. Thanks." Lubna smiled.

Stanley showed up a few minutes later, and Sarah overheard Lubna telling him to check the 12:14 time on the video log and see if it might be his guy. Stanley went to the back office computer station, and Adam came to the desk while he was checking. It was about time to start the closing round, and Adam had that look on his face. It was the *X Files* adventure look, as Sarah had started labeling it in her mind. He was grinning like a kid about to climb into a go-cart. "I see you're pumped. Ready to kung fu anybody hiding in the bathrooms?"

Adam chuckled and looked down at his sweatshirt, "I'm not really dressed for ninja activity. But I'm hoping the sweatshirt makes me look bulkier than I feel. Maybe I should apply for a job as a security guard? I might apply down at the Weather Center. I spend a lot of time there in the OWL room trying to do some forecasting from the student lounge. It's such a new building, though, there's really no creep-quality."

Before Sarah could answer, Stanley walked up to the desk and said, "The guy Lubna said you identified is the guy I saw on my rounds tonight. He didn't really do anything, but I just had a feeling about him and wanted to make sure he was out of the building when I closed. Thanks for tagging him."

"Sure," Sarah replied. "I saw him the same afternoon I got trapped in the elevator. He brushed past me in a hurry when I took the cart of books down to the basement. He didn't do anything but didn't answer me when I apologized for almost running into him with the cart. He just grunted and hurried off. So I looked at him as he walked away and noticed his pants."

"He was there when the elevator messed up that day, and he's here tonight. Probably just a coincidence. I saw him leaving the elevator in the decks when I took the out-of-order signs upstairs to hang them on the doors. The elevator was turned off, so it wasn't going anywhere, but he had apparently tried it and gave up just as I arrived. I told him it was shut down for repairs, but I had the same experience. He didn't really say anything, just hurried off like he was uncomfortable or something," Stanley observed, then turned to Adam and said, "Ready to go on the closing round?"

"Yep," Adam said, and they headed toward the main elevators. Stanley walked with Adam, and Sarah could hear him explaining that they would work their way down from the fifth floor this time. Adam and Stanley stood waiting for the elevator to arrive, and Sarah couldn't help making a mental comparison. Stanley was in his Pakistani/Native American garb and Adam in blue jeans and a sweatshirt. Somehow it brought to mind an Indian guide and a settler about to go hunting, something you might see in a Western painting. Her gaze swung from them to Lubna about the same time Lubna turned to Sarah. She had also been watching them. Simultaneously they grinned and Lubna whispered, "*X Files!*"

"Yeah, the adventure begins," Sarah quipped. "I think they are having *too much* fun."

"I'm glad Adam is so interested in you. It gives Stanley backup. I worry some about him confronting a bunch of fraternity guys. He's got a really laid back demeanor, but I think his clothes might make him the butt of some jokes," Lubna said.

"I remember when I first met Stanley, I thought he was a little wacky. So I get it. But I think you may be underestimating Stanley's gravitas. He's very professional and I think his clothes are more cool than kooky. He's got more of a Johnny Depp vibe."

"You really think so? I like his artistic persona. He doesn't seem to care whether other people like his clothes or not. I think an artist has to be willing to walk alone to really tap his creative self. You know, medicine is both an art and a science. I'm hoping I will be good at it because I'm analytical, but I'm drawn to the artistic," Lubna said.

"I've noticed that you're drawn to this particular artist," Sarah replied, smiling.

Sarah saw Lubna look down and thought she blushed although her brown skin masked it, so Sarah wasn't sure. "Stanley was really kind to the young woman who was upset. He handled it all really well. It was … reassuring and compassionate," Lubna said.

"Good qualities in any person, artistic or not," Sarah observed. It made her think about Adam and what drew her to him. But rather than thinking of his character qualities, she recalled kissing him while the cold wind whipped her hair around their faces. That daydream kept interceding as she and Lubna talked about the shalwar kameez Lubna had given Stanley and about clothes in general.

"You said you thought Adam was interested in me," Sarah finally succumbed to her curiosity. "Do you think so?"

"Really, *really*? You're asking me that when the guy shows up to walk you home at one in the morning? Besides, Stanley keeps saying that Adam is somehow entangled with you. I'm not really clear about entanglements, as Stanley sees them. But it's his way of saying there is something that runs deeper than basic attraction," said Lubna.

"Do you mean physical and spiritual gravitation – to use Stanley's words?"

"Maybe. I think he means more. I think he sees some people as having relationships influenced by past lives or spirits, or something like that, in addition to physical and spiritual compatibility," Lubna explained. "I'm still figuring out Stanley. I think I'll be working on that for quite a while."

Sarah thought about Lubna's remark as she went to empty the outside book drop before they closed. There was quite a heap of books stuffed in the drop, and some had fallen on the foam bedding below and were splayed open. She got down on her knees and began collecting the pile. One book had landed on its back and had fallen open. She'd noticed that it had been written in. It was a pet peeve of Sarah's, not taking good care of library books. She had spent lots of time with her mother as a very young child in the children's section of the public library. She and her mom and sister had attended story times, and Sarah learned to cherish books back then. When her dad got sick, books transported her away from a sick house to places where she could forget about her dad's illness for a few hours. She always hated to see a book that had been defaced by someone; it took away from the private moments she cherished when reading.

That thought made her recall her dad and Lubna's remark about relationships. She wondered if her interest in Adam was spurred by her dad's spirit, which she still remembered feeling that first day of the Frisbee game. As she looked at the book, her heart bumped twice. The writing in the book was pretty nasty. Clearly someone hadn't just been making notes. Sarah walked quickly to the desk and said, "Lubna, I found this in the book drop. It's been defaced, and, frankly, the writing is kind of psycho. Should I leave this for Luke to review? I'd hate to see someone else pull the book off the shelf and then find this stuff inside." As Sarah said it, she screwed up her face as though she had just tasted spoiled food. "This is a book from the children's literature section. I don't think any young kid should see this stuff. It's really anti-women and is a pretty negative rant."

Lubna looked at the book and had a similar reaction. "I would put it on Luke's desk with a note about where you found it. Before you do, let's see who has it checked out. Hmm … it's not checked out. I guess someone stole it and marked it up, then put it in the drop, hoping it would be seen by someone. I think this person is looking for a reaction. Otherwise, why wouldn't he just put it back on the shelf? It's sure creepy," Lubna observed. "I've been working here for three years, and I've never seen anything like that. Usually, most people who write in books are just underlining or making notes."

"Yeah, this is worthy of a television show psycho. I generally think television shows are ridiculously exaggerated. But this kind of stuff makes me rethink that," said Sarah. She walked to the back office and laid the book on Luke's desk, then sat down to write a note explaining where it was found and that it wasn't linked to anyone's library record. As she finished the note, Stanley and Adam came in. Adam walked over, smiling.

"We had contact! I think I saw, well, heard, something," Adam spoke with the enthusiasm of a kid who just got off a rollercoaster. "We were in the old basement, and a whole row of books just fell off a shelf. We were only a few ranges away and when we got there – nobody. We looked at the whole floor, Stanley on one end and me on the other, and nothing, nada. We went to pick up the books and guess what? The books were all about medieval architecture stuff." Adam answered his own question before Sarah could reply. "Stanley thinks it is significant. Only he's not really sure how to interpret it. He thinks it might be a spirit trying to get our attention about something."

"Really? Maybe it was just a bookend that slipped? I've noticed books that have fallen over after someone removed some titles. Maybe someone was there a few minutes before and took a book and the whole shelf just fell over as the spines shifted, a sort of slow-motion thing." Sarah surprised herself because she sounded more pragmatic than she felt. She wanted to think that a spirit might be there and that it might even be her dad, but her analytical bent made her present a logical alternative. She said it before she realized that it might deflate Adam and for a moment regretted her unedited reply.

"That's what I like about you, you're always thinking," Adam grinned and seemed to actually enjoy her skepticism. "It occurred to me that it might be a change in humidity. Tonight, the relative humidity is going up and paper swells. So, you see, I'm not just buying into the spirit thing without critically examining alternatives. But it doesn't explain why that shelf and not others would be affected. I'm open to another possibility until we can prove otherwise. Besides, it feels like I'm in *Ghostbusters*. I consider it homage to Harold Ramis. He was a hero of mine."

Sarah replied, "I liked Harold Ramis, too. I was sorry when I read he died. My dad liked him and Bill Murray, too." Sarah paused and then said, "Let me check with Lubna, then I'll get my backpack and we can leave. I've got Calculus tomorrow morning pretty early." Lubna was turning off the lights and told Sarah it was OK to leave. She and Stanley would lock up. Adam and Sarah bundled up and headed out. It was cold and calm. Adam still seemed pumped and was walking fast. Sarah began to trot next to him. She had long legs, but Adam's were longer. Adam grabbed her hand and took off, jogging along, and Sarah found herself matching his pace and enjoying the brisk, clean feel of the night. He slowed after they had passed several classroom buildings on the South Oval.

"I needed to warm up and burn some adrenalin," Adam said, as he slowed to a regular walk.

"I was beginning to think that you were trying to get away from me as fast as possible," Sarah joked.

"Never, Juliet," Adam replied, with his suggestive eyebrow raise. "Care to go skating?" Adam grabbed both her hands and pulled her toward the street. The sidewalk had been cleared, but the snow had partially melted and refrozen, and the street, untrafficked, was like a skating rink. As they stepped from the curb, Sarah's feet immediately slipped sideways, and Adam grabbed her around the waist. There was a scramble of feet and a push and pull as they each over-compensated back and forth. Sarah began laughing and held on as the struggle to maintain their footing was lost, and both landed on their backs, legs splayed out. The backpacks softened the fall for both of them, and they laughed uncontrollably.

"Well, Romeo, or should I call you Thumper? That was a Disney experience," Sarah said, as she gasped for air between giggles. "A person doesn't need to go to a movie for entertainment around you," she said, as she grabbed Adam's arm and pulled him back to the ice as he tried to rise.

"Hey, do you know that penguins toboggan on the ice on their stomachs and use their feet to push themselves? Like this," Adam said, as he grabbed her jacket sleeve and began trying to dig his heels in and get some traction. Sarah mimicked his foot action, and they slowly began to push themselves along the ice, using their backpacks as impromptu sleds. It worked for about a hundred feet, and then they began to slide sideways as Adam's longer legs delivered more push than Sarah's. Stopped by the curb, they lay for a moment breathing hard. Sarah reached over, grabbed Adam's jacket and pulled him toward her. She kissed him, forgetting that they probably looked strange, lying on the ice in the street. Flashing blue lights reflected on her closed eyes, made her gasp and pull away. She looked over and saw a campus police car. The window rolled down and the cop said, "You two OK?"

"Yeah, we're fine," Sarah yelled. "Just … sledding!"

The policeman shook his head, like he'd seen many similar incidents, "Best take that off-road," he observed dryly.

"Yes, officer. We were just getting up," Adam said, as he scrambled to his knees and crawled to the sidewalk for firm footing. He held his hand out to Sarah and pulled her up quickly. They waved to the policeman who closed his window as he pulled away. Silently, Sarah laughed hard, until she had to take a breath and realized when she did that Adam was also laughing but trying hard to look serious until the light changed and the policeman pulled away. They let loose when the car had moved on and laughed so hard Adam put his hands on his knees for support. Sarah was giggling so rapidly, she felt herself nearly pee in her pants. Neither seemed able to stop. The laughter went on through a change in the traffic light and kept resurfacing as they crossed the street walking toward the dorms. Every time it seemed to subside, Sarah would look at Adam and begin laughing uncontrollably again. She even involuntarily grabbed her sides as the muscles began to ache from the repeated spasms.

They arrived at the dorms. Sarah felt limp. Adam looked over at her again, and unexplainably she cracked up. Again, she and Adam laughed until they gasped for breath as they collapsed on a bench. Sarah couldn't remember laughing this hard since she and Abby, sitting in the back seat of the car on a trip to Yellowstone with their parents, heard her mother describe a friend being so sick that she lost control of her bowels. Her dad had misheard or, perhaps, willfully misheard, because he replied "Lost control of her vowels?"

Sarah's mom started to laugh and correct him at the same time, but Sarah and Abby caught the joke and started laughing, too. Her dad had to eventually pull over, because they all were overcome with laughter that seemed to feed on itself. Later, that phrase often made its way into a conversation as her dad's illness got worse. It was his way of coping when any of them asked how he was feeling. He'd respond, looking very serious, and say, "I had a temperature this morning. It's gone now, but I lost control of my vowels about an hour ago." That usually started them all laughing, and they'd really laugh hard. They wanted to laugh so badly. It was a release from the tension and anxiety they all shared about their dad's condition.

Adam sat and caught his breath, wiping a tear that had been squeezed from his eye by the laughter and the cold air. Sarah said, still a little shaky, "I can't sit on this cold bench very long, all that laughing almost made me pee."

"I can warm you up some," Adam said, pulling her closer, eventually sliding her onto his lap. "This is warmer for me, too," he said, as he pulled her cozily close and began kissing her. Sarah felt the warmth of affection relax her, but she hadn't finished her laugh parade just yet. When she pulled back to take in a deep breath, the recollection of her dad's joke caused her to begin shaking with mirth. She tried but again was lost to laughter. Adam's mind had clearly been diverted to other thoughts, because he chuckled slightly and ran his hand up Sarah's thigh, hoping to rearrange her thinking. But it was no good, Sarah began giggling as she warmed up and couldn't seem to divert herself. After a few minutes, Adam gave up and appeared to rock Sarah like a child, patiently waiting for her to stop laughing and take his foreplay more seriously. He didn't really seem to mind, as he soaked up her warmth and flicked her hair away from her face. Adam definitely wasn't in a hurry, he appeared to be savoring the arrangement.

"I'm still laughing because this reminds me so much of another time, when I laughed this hard," Sarah gasped.

"Tell me about it," Adam said, as he turned to look into her face and shifted her position to turn his direction more."

Sarah told the story of her family's vacation joke, and they both laughed. Adam responded with a story of his own, talking about his family hiking in Yosemite. His dad loved hiking. They'd parked their car at an overlook, and his brother and sister had gotten bored when their dad was taking pictures. They'd climbed the upper side of the mountain road looking for arrowheads on the rocky slope. When their parents finally noticed, their dad yelled for them to come down. His brother started down but tripped on a rock and began running and flailing his arms to keep himself from falling forward head over heels, picking up speed as he went. As Adam sat in the car looking toward his brother and the road, he realized a car was coming around the curve and it looked like his brother would arrive at top speed in the roadway at the same time the car came around the curve. His dad ran toward the road, waving his arms, and yelled, "Slide!" Luckily, his brother had been learning how to slide in Little League and fell backward, slipping on the pebbles and sliding feet-first into a bush by the edge of the pavement. The car's driver never saw him and passed him without even slowing. His mom stood with her hand over her mouth and then yelled to his sister to sit down and wait for their dad to come get her.

Sarah sat up suddenly and said, "What's funny about that? It sounds like your brother almost died!"

"Yeah, that wasn't the funny part. The funny part came later, when we got back in the car and everybody started talking about what happened. We were all commenting on how scared we were, and then my sister said she thought my brother looked like a character in a television show like *Modern Family*. Then everybody in the car started coming up with episodes they liked, and we all started laughing and couldn't stop. I think it was a combination of being scared and being on vacation. But it lasted for about half an hour until we stopped to go to the bathroom. I'll always remember that moment and how good I felt when everyone was back in the car and we were all laughing and safe. We all took pictures of my brother, who posed like he was falling every time we stopped at overlooks. My mom pulled out those pictures last Christmas and it was pretty entertaining."

Adam shifted underneath her, and she realized she must be getting pretty heavy, so she jumped up from his lap and said, "It's pretty late, and tomorrow is Calculus. Thanks for the toboggan ride, I'll always remember it. Too bad we didn't take any pictures," Sarah said, as she hugged Adam and pecked him again on the cheek. As she climbed the stairs, she made a mental note to peck Adam on the cheek regularly. It reminded her of how she always said goodbye to her dad when she left for school every morning. She just couldn't leave the house without that superstitious habit when her dad was sick. Adam had begun to be important to her. She couldn't help it, whenever she cared for someone she created some little habit that she convinced herself was like a protective amulet that would keep that person safe until the next time she saw them.

Sarah wondered how that all fit into her spiritual cosmology, which even to herself sounded a bit mixed up, part voodoo, part agnostic, part who knew. Of course, it hadn't really protected her dad, but maybe it just protected the feel of that relationship and gave her some satisfaction … although a wave of regret about other things she had done enveloped her as that thought emerged. Before she entered the hallway, someone else opened the stairwell and a surge of cold air pushed past her. For some reason, she had the same feeling she'd had a few weeks before on the first night when Adam walked her home and the wind felt like a push from her dad. That push from the cold air this time took her mind off the sadness, and she headed for her room. She saw Jennifer hugging a pillow as she tried to silently get to the bathroom and change without awakening her. She crawled into bed and drifted off, chuckling silently as she thought of Adam on his back like an awkward penguin.

Bernadette looked out at the snow-covered campus from the top turret window. She shared the space with a couple of pigeons that had overcome the attempts of the physical plant workers to exclude them from this dusty, secluded and cold space. It wasn't connected to the big attic but was part of the 1932 structure and getting to this particular space was hidden and often forgotten when physical plant workers retired. The last time the room had been visited was when the roof sprung a leak three years ago, and old blueprints were pulled out as the roofers tried to trace down the drip and repair the flashing that had pulled away from the wall during the last earthquake that modestly rattled the campus. Bernadette couldn't really remember the campus ever having many quakes during the time she had been living there, but she had read that oil well fracking was probably the cause of the recent flurry. They were little quakes, but Bernie always felt even the small ones. They seemed to really rattle her bones down deep.

As she looked out the window, she watched the two students slide on their backs on the South Oval ice and thought about the evening. Whenever Bernie moved in, she always considered a building her home, and she defended it as necessary. Tonight had been a curious mix of events. She remembered waking up on the elevator roof and sensing a figure below, tampering with the elevator panel buttons. Bernie had a sixth sense, or so she named it after she had watched that movie with the kid who saw dead people. She didn't like this individual. Hate seemed to radiate off him, and his movements were furtive like he was trying to get away with something without being seen. Since getting away without being seen was one of Bernie's well-developed skills, she recognized a fellow sneak when she saw one and wondered what he was up to.

Patience was a virtue she had. Long days of sitting still, quietly observing campus life on the South Oval had imbued her with a variable time sense. She could watch ice melt and often did.

Granted, her attention span wasn't that long, but she often found herself watching something, fading out, and hours later still sitting and watching. It gave her an appreciation for small changes and subtle developments, kind of like time-lapse photography.

The guy Bernie had watched in the elevator smugly sauntered away, looking both directions. Bernie stretched and prepared to drop down through the service hatch to see what had been done to the panel. The sound of footsteps stopped her, and a young woman entered the elevator. The door closed, and the elevator failed. The young woman tapped her cell phone, set the flashlight and dialed the campus emergency number. Most coeds had the number on their contact list after dorm orientations. Calmly she waited, while Bernie leaned on her elbow and watched silently through the crack around the hatch. Patience was Bernie's close friend, but planning an escape route that avoided the elevator service crew occupied her mind. She couldn't get off the elevator roof without dropping down the hatch or waiting until the elevator moved to the top floor, giving her a chance to exit into the attic and hide among the barrels of old nuclear war survival rations from the 1950s. If the elevator didn't engage before the repairman entered the attic, it could be dicey trying to hide without being noticed.

While having these thoughts, her ears pricked at the sound of scratching, and she saw the girl go on alert. She looked down through the cracks at the bluish light of phone LED. Another scratch, then tapping could be heard. She had to acknowledge that the creep was subtle. The coed called out, and it went downhill from there. After some yelling and another call, the security guard arrived and the door opened. Bernie wanted the guard to leave quickly so she could follow the creep and get out of the way of any repair person. Antsy, she must have unwittingly made a sound, because the guard looked upward and seemed to focus on Bernie's position. His look was quizzical, and Bernie might have worried, but for the coed's near hysteria, which distracted him. He escorted her away, taking one last, long piercing look at the elevator ceiling after locking down the elevator.

As she dropped through the hatch and landed softly on the floor below, Bernie thought she heard footsteps fade on the floor above. Because the decks were an old architectural wonder in which the glass floors were suspended on the book stack structure, it was easy to hear walking above, because the stacks themselves actually penetrated each floor, leaving gaps between the glass slabs and the book shelves. Noise from above or below was easily tracked, and, depending on the lighting, even shadows of people on the floor above could be discerned, if one was watching carefully. The old brick walls separating the stacks from the Great Reading Room had been painted white, to make it seem less dark and eerie, and emergency phones had been installed, but the stacks character wasn't so easily dispelled.

The books themselves added to the feeling of age, dust and secrets long kept. Anyone walking through the stacks alone seemed to sense that the stacks had seen many a student come and go. It smelled like history, if you could believe that history smelled.

Pissed, miffed, irritated, all these described Bernie as she tried to track the direction of the sound. A pissed Bernie was a dangerous Bernie. How dare this creep invade *her* library. Sidling quietly to a book aisle, Bernie pretended to scan the shelves in search of a book while listening for activity on the floor above. Bernie was practiced at looking casual and innocent. She marked the footsteps above. Putting on her middle-aged professor persona, she climbed the metal staircase and got a clear look at the creeper. He looked smug, a young man with a freckled face like a Howdy Doody puppet. Bernie observed that hanging by the elevator had given him an adrenalin rush. That adrenalin addiction was a mistake, because that little mischief celebration let Bernie tag him, and Bernie was ruthless when she felt her territory was threatened. She'd plan a special treat for this creep.

It wasn't Bernie's first experience with pranksters and creeps. But still Bernie felt surprise at the ordinary, rather pleasant face of the creeper. Somehow they never looked greasy or malevolent, like Hollywood characters. Only in the movies do creeps look like creeps, she thought. It was scary sometimes how the nastiest types often had the most innocent expressions. She wondered what this guy did in his spare time when he wasn't scaring women in the elevator at the library? Probably it was something unsavory and maybe something hurtful and destructive. Hmmm, she knew he'd be back.

They all came back whenever they needed another adrenalin rush. As she watched the creeper head through the doors to the reading room, Bernie thought again about the security guard who had seemed to hear or sense her presence. Frankly, Bernie couldn't remember the last time anyone had even noticed her, much less stared in her direction. No, wait, she did remember that an odd Asian woman had hurried away nervously when Bernie stood in an adjoining aisle in the book stacks.

She'd used her most practiced middle-aged professor persona that day, but the parasol lady still seemed unsettled. Surprised, Bernie had considered changing her outfit. Fashion wasn't generally on Bernie's agenda. Maybe she was looking unkempt or strangely dated? You could stand out sometimes by just not attending to details. Her attention span being what it was, Bernie wandered off to go find a copy of the student newspaper to compare her outfit with photos of what students were wearing these days, temporarily forgetting about the guard, the parasol lady and the creeper. She could just detect the smell of coffee emanating from the Chaucer Variorum office in the basement and took the old stairwell. As she slowly walked down the staircase, she looked up at the old painting of angels that had been in the stairwell for nearly a century and bemusedly thought her own outfit might be a bit drapey – a little too much like one of the winged spirits rising into the air. How on earth did a painter decide what an angel should wear anyway?

Chapter 6

"The man who does not read has no advantage over the man who cannot read."

--Mark Twain

The bowling alley was under renovation, so the carpet was patched where the shoe desk had been. As they entered, the crew looked up at the new scorekeeping displays installed in the lanes. Animated characters moved over the display, making comments on the last ball played by the birthday party of kids at one end of the building. Sarah, Lubna and the guys walked over to the new shoe desk. Sarah had not completely overcome her aversion to wearing shoes worn by other people, and she hoped the new desk meant new shoes. She hesitated but convinced herself that the thick winter socks would likely protect her from someone else's foot fungus. The attendant was spraying Lysol into a pair of shoes and turned to place them on the shelf. Sarah relaxed and then wondered if she was getting a little too much like Patty Nakamura? That niggled at her as she told the attendant her shoe size, and she could only think, "Crazy is as crazy does...."

Lubna animatedly grabbed her arm and pulled her toward the rows of balls. "Start sticking your fingers in the balls, and pick one that seems to fit without being too tight. Your fingers need to slip out easily when you throw the ball," Lubna said. Obviously comfortable in her surroundings, Lubna steered her toward the lighter weight balls, explaining that Sarah would probably want a lighter ball but needed to be careful about sizing the holes for her fingers, since the lighter the ball the smaller the holes. "If your fingers stick, you'll end up in the gutter," Lubna explained. Lubna took control, seeming to enjoy the process of outfitting them and describing how the score was kept. "Of course, the new displays do the scorekeeping automatically, so you don't have to do the math yourself." Adam listened and then admitted he had played a couple of times, but elaborately lowered expectations by focusing on the number of gutter balls he'd thrown.

Stanley seemed unconcerned, "I like the design above the alleys; it's got a retro 1950s feel to it, and did you notice that the scoreboards have cartoon characters that pop up when you have a gutter ball? I wonder what company designed them."

Adam replied, "Interesting. Lots of companies out there that focus on gaming and service screen design these days. Could be an interesting specialty for someone with an art degree. Do you have to take courses in web and computer design?"

"Some, but I'm beginning to think that I'll minor in web design or computer-generated imaging. Job opportunities are better. There are art students who look down on graphic design, but I figure the more you get your art out there, the more cultural influence you can have, even if no one recognizes your work," commented Stanley. "Think about it. We're being impacted right now by the graphics on the wall, the carpet design and all the colors. That makes a difference. Lots of research these days on visual design and human behavior."

Don't forget the smells," said Lubna. "The smell of a bowling alley always makes me feel good. We had a bowling alley close to our house in Lawton, and my family went there twice a week. I remember experiencing some racism when we first started going, and I was really awkward. I whined to my father, but he just persisted and even got us lessons and enrolled us in the kid's league play. Once I got better, I felt I earned some respect from the other kids, and they stopped harassing me in the bathroom. From then on, I liked coming and smelling the sweat, stale shoes, alley wax and French fries. They smell like victory." She grinned as she paraphrased *Apocalypse Now*.

"I feel that way about being outside with a Frisbee. My dad and I spent hours on a Frisbee golf course he designed in a park by our house. The sounds of kids playing on playground equipment, and even the smell of dog poop, does it for me," Sarah smiled back at Lubna, who giggled.

"Dog poop, that makes an easy gift idea," Adam grinned back. "My dad's a big walker. Our family took a lot of hiking/backpacking vacations in national parks. Packing a backpack with Twizzlers and Nutty Buddies is a smell I remember that always got me excited as a kid. Campfires and s'mores are another smell and taste that make me feel good. I remember always playing with the fire and ending up with ember burns on all my jackets. My mom would just shake her head when she pulled them out of the dryer. I guess all that and the smell of pines and mountains does it for me. What about you, Stanley?"

"The smell of fry bread, beans and grape cobbler, and the sound of a stickball game give me that feeling. We attended powwows and family reunions at the same time every year," said Stanley, who moseyed down the alley and released a ball with more grace than accuracy. The game generated lots of laughs. Sarah and Adam were the least able, and Lubna quietly made suggestions after several balls rolled directly into the gutter, "bend your knees more" or "hold your hand so your thumb points toward an arrow on the alley guide." Stanley was light on his feet and seemed to quickly get his ball under control. Lubna was a petite powerhouse who released the ball so close to the floor it barely thumped. She was a pleasure to watch, quiet and smooth with surprising accuracy and the ability to pick up some difficult spares.

"Fine, very fine," said Stanley admiringly. "She's so graceful she makes it look natural, like she was born to it." Lubna turned back, clearly uncomfortable with the praise.

Diverting the conversation, Lubna asked, "Stan, did you decide if the elevator incident was a prank or a spirit, or something more sinister?"

"Actually, I got some pretty mixed vibes that night. I felt a real presence in the elevator when I opened the door. I'm sure the

94

elevator was messed with but not by a spirit. We had a security guard meeting yesterday, and Luke said the repair people found it had been tampered with. I can't define what I felt exactly. It wasn't nasty or brooding, but it was there. The panel had definitely been compromised by a living person, though," Stanley said.

Sarah jumped in, "What about the books that fell over? Do you think that was related to a real person or to the presence? Could it be a spirit that is associated with the girl herself? Do you think spirits can move real objects?"

"I'm positive the feeling wasn't about the girl. The feeling was strongly tied to the elevator. As I walked the girl downstairs, I definitely felt the pull fade as I walked away from the elevator," said Stanley. "The guards are going to put that elevator on surveillance. There's a camera installed in the elevator, but it wasn't working. It seems to go on the blink a lot. The high-pants guy might have something to do with the tampering," he added, hesitantly.

"I've been thinking about the books that fell over and still think that was more than relative humidity changes," said Adam. "I don't think it was coincidence that the books were all about gothic architecture. Maybe that was the act of a spirit and shows physical objects can be manipulated?"

"Do you think the defaced book I found in the book drop is tied to any of this?" Sarah asked.

"Like I said, I'm getting multiple vibes on all this, and I can't say. Luke is reporting it to campus police because he thinks it is pretty threatening, psycho stuff. Jeff, the afternoon guard, said the writing reminded him of some graffiti in the third floor men's room that was painted over a couple of months ago. Similar wording, similar threats to women," Stanley said. "Could be different perpetrators, could be totally unrelated. I'm thinking the vibes I got in the elevator are not likely to be associated with the writing. I just didn't get a feeling of menace or anything like that. In fact, the vibe I got was female … ish."

"What's female … ish? Are you saying it's a transgender spirit?" Adam asked, lifting an eyebrow quizzically.

"You are asking me for spin, and I'm going too far into this trying to interpret. I don't think spirits focus much on gender identity. I'm just saying that the vibe I got was like standing next to Lubna or Sarah, not like standing next to you," Stanley answered.

Lubna interrupted, "Let's continue this analysis over a banana split. The yogurt place on campus corner makes a great one. Since you all came bowling with me, I'm willing to treat."

"How can we say no to that? I'm into caramel and marshmallow crème. How about nuts; I like lots of nuts," Sarah remarked, as they headed for the door. "Seems like we should have some nuts, since we're talking about another kind of nut...." Silently, Sarah wondered about nuts in general and was again reminded of her avoidance of germs and whether she was more like Patty Nakamura than she hoped. Adam's smile in her direction changed her mood, and she began a discussion comparing hazelnuts to pecans and almonds and walnuts. She'd read on the Internet that walnuts were really good for you, lots of antioxidants. The rest of the evening was a delicious discussion of health foods, pizza, gluten and the multitude of contradictory information on the Internet. Sarah felt more relaxed than she could remember being since she was a child at a family picnic.

It seemed like Lubna, Stanley and Adam felt like a little family. She wasn't sure why exactly, but she thought it might be how she felt about her three companions. Somehow they had formed a bond of friendship and caring. She'd text her sister about the evening when she got back to her dorm room. She was sure Abby would like Lubna and particularly hoped she would like Adam. She and Adam opted to walk back to the dorms and left Stanley and Lubna discussing worldwide tattoo art and their theories on why tattoo art is so popular these days. Lubna was on the side of tribal needs, and Stanley was arguing about the transitory nature of personal statements and the feel of permanence that body art inspired.

"Did you hear that TED Talk on posing?" asked Adam. "It was pretty engrossing. The woman who gave the talk has done research on posturing – like 'standing tall' kinda like assertive yoga stances. She actually found that standing in an assertive pose in a bathroom for two minutes before a job interview lowers your stress hormones and makes you more appealing in a job interview."

"You're kidding. What kind of posing?" Sarah asked.

"Well, the example she used was Wonder Woman, with her fists clenched, hands resting on her hips, looking strong," he replied, as he lifted his eyebrow in that typical quizzical challenge. "It's also supposed to raise your testosterone levels." As he said it, he stopped midstride and stood like Wonder Woman puffing out his chest."

Sarah giggled, "So that's it, you just stand like that, and your hormones change and you become a job interviewing god?"

"Sex god, if you don't mind," Adam replied, beating on his chest and grabbing her. He leaned her backward in an exaggerated dance pose, while kissing her. She wanted to cooperate, but couldn't help laughing.

"Hey, I want to try!" Sarah broke away and stood like Wonder Woman while Adam watched. After a moment, she grabbed Adam and tried leaning him backward. The kiss happened, but she didn't have the same leverage and they both teetered, just barely catching themselves before they collapsed on the ground. "Guess I'm not a candidate for *Dancing with the Stars*," Sarah mused.

They walked over to their favorite bench, and Adam pulled Sarah into his lap as he had done the night of the penguins. After some time had passed, Sarah looked at Adam and said, "I had a great time tonight; in fact, I'm still having a great time. Thanks."

"I wish I'd said that first, but consider it said. In fact, I expect I'll think about tonight over and over again and have a good time every time I remember it. I think I will even enjoy throwing the gutter balls. You know, they say that every time you remember something, you change it and it becomes a different memory just because you recall it."

"You are full of fascinating trivia tonight!" Sarah countered. "I'm gonna remember fewer gutter balls then, and maybe I'll believe I can actually bowl. But I'm thinking I'll remember more kissing."

"I can remedy that," Adam said, while pulling her closer. "This way you don't have to use your imagination."

"I'm thinking I'll be using my imagination anyway," Sarah replied.

Adam pulled back and looked into Sarah's face, "So are you interested in more reality?"

"How about you?" Sarah asked tentatively.

"Hey, I'm 19 years old, and I don't have to stand in any poses to generate testosterone. I'm always interested," Adam stated frankly. "I'm supposed to be interested. That's what guys do."

"Women have hormones, too. But ...," Sarah replied.

"But...."

"But I like you; I like being with you. I don't want to get into something that ends our friendship. Besides, I'm not really ... experienced, and I don't want to seem like a dork," she said explosively, like she'd dropped a bomb. She actually felt some weight drop from her shoulders with the admission, and she looked at Adam anxiously awaiting his reply. "It's not like I haven't seen movies and am ignorant. It's just that ... I'd like to know you better. I'd like to be sure that I can count on your friendship before I count on your, you know," Sarah rushed on, "I've spent the last couple of years getting through things I thought were really hard. I'd like to do more than just get through. I'd like to take time."

"Well, I am a guy, and I'm trying real hard not to ask myself how much time are we talking and how can I arrange this so that it is as little time as possible?" Adam said, lifting his eyebrow. "But I'm not exactly Mr. Experienced either. We are freshmen, and it's not like we have some fatal illness. Am I really saying this? I'm beginning to wonder if I do need to do some posing to get my testosterone levels a little higher...."

"I think your hormones are just fine," Sarah laughed. "I'm pretty sure mine are, too, based on how much more attractive you look right now. I'm thinking that my imagination is going to make you look even more compelling while I lie in bed tonight."

"Hmmm, well keep the expectation bar down to something obtainable. I don't want to be competing with myself and losing," Adam muttered with a small hint of irritation.

"You don't need to worry," Sarah said softly, touching Adam's face.

"Hmmm ... watch out. I'm secretly going to be posing every time I go to the bathroom," Adam said.

"Well, I guess you'll be getting a lot of job offers," Sarah laughed, as she felt Adam chuckle.

"I'm going home to see my mom and sister tomorrow. I have a ride with Jennifer. We're going to leave early. See you Tuesday?"

"Probably. I'll text you. I have that presentation in Meteorology. I have to do some predictions using the Mesonet system data and OWL that's due Wednesday morning. Good night ... Wonder Woman."

"Night, oh captain, my captain," Sarah whispered.

"*Dead Poets Society*?" Adam queried.

"I watched a lot of Netflix when my dad was sick. He'd lay on the sofa too sick to do much else, and we would watch movies together. I tried to pick inspiring movies, but I should probably have focused more on funny ones or maybe it's just pirate speak," she observed, as she turned toward the dorm. Adam stood and watched her enter the lounge door and then slowly turned himself and headed to his dorm.

Sarah opened the door to the dorm room, expecting to see Jennifer in her bed with the computer lighting her face. Now that Jennifer was in the room more, she had a habit of studying with the lights out by just the computer screen. Surprised to see the room empty, Sarah's anxiety immediately surfaced. Before she got into bed, she checked her phone. She found a text from Jennifer. It said, "Staying at Zach's, be back to pick you up in morning...." Sarah sighed. At least she wouldn't lie awake worrying about Jennifer being hurt, but she knew she would still worry.

It had been really nice to see Jennifer returning to herself and focusing on school again. Sarah liked things orderly, and she had begun to appreciate the lack of drama. It was unsettling to see Jennifer reunite with Zach, because she feared that Zach had sought Jennifer out to bolster his ego and have a ready source of comfortable sex. She didn't trust Jennifer to assert herself. Zach would be the pilot and Jennifer, well, maybe she had learned something from the breakup. Sarah lay in bed wondering about herself and Adam. What if they did take their relationship to the next level? Would she change? Would Adam change? Right now, she wanted Adam as a friend more than she wanted the other. She loved being with Lubna and Stanley and Adam as a team. It felt like family. She nodded off, making a mental note to watch Lubna and Stanley's relationship and see how that affected the group. Sarah was sure about one thing, she didn't want what Jennifer had with Zach. It still creeped her out. And what about the creep that was running around the library? That was disturbing. Somehow, though, she thought Stanley had something that made her feel empowered and Lubna, well, Lubna was a force to reckon with. She grinned as her eyes closed, and she remembered her first, non-virtual strike.

Chapter 7

"Any sufficiently advanced technology is indistinguishable from magic."

--Arthur C. Clarke, *Profiles of the Future: An inquiry into the limits of the possible*

He was back. Bernie had been dozing on top of the elevator. Sleep came easy whenever she entered the warm building on a cold day. It seemed like she had barely lifted herself onto the elevator roof, when she folded her legs and curled into a cozy little spot next to the warm engine. It could have gotten hot, but the elevator was used so rarely that it emanated just enough warmth to encourage sleepiness and a sense of relaxation. Her eyes opened, and she instantly felt the raw anger that permeated from the elevator cabin below.

The buzz of a battery-operated screwdriver confirmed his presence. Bernie hated to be awakened suddenly from a good nap – who doesn't get a little irritable when you are startled awake? Sometimes creeps were especially irritating, and Bernie couldn't contain her immediate response. She thumped him, whacking the floor beneath her and causing the elevator to shudder. He jumped like a rabbit, looked up and ran the minute the elevator door popped open. The button panel was left leaning against the elevator wall and the panel wiring was exposed with a thumb drive protruding from the USB port inside the panel. That was fun! She'd scared him enough to abandon his thumb drive. Maybe that would be enough to expose him to the campus police and get him out of her library.

Before that thought coalesced, she heard footsteps creeping back and watched him slowly move in, looking at the ceiling of the elevator, warily eyeing the security camera. The creep was back! He stepped into the elevator, grabbed the thumb drive and skedaddled. Humph. Bernie didn't know that the elevator wiring had been refurbished and now operated from programmable panels. Apparently, the upgrade was done in the summer months, when she rarely went inside, preferring to roam the campus gardens. Now it was clear that the creep had some expertise that made it possible to mess with the panel functions.

Perhaps she would have to enlist some help? Bernie herself had managed to disable the security camera so she had contributed to the problem. After all, you couldn't be climbing through the ceiling of the elevator with the security camera pointed directly at you. She'd rationalized it but was feeling a bit guilty now that the creep had capitalized on the blind spot. The building was in Bernie's bones, and she felt somehow that she'd let it down, this place, this sanctum. Her sanctum. And, frankly, the sanctum of countless students.

Bernie had been watching students come and go for decades. Occasionally, she latched onto one particular student and followed, like the lanky, intense young woman who had gotten her off her butt after a long hiatus of sitting and watching the world transpire. It seems she would have to get the lanky girl's help, as the creep wasn't easily scared off. Bernie assumed the creep would look for a different spot in the library to play his games, but she would start cruising the decks at night in an effort to identify his patterns and construct her own game plan. This could be fun.

First, Bernie dropped down through the elevator and sparked the emergency stop. An alarm sounded, and she moved toward a book aisle and calmly scanned the shelves, looking at books. She found a shelf with a loose book end and pushed, causing the contents of the shelf to slide to the floor. Then she moved over a couple of aisles and waited. It took almost 30 minutes for a security guard to appear. The young woman, with a radio in hand, entered the elevator and pushed the emergency stop. The ringing of the alarm ceased. She looked anxiously at the panel cover on the floor of the elevator and stepped gingerly out the elevator door, almost tiptoeing. Then she turned and noticed the pile of books on the floor in the aisle across from the elevator.

Bernie could hear her whisper, "Whoa. This is weird." She pushed the radio button and a voice answered.

"This is Luke."

"Luke, this is Rachel. I'm on deck 3 at the west elevator. I found the emergency stop alarm was pulled, and the elevator panel cover has been removed. I also see a mess of books on the floor in this area. Can you check the elevator camera video and tell me if you see anything happening here in the last 30 minutes?"

"Sure, Rachel, hang on," Luke responded. The young woman walked over to the mess of books, looking at the shelf where they had been. She pulled her phone out and snapped a picture of the mess. She set the radio down on a nearby shelf and began rearranging the books in order. She was quiet and seemed to look through the book stacks in both directions while she worked, as if she expected to see someone or something. Before she finished, a voice emanated from the radio.

"Rachel, it looks like that camera isn't working. I've got nothing. I'll call the service people and get them to fix it. How bad is the mess? Is the elevator working? Do I need to call the elevator repair people, too? We've had a lot of trouble with that elevator. I'm on my way up," Luke said.

"I don't really want to test the elevator with the panel cover removed. It looks like someone might have tampered with it. I think you should notify campus police. I don't think it is anything too serious, but something doesn't feel right around here, and I don't know if someone was trying to – well, rig the elevator is some way," Rachel theorized. "It's a little sinister."

"OK, don't touch anything in the elevator. And, Rachel, move away from the elevator and stand behind some book stacks. Stay in the area and don't let anyone get on. I am on my way, but I am going to stop and pick up some ribbon to cordon off the area until it is cleared by the campus cops and the camera is operating reliably. Don't go into the elevator and don't try to key it off. You never know …," he speculated. "I don't want you to touch it."

"I hear you loud and clear. I'll be standing in the aisles by the doors to the 1952 addition, close enough to direct people away from the elevator and far enough away to be safe if anything explosive happens, I hope." she said, swallowing audibly.

Bernie was pleased. The alarm and book mess had the results she hoped for, maybe even more than she imagined. She was almost floating when she quietly walked into the lounge area but stopped suddenly when she realized that the creep was sitting in the most comfortable of the overstuffed chairs, pretending to work on his laptop. Not wanting to call attention to herself, she walked through the lounge into the Great Reading Room and stood near the doorway, scanning the shelves of dissertations. The creep sat by himself, looking up as Luke and another student worker hurried up the staircase with two rolls of yellow caution tape. As they rounded the corner into the decks, Luke called Rachel, "Rachel, we're here in the lounge, and I'm putting up the tape on the lounge entrance doors."

"I'll stand in front of the doors from the 1952 addition, but we probably need someone to tape off the staircase from the fourth deck," she replied.

"OK, I'm sending Fotis with some tape to go up the two staircases and tape them off. Stay by the doors until I come get you," he advised.

The sound of several footsteps coming up the staircase caused the creep to tense slightly, but he started typing on his laptop like he was really serious about studying. Moments later, two campus police topped the stairs and surveyed the lounge. One walked over to the creep and said, "Sir, I need to ask you to leave this area. Please continue your study in another part of the building."

"What's wrong, officer? This is my favorite study spot when I have a test. I can usually concentrate here," he lied.

"Nothing serious. We're just clearing the area temporarily. Please move downstairs into the newer addition."

The creep made a show of picking up his backpack and packing his computer up. He stood up, pulled his pack from the floor and placed it on the chair. He unplugged his computer from a nearby outlet and slowly rolled up the cord, stuffing it into the pack. Bernie could see his face because he had turned away from the officer to complete the task, and she was sure he was suppressing a grin of excitement. Bernie was livid and wanted to point to the creep and shout a warning to the police, but that would have broken her lifelong campus MO. Never, ever call attention to yourself. Always stay under the radar.

She fumed as she watched the creep head down the staircase. Both officers walked over to talk to Luke and began asking about the situation. Bernie wanted to stay for the show, but her curiosity about the creep overwhelmed the entertainment value of the elevator incident, especially since she already knew that there wasn't a bomb or anything substantial to be found. She slipped down the staircase following the creep. He was headed for the exit and left through the old entrance. Bernie hesitated. Once she had staked out a building, she rarely left. The cold air that swept into the atrium discouraged her from trailing The Creep.

She had settled on naming the lowlife The Creep or TC for short. She didn't want to know his real name. This name would do. As she stood in the atrium watching him walk southward toward the Physics Building, Bernie smelled stale coffee in the Library School offices. She sighed and inhaled deeply. She wondered if he was coming back. That kind of attention usually discouraged ordinary miscreants, but this one had surprised her. His addiction to excitement had caused him to park himself in the lounge, even when he must have heard the elevator alarm – or maybe because he heard it? Hmmm … that was creepy and certainly convinced her that her nickname was appropriate.

Bernie slowly turned and followed her nose. It was almost five and the Library School office would be locked soon. She looked into the doorway and noticed the secretary at the copy machine, engrossed in changing toner. Bernie floated silently through the office back into the dark conference room and entered the turret bathroom. She'd hide here until the office was closed and then help herself to the old coffee and crusty, day-old doughnuts.

Bernie had come to love this particular secretary, because her habit of putting off the cleanup until the morning always afforded Bernie an opportunity to clean up herself. There were several other offices and a staff lounge in the library, but this particular office was Bernie's favorite. She was a carboholic, and anything sweet was irresistible. Apparently, she shared her love of carbohydrates with the office assistant because there were always cookies or doughnuts or leftover Halloween candy or some sugar-laden something to be had. Fifteen minutes later, the secretary turned off the lights and locked the office door. Bernie stepped out of the bathroom, lying down on the conference table. She needed to collect her thoughts.

As Bernie focused on the problem, she recalled the lanky female student who she had originally followed into the library building. Bernie surmised that working with the young woman would help her execute a more complicated strategy to evict The Creep. It would have to be subtle, but she could do it. She'd done something similar back in the 90s. There had been a transient who had taken up residence in the library, hiding a sleeping bag in the old stacks. Bernie had "haunted" the guy in the late night hours and eventually spooked him into moving on. That was back before all the cameras and motion detectors so it had been easy to move around. She'd enjoyed ghosting him.

Spring was getting close, this would be a lovely way to usher out winter and clear the decks. She rolled over and looked out the tall casement windows at the stars, surprised that darkness had settled. A snooze would be perfect. She often awoke with a plan when she slept on a problem. The table was cold and hard, and Bernie felt like her bones were aching. She slipped off the side of the table and crawled under it, comforted by the padded carpet and the secretive darkness under the heavy oak conference table. She loved these tables. They had been made for the original library building and matched the gothic décor in the Great Reading Room. The carved wood embellishments above the book stacks and her friends, the seraphim, who inhabited the beams of the domed ceiling, were all made of oak. Now that she thought of it, the angels had many eyes. Between the security cameras and the watchful eyes of the carved faces who looked down on everyone, Bernie felt the task of discouraging The Creep from further nastiness would be simple, a party really. A smile formed as she drifted away, warmed by the old steam radiator.

Sarah was running late and hurried toward the library from the Chemistry Building. It was quicker to enter at the new entrance, but her superstition about the library made her walk the extra steps to go around and enter from the south, looking up at the gargoyles and greeting them silently, maintaining her ritual of befriending the building's guardians. After her nap, Bernie had been hanging around the south doors, lolling on the settee in the lounge just inside. She perked up when she saw the lanky brunette and stood up, walking toward her. Bernadette said, "Excuse me, can you direct me to the coffee shop?"

The young woman seemed confused, paused with an unsettled look and then walked through Bernadette, visibly shuddering, but hurrying along as if she was late for something important. Bernie felt as if the particles of her bones shifted and swirled like a pile of leaves swirled by an eddy in the wind. She was spooked. Did that really happen? Did the young woman walk *through* her? It was weird, and Bernie stumbled toward the settee as she felt her way back to some semblance of coherent shape and substance, her billowy garb seeming to float like a ruffled flag, refusing to settle quickly. Sarah - that was the girl's name. Bernie gained some intimate knowledge with the encounter because she now knew the girl's name, her work schedule and understood her preoccupation with her father's death and many more thoughts.

It was so invigorating! She felt herself stir with the energy possessed by youth. Thoughts of a young man, Adam, warmed her bones in ways she had forgotten long ago. It was both disorienting and intriguing. She sat for some time, trying to corral her thoughts or Sarah's thoughts. Her thoughts seemed to blend together with Sarah's like a pot of soup when you added an ingredient and stirred. The longer Bernie sat and tried to grab the additional thoughts, the more she felt like she was reaching for a fluttering butterfly. She was mesmerized when a thought settled, and she could examine it and then be drawn toward it as the thought took flight, leaving her to watch it become fuzzy and distant. She concentrated, and, as each thought occurred, she focused on incorporating it into the soup of her consciousness. Time passed, days passed. As Bernie incorporated the fleeting thoughts, she became more time-aware.

She now began to realize that her naps could run for days, and she humbly began to understand that she wasn't quite as clever as she thought. It wasn't her clever behavior that had allowed her to sneak around the campus. She was insubstantial, another being altogether, and it frightened her to know that she had dallied on campus for years – who knew how long? She was just now realizing that she wasn't sure how she had been counting time, but she knew now that she could feel time on a human scale. Who was she? What was she?

Two days passed as Bernie collected the thoughts like a butterfly collector with a net. Slowly, she brought herself into the present and stood up on shaky legs – did she have legs? She looked down at herself and noticed legs, but as her mind (if she had one) considered the thought that she might not have them, her legs seemed to waver and grow transparent. So, what I think I am, I am? Do I actually have thoughts if I am insubstantial?

The conundrum of particle physics and personhood defied Bernie's attempts to understand, but the youthful energy that coursed through her made it seem like a problem she could address later. Now, the present, buoyed her spirits, and she decided to undertake the adventure of discovering who or what she was and how Sarah's energy made this self-realization possible. In fact, she felt a giggle well up inside her and lift her incorporeal self up to the rafters. She floated and found herself giggling and somersaulting in the air above the students entering and leaving the building. Whatever, whoever, whomever, he, she, it … the feeling was exhilarating and inspiring, and a kernel of gratitude and affection grew in her for Sarah.

Whatever that girl needed, Bernie would provide, if she could. Sarah's anxieties and grief for her father had come through in the encounter, and Bernie felt she could assuage some of those feelings if she put her mind to it. In fact, was it her mind or Sarah's mind? Had she cooked the pot of consciousness so long that she was no longer a separate entity, but part Bernie, part Sarah? Was her time sense Sarah's or was it the new Bernie, part Sarah, part Bernie? Or ... the introspection began to tumble around in a confused mess and Bernie paused. Go with it, was the thought that emerged, and so she floated through the library like a child at Disneyland for the first time, looking at the building, the people, the books from a whole new perspective, and Bernie grinned, a wholesome, unchecked grin of pure wonderment and joy.

Sarah had a wave of nausea as she turned the corner by the display cases and headed for the circulation desk. A momentary feeling of disembodiment passed over her, and she seemed temporarily disconnected from her legs. There was a feeling of time slowing and then speeding up again. It was awful, it scared her. Immediately, Sarah thought of Patty Nakamura and wondered if she was losing it. Maybe it was just her period. She'd started it yesterday afternoon and was bothered by cramps for hours. She'd eaten breakfast, but maybe the oatmeal hadn't been enough. Perhaps her blood sugar was low. She grasped at any explanation that would make this feeling seem normal and not, well, crazy.

Truth be told, Sarah thought she'd heard a voice when she entered the library. She even thought a form momentarily, shadowy, appeared and "touched" her. She wondered if she was hallucinating. She pulled her phone from her pocket and texted her sister. Abby was always grounded, and she asked her if her period had ever produced any similar experiences. Sarah had three minutes to clock in, but she stood still momentarily, hoping for a reply from Abby. "Eat something," was the cryptic reply, and that settled Sarah and she headed for the sort room. It was probably lucky she was starting work. It would take her mind off this odd feeling and give her something to focus on. Thoughts of her dad surfaced as she threw her books into the locker, and she grabbed a cookie from a tray of stale treats that were left over from a staff meeting and put out for the student workers.

Chewing, swallowing and crunching all grounded her, and the odd feeling of being insubstantial was passing. There were moments Sarah felt unsure about herself. When Stanley was talking about spirits and Adam seemed open to possibilities, Sarah hesitated to fully examine the ideas because she wanted to be grounded in what was real. She remembered having feelings when she'd read *A Wrinkle in Time*, feelings that made her drift away from the everyday and ponder the universe and the non-linearity of time as some science fiction writers and even some scientists proposed. As she began sorting books, she kept thinking about Physics class and the concepts put forth by her professor about quantum mechanics. If a person is more space than substance, molecularly speaking, how did that jive with feeling substantial? If you cut your finger and the molecules don't really touch the knife, why do you bleed? Had she just experienced some kind of molecular collision or shift in time or was her blood sugar just too low?

Sarah remembered talking to her friend Donna when they were both reading *A Wrinkle in Time*, and how Donna had told her that it made her nervous to think that she could see alternate realities. Sarah quietly agreed and wondered when she sometimes dreamed of flying and woke with a start, if that was what if felt like to hallucinate? Are crazy people just perceiving alternate realities with some extrasensory ability like Stanley's shaman-sense, or were they just crazy with mixed up neurotransmitters? That's why she had picked Engineering over Physics. Sticking with real world perceptions was easier than dealing with the floating anxiety she experienced when she tried to wrap her mind around quantum mechanics. If you let go of what was substantial in daily life, where would you end up? How far down the rabbit hole could you go before you got lost? What did she really feel and see in the hallway a few minutes ago?

Sarah pushed the loaded cart out the door and headed for the elevator. She hoped the physical exercise of wrestling with the cart would move her away from these thoughts. Exchanging ideas with Stanley was more grounded than wrestling with these ideas by yourself. Somehow Stanley seemed comfortable with alternative perceptions and ideas. He seemed to live in multiple worlds, and Adam was OK with that. Why did it unsettle her? It could be an opportunity to communicate with her dad, like they did in séances.

She knew why. It was because she thought people who believed they could talk to the dead through a Ouija board were crazy, and she thought the people around her would think she was crazy, too. Plus, she mused, how different was it from looking for Sasquatch? She paused and looked at the book she was about to shelve. *Nanoplasmonics,* that's what she was thinking about, it was a sort of rabbit hole, but, at the same time, it was a field that encompassed Engineering and would probably develop into an area she might have to master as new solar cells were developed based on Plasmon's.

Somehow the realization that she had talked herself through that unsettled feeling actually piqued her curiosity. It felt good. She'd conquered that anxious feeling and found herself putting the book back on the cart, intending to check it out and take it back to the dorm room. As she began pushing the cart back to the sort room, she turned her head, looking down the aisles. A young woman in a skirt and tights was absorbed in some books she'd pulled from the shelf, oblivious to her surroundings. The next aisle caused Sarah to slow, and as she did, the high-pants guy, who was lying on the floor with his head stuck through the bottom bookshelf seemed to crane his neck to look up the skirt of the girl in the next aisle. His eye caught the movement of the cart, and he hustled to sit up when his eye caught Sarah's.

Momentum kept Sarah moving, and she had passed two aisles before she put together the scene she had just passed. The high-pants guy was looking up the girl's skirt! She couldn't believe it and wasn't sure what to do about it. She knew she should report it, but decided to park the truck and go back and tell the young woman she was being victimized. She walked back quickly, and the high-pants guy was scrambling down the aisle with his shoes in hand. He turned the far corner of the aisle just as Sarah passed, and she stopped. He was headed for the north staircase and was moving pretty fast. She saw no reason to alarm the girl now that the high-pants guy was leaving. As she stood by the cart, she thought about his hurried escape and concluded that he had taken his shoes off to keep from being heard as he crept up behind the young woman. She turned quickly, leaving the cart parked, and hustled downstairs and back to the office. Luke was sitting at his desk.

"Luke, I just saw something I need to report to security. There was a guy upstairs that I saw sprawled on the floor with his head stuck through the bottom shelf and he was trying to look up the skirt of a coed in the next aisle."

Luke responded, "Did he have his pants hiked up to his chest and dark glasses?"

"Yeah," she said, curiously deflated by not being the first to discover the activity. "He is the same guy that we caught on camera the other night, because Stanley thought that he might be involved in the problems with the deck elevator."

"That's good news," Luke said. "So you think Stanley can find him on the camera history?"

"I'm sure of it. He marked the video a few days ago," said Sarah.

"This guy has been hanging around for several months, and I have had reports from other shelvers who felt they were being watched. I got some descriptions but wasn't sure we'd be able to identify him. Did you confront him or do you think he realized you saw him?"

"He got up really fast and headed toward the north stairwell. I'm pretty sure that he knew that I knew," Sarah reasoned.

"We generally have a few lonely, somewhat twisted dudes that hang around every year. Once the jig is up, they usually disappear. Sometimes they end up over at the public library. I'll get with Stanley, and we can email a still from the video. Hopefully, the camera got a pretty good shot of his face. I'll post the image on our security network and see if one of the guards can catch him. Thanks for being observant. If you ever see anyone else engaged in *questionable* activity, try to avoid a confrontation and get down to the office as quickly as you can.

We can usually catch them on the security cameras exiting and tag them. If he isn't a student, the campus police can execute a trespassing warrant, and we can keep him off campus. If it's a student, then we'll work with the student disciplinary system. My guess is this guy isn't a student, just a twisted dude," Luke surmised. "Maybe you'd like to become a security guard? You seem pretty observant. Next time I have an opening, I'll let you know. You'd make more money," he said, in an attempt to sell the idea.

"I hadn't thought about being a guard, but more money sounds good," Sarah said, somewhat hesitantly. "Does this kind of thing happen a lot?"

"Not really a lot. There's probably less weird activity here than in the bus station or another public building. The thing is, we're open a lot of hours and the building is a big place with cute coeds walking around. So it has a certain appeal. These days, what with school shooters and what not, we've got pretty thorough security and lots of technology. We're equipped and better integrated with the campus police so we're able to catch problems pretty quickly. This guy sounds like a voyeur, not like someone who would be seriously threatening. But it's good to know we got him tagged. I think he's probably going to stay away now that he suspects he's been found out," Luke said. "I've got a meeting in five minutes, but why don't you wait here in the office. Stanley's shift starts in five minutes, and he should be here. You can fill him in, and he'll get the report written up," Luke said, rising from his desk and gathering a pad and pencil.

"Sure," said Sarah. Luke's matter-of-fact attitude and lack of alarm about the situation calmed her. While she waited, she thought of conversations she'd had with her dad in the park when they were playing Frisbee. He was always alert to adults in the park who weren't with children and was always giving her lectures about not talking to strangers and trusting your instincts. She remembered that when she'd first seen the high-pants guy, she'd thought he was odd, not quite right. Maybe her instincts were pretty good.

"Hi, Sarah," Stanley said, as he walked up to the sign-in station and saw her by Luke's desk.

"Hi, Stanley. I'm waiting for you. Luke told me to report an incident to you about the high-pants guy. He said you would write up a report and get a picture from the video cameras to distribute to the campus police," Sarah said.

"Hmm, sounds like an interesting way to start my shift. Give me a minute, and we can sit at the security terminal. Do you mind if I record your description of the incident?"

"It's OK," Sarah said, surprised at the formality and Stanley's matter-of-fact attitude that seemed to mirror Luke's. She guessed this wasn't much out of the ordinary, but she sensed a high level of alertness in Stanley's calm exterior.

"OK, I'm going to ask a few questions to get you started, and then you just tell me what you saw, what happened," said Stanley. "About what time did the incident occur, and where did it happen?"

"I was on the third floor in the 1958 addition, shelving books about 1:30 this afternoon, and I was pushing my cart …," Sarah narrated the incident as she had told it to Luke. Stanley interrupted every so often to get more details about the victim and whether there was any interaction with the coed and the high-pants guy. After about 15 minutes of recording, Stanley hit the transcribe button and asked Sarah to read the report and confirm that it was correct. She watched Stanley peruse the video archive. He found the high-pants guy exiting at the place he'd marked a few weeks before and asked Sarah to confirm it was him.

"Yes, that's the guy. He had on a dark shirt and pants today but the same glasses," she observed. "Do you think this is the same person who has been tampering with the elevator?"

Stanley replied, "I kind of doubt it. This type of person usually is into his thing, so to speak. If that's what he does, it's generally what he concentrates on. It's what gives him the thrill. This guy seems to get off on observing and not being observed. The elevator is a little different. That person is trying to interact with the victim, actually scare them. I'm not a psychologist, but I think this guy's a lurker. Anyway, that's my spin," Stanley grinned.

"I guess this makes the spirit idea less likely. Seems like we just have some real live lurkers," said Sarah, borrowing Stanley's moniker. It made her feel better about the earlier incident when she'd felt like she may have hallucinated. Probably just low blood sugar and her period, she reasoned, comforted by the solidity of the explanation.

Stanley tilted his head and paused. "I don't know, I try not to discount anything." Stanley took a long look at her and slowly said, "Did this situation upset you?"

Sarah thought and replied, "Not really. I was surprised when I saw the guy on the floor and wanted to be sure I protected the girl, but I wasn't really upset. Do I look upset?"

"You've got a disturbed aura. I'm not much of an aura guy, but occasionally I seem to see flashes of light and color around some people. My grandfather had that ability and talked about it quite a bit. I saw something around you when I first walked in, but after you mentioned the incident, I figured it was associated with that," Stanley replied.

Sarah hesitated, but decided she would mention the earlier incident since she was in the security office and there was some privacy. She didn't want anyone to think she was a Patty Nakamura, but she felt a desire to confide in Stanley. After all, if anybody would be nonjudgmental, it would be Stanley with his shaman sensitivity. And she yearned to feel more solid, less confused, now that the diversion of the lurker was past. The odd disembodied feeling seemed to reassert itself.

"Well, do you have a few minutes? Something happened to me this morning, when I walked in the south entrance."

"Sure, we can be in here for the next 15 minutes. I need to go on a round on the half-hour, but we can stretch this interview a bit," he replied, encouraging her with his calm discussion of auras, like they were just part of everyday life and not weird at all.

"I thought I saw a shadowy figure and heard a voice as I came in the library, and it made me feel a bit dizzy and nauseous. I figured I just had low blood sugar or some biochemical, hormonal thing. But I'm still feeling funny, not really myself. I can't shake the feeling that something else is there." Sarah stopped, not entirely comfortable, waiting for a reply. She squirmed and trying to sound rational said, "I'm sure I just didn't eat enough this morning, and I haven't had any lunch, either."

Stanley was slow to respond. His eyes focused on her, and he breathed audibly, deeply. "Like I said, I'm not much of an aura guy, but this seems like really positive energy. Of course, eating is a good thing, but shamans often fast to get in touch with their spiritual selves. Maybe you were just more available to input when you walked in and saw something others couldn't see because they weren't. You know me, I don't want to spin it. But I wouldn't worry about being receptive to positive energies, whatever they are. Maybe you've got some shaman in you," he said, grinning. "Seriously, one of the shelvers, Jim, is getting a doctorate in particle physics. We have some pretty interesting discussions. Last time we talked, he said anything is possible and that's from the physical side of things, not the spiritual. Of course, it could be the flu," he said, shrugging his shoulders.

"I don't feel sick, just ...," Sarah struggled for a word that could capture how she now felt, "kinda shiny ... brighter ... lighter... warmer maybe."

"That all sounds like positive energy to me, and, frankly, it looks that way, too. Lots of steady emanations," he concluded, studying the space around her. "Let's plan on getting together after our evening shift tomorrow. Can you bring Adam? I'll check with Lubna, and we can have a late night pizza thing or something. I'd like to see how you are feeling in another day and whether I can still see your aura when we both have a full stomach. Like I said, this is pretty unusual for me. Auras aren't my thing."

"Adam's already planning to meet me at the end of my shift, so I'm sure pizza will be welcome. He's working on some project analyzing Mesonet data. He's planning on getting a lot done in the evening and celebrating when I get off," Sarah replied. "Stanley ... you aren't going to tell anyone about this, are you? I don't mind discussing it with Adam and Lubna, but I'd rather no one else thinks I'm a handyman for Patty Nakamura's wheelhouse," Sarah said, as she pictured Patty's gloves and odd demeanor, and remembered what she thought when Patty imagined germ warfare.

"Understood. It wouldn't be ethical of me. No worries," Stanley replied, getting to his feet.

"Thanks." Sarah smiled crookedly as she left the office and returned to the sort room to get another cart of books. She had another hour on this shift and needed to beef up her shelving stats since she'd lost time. Now that Stanley had made her feel less anxious, she could feel her worry fading. She was glad for the energy that seemed to accompany the sensation and pushed the cart with some enthusiasm out the doorway. Maybe it was a good thing … maybe crazy wasn't all bad or maybe crazy wasn't crazy, but something else. She grabbed another stale cookie, though, just in case.

Chapter 8

"To study courtesy, courtliness and chivalry in their various permutations in courtly literature ... is nothing less than to survey the history of thought on civilization."

--Kristina Marie Olson, *Courtesy Lost: Dante, Boccaccio and the Literature of History*

As Bernadette floated through the library, no longer obliged to delude herself about the corporeal nature of her existence, she watched students, professors and library staff go about the business of academia. There were moments of anxiety fleeting across her consciousness. These seemed tied to realizations, previously unfamiliar. For example, she was thrilled to realize that she wasn't really hungry but disappointed that savoring sugar-laden cookies had been a figment of her imagination. She didn't eat, hadn't really ever eaten that she could remember, but she'd enjoyed the idea of eating with gusto. What was she to look forward to, if the little pleasures of her "life" were not actually there? This was going to take some serious reeducation, nothing short of revolutionary.

One benefit she realized as soon as she "felt" sleepy was that she could go anywhere, even to the roof of the old elevator without difficulty. No longer bound by the physical world in her mind, she simply floated upward. With her senses, whatever they were, she could see the molecules of metal as she passed through them. Her own sense of cohesion relied on focus. If she let her thoughts drift as she floated through a structure, she could feel herself becoming solid, a part of the structure. If she focused, she passed readily through the structure and emerged as Bernadette on the other side.

Perhaps the tendency to merge with other objects was why she had taken on personhood. Assuming she was a human forced her to avoid merging with solid objects and emphasized a tie with the human world. Perhaps, long ago, she had gotten into the habit of thinking of herself as alive and simply forgot, after years passed, that she wasn't bound by human conventions? But, if that was so, just how many years had passed before she'd forgotten? Ten, two, maybe centuries? That was unsettling. How long had she been in existence? And just exactly how did she exist? She didn't have any gray matter, no real brain. But she had thoughts – she was unshakable about that.

Bernie began to classify those attributes. Thought, purpose, ability to observe the real world, and now the ability to merge with Sarah's thoughts and somehow retain them or maintain a link with the child. She'd begun to think of most of the humans walking in and out of the library as children, as she came to the realization that her own existence might have lasted through multiple human lifetimes. Classically, Bernie's attention span was her undoing. Floating back down the old staircase, now unworried about being observed, Bernie smelled the stale coffee and found herself drawn to her old familiar habits.

This time, she knew she wasn't drinking the coffee, but she reveled in the aromatic molecules, twirling in the air like a dog rolling in some particularly savory cow manure. She became the coffee, toying with the molecules. It was like drinking and digesting but with no need for a cup or a stomach. As she passed through the cookies, the sugar's crystalline structure fascinated her, and she felt angular, but brighter, like a diamond reflecting and magnifying light. She became light as it and she bounced within the sugar crystals. But as she did so, she began to lose the connection with Sarah, and she hurried out of the room, hoping to preserve the tie. Perhaps that's how Bernadette forgot herself? She'd reveled one day too long in some cookie or ceiling or other structure that caught her attention and then held it for how long? Days, weeks … maybe years …?

Sarah entered the library for her evening shift looking upward in her superstitious ritual of passing through the old oak doors of the south entrance. As she passed by the settee, Bernie emerged from her cookie fest and spied Sarah's lanky form headed toward the circulation offices. She followed, floating behind, studying the young woman. At the same time, Sarah felt that warming sensation and, just for a moment, stumbled. It freaked her out. For a brief instant, Sarah seemed to see herself from behind. Ugh, what was happening? Sarah paused and grabbed a chair next to a study table to steady herself. Patty Nakamura, here I come, was the thought that overwhelmed Sarah as she breathed deeply, hoping the feeling would pass. It did and, surprisingly, Sarah felt unusually refreshed and invigorated. Actually, she felt sparkly. It was weird, but she felt like she did when she was a child making greeting cards with cylinders of different colored glitter. She always got up from the kitchen table with glitter in her hair, on her clothes, glitter everywhere. Sarah loved glitter, and somehow the sparkle always made her smile inside.

Bernie had touched Sarah from behind and immediately sensed her discombobulation. She pulled away quickly and pushed the sensation of light that she had experienced in the sugar crystal. She was pleased when Sarah seemed to calm. It appeared to Bernie that if she got close to Sarah, without actually touching, molecularly speaking, that she could feel Sarah and Sarah had some sense of Bernie's energies. Keeping her "distance," though, clouded Bernie's perceptions of Sarah's thoughts. From a distance, Bernie couldn't get a clear read on what Sarah was thinking or how her experiment at pushing sugar crystal feelings was affecting Sarah, exactly. The child rose slowly and began walking toward the circulation offices. She seemed OK, and a tentative smile hovered at the corners of her mouth. However, Bernie could tell Sarah was wary and hyperaware of her own perceptions.

This made Bernie hesitate. She was desperate to keep this tie. Touching Sarah was better than rollicking in coffee and cookie molecules. Bernie vibrated with a living frequency when she touched Sarah, and the feeling was addicting. But Bernie had some distant sensation that she'd had that feeling before and had made mistakes. A memory was emerging, but it wasn't easily recalled, and it nagged her and made her stay several feet behind Sarah. Bernie tried to recall the memory, but it was more a feeling than a recollection and seemed to elude her like a mosquito buzzing around your head as you try to sleep. One moment it seemed close, the next gone. Yet it was difficult to tell if you or the mosquito drifted away.

Sarah arrived in the offices and checked in. She made her way to the sort room and began sorting a cart of books. She was anxious, but kept recalling a glitter-filled Thanksgiving many years ago when she and her sister, Abby, spent hours at their kitchen table creating Christmas cards for the upcoming holiday, while her dad read the newspaper on the couch nearby. It was a memory that always felt good. She clung to it when that other sensation intruded, the feeling of being disembodied. She shuddered and then, thankfully, the recollection of glitter-filled laughter came back, and she gave the cart a push out of the sort room. Just then, Stanley rounded the corner and full-stopped as if he had run into an invisible wall. Sarah automatically raised an eyebrow and said, "Hi, Stanley. Something wrong?"

"Uh, no …. Are you feeling OK?"

"Sure … well, yes and no. Remember the other day when I mentioned that funny feeling? I had a very similar feeling coming in the entrance again for this shift," Sarah explained. "How's my aura? You looked surprised when you saw me."

"I really can't see your aura today …," Stanley hesitated.

"I'm surprised; I feel extraordinarily sparkly, positively glittery today," Sarah smiled, feeling pervaded with the warm feelings of childhood holiday recollections. Bernie nudged Sarah steadily with faceted sugar feelings, somewhat enthralled by how Sarah was interpreting Bernie's intrusions. She was recasting the sugar crystal feelings into her own experience. Bernie supposed it was natural to do that, given that her own reality seemed less an objective state and more an interpretation based on her mood – she had legs, she didn't have legs. As that thought passed through her mind, she noticed Sarah blanch and she hurriedly pushed sugary thoughts again, realizing that her musings may have made their way into Sarah's consciousness. She was going to have to be really careful. It was easy to accidentally push a thought that would be hard to interpret or that would be just plain scary. Bernie focused and backed away from Sarah, slowly disengaging.

"I came by to confirm that we're headed for pizza after our shift ends," Stanley said, as he eyed her cautiously, his eyes moving toward the space behind her. Sarah turned her head, expecting to see Lubna heading to the sort room from the desk area, but no one was there. "What are you looking at, Stanley?"

"I'm not sure. Just thought I saw something for a minute. Is Adam coming?"

Sarah smiled, "Yes, he was planning on coming from the Weather Center about eleven. Said he was interested in walking with you, if you wanted the company. If not, he figured he'd get in some study time until we close."

"Lubna's in, too," he replied. Hearing her name from the front, Lubna ducked her head around the room dividers and grinned.

"My ears are burning, and my stomach is talking at the same time. It's a veritable body concert," Lubna quipped. "Pretty soon I'll be smelling pizza. This is going to be a long shift."

"Down, girl," Sarah laughed. "I've got a granola bar in my backpack if you need it." Lubna's hands came together in a prayerful way, and her head bobbed in agreement.

"OK, OK," Sarah said, as she turned toward the locker room to retrieve her backpack.

"What's up, Stan? You look confused or worried or something," said Lubna, as Sarah moved out of earshot.

Stanley seemed focused on something behind Lubna and started to reply, but as Lubna turned to look behind her, she noticed someone at the desk and left to help. Bernie hovered a few feet away, watching the male child carefully. He sensed she was there, she could tell. She floated toward him, and he tensed but stood still, breathing deeply. She touched him, expecting to learn him, as she had Sarah. Nothing. He saw her, but she couldn't seem to reach his consciousness like she had invaded Sarah's, however inadvertently. This child was different and it confused Bernie. She tried again. Again nothing or something. She felt something solid, grounded, not unwelcoming but impermeable, dual.

"I host a friend already, sparkle queen," said Stanley, quietly. "My friend doesn't want to share but may talk later. Please be gentle with Sarah." Stanley quickly turned and silently padded away in his moccasins, leaving Bernie to ponder. Frankly, she was blown away. It seemed as though this male child knew another like her, very well indeed. Seemed like she could be hosted? It was all so confusing. She floated upward until she reached the attic. She needed to chew on all this in a quiet place. She needed space. Bernie had lost a bit of her nerve and retreated to a long-held secret space, curling up next to the elevator motor. However her consciousness worked, she needed it to focus. She had lots of questions. How did this male child "host" a friend? There was still that mosquito of a feeling that she'd been here before and no good had come of it. Luckily, the humming of the motor gave her a sense of peace, and she spent the evening thinking. The rhythm of the motor helped concentrate her short attention span until she lost focus and the mosquito drifted away.

Sarah handed Lubna the granola bar and turned to a student who had come to the desk inquiring about class reserves. After she helped him, it seemed like the evening flew by. Lots of students were studying, lots of questions to answer. There was a small break in the steady traffic but little time to talk. Both of them took bathroom breaks, and the night students rushed in, all anxious to prepare for upcoming midterm exams. She must have checked out a packet for Comparative Vertebrate Anatomy 20 different times. Sarah asked one of the students about it and got an earful of concern about an upcoming lab test.

Lubna stood by listening and nodded. When the student left, she said, "That class nearly ate my lunch. The labs are long, and the graduate students who help don't always know the material themselves. I was lucky I had a good table of lab partners. Are you getting hungry?"

"I doubt I am as hungry as you. You've been talking about food all night! But pizza sounds most excellent," Sarah commented, as she emptied the return bin. "I'm glad it's closing time and glad it isn't a full moon. For some reason, I am ready to get out of the building and connect with the non-library world." Lubna looked up as the second floor lights went out, and Sarah recalled the two partially undressed students who had run out of the building at closing several weeks ago when she was a newbie.

This night was uneventful. Adam and Stanley walked up to the desk after the last bell sounded, and Adam stood talking with Sarah about his weather forecast for the upcoming week. He was hoping for an A and was pumped to see if his forecast the past three days was accurate. That was the challenge.

"These days, with satellites and radar, a few days are easy to forecast, it's the week-long forecast that's harder. We're in for it tonight. Expect freezing precipitation." Adam continued.

Stanley finished the lock down, phoned campus security and engaged the security system. They had 30 seconds to exit and didn't dally. Lubna, still hungry, excitedly talked about various pizza toppings with undue reverence, and Stanley reminded her that they would have to get at least two pizzas because he wasn't eating greens alone, he wanted some meat. They texted in their order, and the two walked ahead, debating about the best pizza in town. Adam and Sarah followed as they headed across campus to Campus Corner. They walked briskly, no stars to look at because it was overcast and just beginning to drizzle. The drizzle began to turn to small ice pellets as they arrived at the restaurant, and Lubna invited them all to her apartment which was a block away. It was beginning to turn into a treacherous walk. As Adam and Stanley carried the pizza and liters of root beer between them, Lubna and Sarah held on to each of the guys, providing additional balance as they all began slipping and sliding over the ice pellets. It had started to feel like walking on ball bearings.

"Maybe you should lie down on your back and push off with your feet like a penguin? We could put the pizza on your stomach like a baby penguin," Sarah quipped, recalling the night they played in the snow. Before Adam could respond, Sarah fell just as they started up the metal staircase. Adam dropped a liter of soda and grabbed for the handrail with one hand and Sarah's jacket with the other. Sarah went down, whacking her ankle on the riser, but didn't fall flat due to Adam's quick thinking. Sarah sat on the stairs rubbing her ankle while Adam gingerly retrieved the soda, which had rolled into the nearby parking lot and under a parked car.

Lubna quickly asked, "Are you okay, Sarah? Do you think you broke anything?"

"I'm not sure. I whacked myself pretty hard just around my ankle, but I think it is just bruised," she surmised, as she pulled down her sock revealing a sizable lump and some scraped skin. "No blood, but I'm sure I'll need some extra pizza. After all, healing takes lots of energy," Sarah quipped, quoting a remark Lubna had made weeks before when she was waxing on about medicine and Ayurvedic history. It hurt, but she focused on walking it off, as she limped up the last of the stairs, holding the handrail on one side and Adam on the other.

Stanley put the pizza boxes on the table, and Lubna grabbed a piece without ceremony, indicating they all should dig in while she got glasses for the root beer and pulled some hummus out of the fridge. She put that on the table and some plates, then handed Sarah a bag of frozen peas. Sarah raised her eyebrows, and Lubna grabbed her ankle, rested her foot on the coffee table and nestled the bag on her ankle, while devouring a pizza slice

"The ice will keep the bruising down and so will keeping the foot elevated," Lubna stated, as she came up for air and grabbed another slice of pizza. Good thing both pizzas were large because they had demolished one in about three minutes, Sarah thought. Her ankle throbbed as she warmed up, and a brief quiet descended on the group as they took their pizza as seriously as most college students.

Spooning some hummus on his next slice, Stanley said, "You should try this. I'm addicted to Lubna's hummus. It makes me feel like pizza is healthy." He grinned with his cheeks bulging like a squirrel with a load of acorns. The invitation was accepted with enthusiasm, and another quiet interlude settled on the group as they all warmed up and ate. No conversation was needed, and none was offered except for some minor polite murmurings when two hands started to grab the same piece. "That last piece is yours, Sarah," said Lubna. "I'm a pizza hawk; I count how many pieces everyone has eaten. And don't say you don't want it. No need to try and be polite. I'd eat it if I hadn't already had my share."

Sarah looked around. "After all, I am wounded," she said, as she spooned a small mountain of hummus on the last slice. Sarah was glad Lubna had no gender constraints on food portions. Although petite, Lubna could eat like a grizzly bear. Sarah savored this last piece with true pleasure. The others bussed the table, and Stanley retrieved a pack of cards from his jacket. They were all there to learn bridge.

"You know, Lubna, this will be the second non-virtual gaming experience I've learned from you," said Adam. "Do you have a problem with non-virtual reality?"

"Actually, this was my idea, Adam," said Stanley. "Lubna and I both game, but sometimes I think too much gaming exposes us to too many EMFs. I like to intersperse my virtual and non-virtual experiences. Give my personal electromagnetic field time to regroup. Use a different part of my brain, man. Lubna's the teacher tonight, but I'm glad to be staring at real faces. I was on the computer all day working on my senior project in graphic design. I prefer looking at beautiful brown eyes tonight," Stanley glanced over at a smiling Lubna who fluttered her eyelashes coquettishly and then guffawed

"He's just hoping for more hummus," Lubna said. "The man's a hummus addict. I make big batches and keep it in my fridge. It's useful. It got my oil changed. In fact, I'm thinking of putting it up as an alternative monetary system, like bit coin."

"I think that would have to be a commodity, rather than a currency. Kinda like tulip bulbs or pork bellies," Sarah answered, with a wince. As she shifted her foot, she realized it had stiffened up and the peas had warmed. Lubna picked up the bag, returned it to the freezer and came back with a bag of edamame and a bottle of ibuprofen. "I'm beginning to doubt that I can walk back to the dorms on this foot – at least it would be slow going," Sarah speculated.

Lubna parted the curtains and looked down on the parking lot below. "I think it would be slow going for anybody. I'd offer to drive you, but I think you are all going to have to spend the night. The cars are coated in ice, and there's a guy down there who's rocking his car but isn't getting any traction. Don't worry. I have some air mattresses in the closet. I bought them for the swimming pool when they were marked down at the end of the summer. Adam, you did a forecast, what do you think?"

"It's gonna get worse tonight, but the temperature should rise above freezing tomorrow. I expect by two in the afternoon the streets should be passable," Adam said as he got up and looked out the window. "Look at that power line," he said, pointing across the street. "It's beginning to droop. Ice is pretty heavy, and it's not coming down in pellets anymore; it seems to be really coating things. I hope we don't lose power, that'd be a bummer."

"We could tell ghost stories and turn it into a slumber party," Sarah said, remembering the odd feelings she'd talked about with Stanley and wondering if Adam would think she was crazy if she brought the subject up.

"I've got a pretty good *story*," said Stanley. "Let's play a couple of rounds of bridge and then decide what to do. We can't stop the ice storm, and we're in a warm spot with some of my favorite company. What's not to like?"

"There's whipped cream in the fridge and my favorite instant hot chocolate, a whole box, in the cabinet. I'll heat up some water. We've got the gas fireplace, too, in case the power goes out. Who knows? Maybe we'll make this a marathon bridge session," Lubna replied happily. Sarah shifted her foot as she texted Jennifer. She doubted Jennifer was in the dorm room because she was Zached again, but she didn't want her worrying if she happened to be there. Sarah could miss classes tomorrow if she had to. Jennifer texted back OK, and Sarah checked her calendar for assignments or quizzes. The throbbing in her foot was subsiding, but she was glad that she didn't have to try and walk the six blocks back to the dorms. She looked at Adam, and he looked back with that sidelong glance he adopted for *X Files* adventures. They grinned at one another, and he bid one no-trump, eliciting a lengthy commentary from Lubna on the points necessary for such a lead bid. Adam simply replied, "If you want to swim, you've got to get in the pool."

About 2:30 a.m., the lights went out, came back on and went out again. Lubna got up and turned on the gas fireplace angled in the corner of the room. The apartments had been built in the 70s, and the fake fireplaces had begun to be included in even the quick-built, student-oriented complex. It might have been a thoughtful landlord strategy because it was a way to keep pipes from freezing in just this situation. Stanley jumped up and opened the cabinets under the kitchen sink, then went into the bathroom and did the same.

"I don't think I have any candles, and I'm not sure I can see the cards well enough to play in the light from the fireplace," said Lubna. "Maybe it's time to hear your story, Stan. Let's turn the couch toward the fireplace, and I'll get the air mattresses. We can partially inflate them and push them against the wall. That will make a comfortable place to sit and listen. It will be like sitting around a campfire. That should make any story sound better."

"Are you suggesting my stories need atmosphere to enthrall? I'm an artist, I can create my own landscapes, use my verbal skills to create a vivid picture. I'm disappointed," Stanley opined, exaggerating his plight with some physical melodrama.

"Hey, they turn out the lights in movie theatres, and most scary movies are shot in dark hallways," Sarah said, consolingly. "Even great directors need some atmosphere to set the stage. I saw one of the student productions this fall at the theatre, and it was done with a minimal set. I guess I'm a sucker for atmosphere, but I was having trouble staying interested with nothing to look at but a couple of chairs and a card table. It made me feel a bit like … an engineer," she concluded, chuckling. "I know engineers get tagged for being humanistically unimaginative, but I'm thinking most people have a little trouble generating interest in that kind of situation, especially since we've all become dependent on special effects."

"I'm with you," said Adam. "I'm a sucker for games with great graphics and movies that awe."

"Well, we've set the mood," said Lubna, as she handed out a couple of blankets, pillows and cups of hot chocolate. "Weave your tale, storyteller. It's clear you'll be needing all your verbal arts with this crowd of virtual campfire dwellers. Maybe I should just turn on the TV and bring up a picture of a fire … oops, no power."

Adam said, "Wait a minute," as he pulled his phone from his backpack and checked its charge. "I'll bring up some crackling fire sounds to accompany the gas fireplace."

Sarah had to admit the sound of the fire emanating from Adam's phone did make the gas fireplace cozier. She remembered a camping trip with her family before her dad got sick. The smell of the hot chocolate and marshmallows added to the memory, because they had made s'mores, and she and Abby watched the embers burn down as they lay in the back of the pickup camper. Their mom and dad sat on lawn chairs and talked quietly into the night, retreating to the tent only after the girls had fallen asleep. Sarah woke late in the night and looked over at her parents, comforted by the paired sing-song of their snoring. The stars were bright, and a faint light emanated from the embers. It was the best; maybe because it was before her dad became sick and her life became dominated by anxieties about his illness.

"Sarah and I were talking today in the sort room," Stanley began. Sarah immediately went on alert and began wondering if he was going to reveal her confession. "I saw something that seemed to be lingering there. Something I don't think could be seen by just anyone. You might say it was my shaman-sense, but I got the same feeling I had about the elevator several weeks ago. I think the library is inhabited by a spirit guide."

"What do you mean when you say "spirit"? Do you mean ghost, entity, something scary or something good? I need some parameters here to process this," said Adam, with that eager skepticism he seemed to take on during *X Files* moments. Lubna merely looked to Sarah and pantomimed an x with her forefinger and grinned. Sarah knew Lubna was making light of the revelation and implying there was an element of geek adventurism to the tale, but Sarah knew something Lubna didn't, and she couldn't quite summon a grin.

"Well, that's where the spin comes in. I use the phrase spirit guide because that's in my lexicon. I have to call it something. Others might call it angel or demon, low blood sugar or schizophrenia. It all depends on your perspective. From my vantage point, it was a spirit guide. That's mostly because I … have one myself," Stanley said quietly, with a very slightly detectable defensiveness as he looked toward Lubna. "This isn't something I want just anyone to know, and I'm sharing with all of you because it's part of who I am. In fact, it's an important part of who I am.

Sometimes I think I am nuts, and other times I think I've been given a gift. Mostly, I keep it to myself because it's hard to explain, and everyone brings their own spin to the concept. Some of those spins aren't much fun to deal with. My mom, for example, sent me to a psychologist when I was ten. She's finally gotten used to it, sort of, since I haven't gone postal. Also, my grandfather had a long talk with her when he heard about the psychologist. Let me just say that she came around a bit after he told her about his own experiences. I still think my mom looks at me some days and worries. That hurts, but I can understand how hard it is to acknowledge that there may be spirits, entities or beings outside of our sensory perceptions. Especially since Hollywood makes so much money off horror movies. That's bad spin, and it's hard to counteract. But my grandfather has given me lots of pointers, ways to stay grounded yet be open to the journey."

"Does this mean that if we make love, someone else is in the room watching? Can he/she/it hear me fart when no one else is in the room? Exactly to whom am I making love? To you, your spirit guide, an amalgam of the two? I've got some real ménage-a-trois questions," Lubna panned, with a quizzical and comedic look in her eye.

"The fart question and similar ideas entered my mind when I was ten and first saw the spirit guide. That's when I first started masturbating, and you can imagine my concern about having someone or something know about my ten-year-old sexual thoughts. I was pretty uncomfortable. Turns out it's a common concern because it was something my grandfather talked about."

"Oh my, I've got the sexual maturity of a ten-year-old boy …," Lubna crossed her eyes as she said it, and Sarah and Adam guffawed.

"Apparently we all do, because I thought of pretty much the same thing," said Adam.

"Me, too," Sarah sheepishly admitted. Her concern was more personal, and she was beginning to get the drift that Stanley might have brought this up because of her admission the other day. He might, she thought, be trying to help me get a handle on what I felt. So she "jumped in the pool" and asked, "Did you see the spirit guide by me in the sort room?"

Stanley hesitated, "Yes, what I saw was next to you." Sarah couldn't look directly at Adam who had turned toward her.

"Do you think it's a spirit like yours?" Sarah asked. "How did you feel when you were ten and first … made contact?"

"Honestly, I thought about my dog, Blanche. I had a dog, a blond Labrador that went everywhere with me. She walked me to school and was my best friend. She died when I was ten, and I thought the spirit guide was Blanche. That's the context I put it in because that's the context that worked for me as a ten-year-old. In fact, animal spirit guides are common in Native American mythology. As I got older and spent more time with my grandfather, I began to see it differently. But I've come to believe it's influenced by your perceptions in the physical world. I once thought my spirit guide looked like Legolas, but that was when the hobbit movies started coming out, and I figured out that your current physical context can really influence how you personify the guide."

"Man, I have a million questions," Adam blurted out. "Does the spirit help you? Can it physically move objects? Is it affected by atmospheric changes? Can you see it all the time? Does it come and go? Can you call it when you need it? Can it see the future and tell you about it? Could it protect you in a fight, like an invisible ninja? Can it walk on bamboo like they did in *Crouching Tiger, Hidden Dragon*? Can it make you think certain thoughts? Was it once a human being? Is it a ghost? What did Sarah's spirit guide look like? Does it occupy space? Is it dependent on time?"

"Whoa, partner," said Lubna. "How do you know what Stan saw was Sarah's spirit guide? Maybe Sarah isn't comfortable with that idea. It's a bit hard for me to think that Stanley has a guide that might be looking over his shoulder, although it could be kinky. Maybe Sarah's not into this." Lubna looked over at Sarah and said, "Romans had a lot of gods, a regular pantheon. That's one context to consider. I'm thinking others may have seen things and interpreted them as gods. Maybe that is one way to spin this? Maybe all the mythologies are built around spirit visions or perhaps, I don't know ... it's one plausible idea, anyway. Roman gods were always running around on Earth interacting with people. The Hindus have a pantheon, too."

Sarah could hear Lubna struggling to fit the idea into a context that she could grasp. Sarah knew Adam had turned to her expectantly, but she needed a moment. Staring into the fire, all she could think of was her dad. If only the spirit guide was her dad, then she could handle it. Maybe she could just make it her dad, like Stanley made it his dog? It would be her chance to talk to him, tell him she was sorry and know that he heard, or would she just be fooling herself into believing he heard? "I'm open to the possibility ... but I'd like to hear the answers to Adam's questions."

"All good questions, but they don't all have answers," Stan said, "or they may have answers and I may not know them. I think I have a genetic predisposition to "see" spirits. I'm not sure I have the spiritual chutzpah to understand them. Maybe they aren't spirits, as we think of spirits. Maybe they're another life form and a few of us have an enhanced sensory perception that makes them visible?"

"You mean like 'I see dead people?'" Adam quoted.

"In a way, but they may not be dead people. They may be something else entirely that lives and dies independently of our physical world. Or they may be like bacteria in our microbiome, they're always there and always have been."

"I need some processing time for this, and sleep usually helps me do that," Lubna said, stifling a yawn. She got up and looked out the window. "It looks positively impassable out there. Stan, my electric blanket isn't working, and I'm going to need something to keep me warm. Sarah, you've got the sofa, and Adam, you've got the air mattress. You'll be warmer in here than we will be in the bedroom, what with the fireplace. We may end up dragging the mattress out here if it gets too cold. I'm going to dream about spirit guides and see if mine doesn't help me sort this out. Let's sleep on this and talk about it at breakfast." She smiled as she reached for Stanley's hand. "Good night."

"If you'd prefer the couch, I don't mind an air mattress," Sarah offered Adam.

"I'm good," said Adam, as he arranged the mattress so his feet were warmed by the fireplace. Sarah headed for the bathroom and brushed her teeth with a toothbrush from a package of children's toothbrushes that obviously had been on a sale rack and met the whimsical preferences of Lubna. She picked the blue mermaid and looked hard in the mirror, squinting. Hard as she tried, she saw nothing hovering behind her, and her throbbing ankle made her give up the effort. She needed to lie down and get it elevated. As she sat on the couch, Adam headed for the bathroom, and Sarah's head hit the pillow immediately after she kicked her shoes off. She guessed it was the pain in her ankle, but she didn't seem nervous or preoccupied with sleeping in the room next to Adam. Her mind kept coming back to the spirit guide and, more pointedly, she wondered if Adam was weirded out?

She heard the plastic air mattress whooshing and opened her eyes, turning toward Adam. She smiled and said, "Adam, was the discussion tonight too weird?"

He looked up at her, turned toward her and said, "More like too interesting! What if there is another life form that lives a parallel existence?"

"What if Stanley is just a little nuts, and I'm a little too much like him?" Sarah sighed sleepily. "I don't want people to think I'm like Patty Nakamura. I particularly don't want you to think that."

"Don't worry, Juliet. Stay focused on school and on me. My dad always says on hikes that getting to the top of the mountain is important but that what you see along the way may turn out to be the best memory. Tonight was fun, don't overthink it," Adam reasoned. "Good night."

Sarah watched Adam turn toward the fire and found herself watching the flames. "Good night, Romeo." Adam's reasoning sounded like something Abby would say, and it helped her relax.

"Glad to hear that moniker. I didn't want you thinking that I was short on testosterone because I wasn't over there hugging on you. I did some posing in the bathroom, you know," he joked. "But I figured it wasn't chivalrous, messing with a wounded maiden in distress. Besides, I'm just too tired to be my most manly."

"Thanks, that makes you even more charming. I guess we both have a closet full of anxieties. My ankle hurts too much to be romantically inclined, myself." Sarah said, drifting toward sleep. Moments later, she could hear the ice pellets tinkling as they hit the window and the deep breathing of sleep coming from the air mattress. Her breathing slowed, and soon she too was oblivious to world worries.

Chapter 9

"What if the pyramids, mounds and henges ... were built on ground where certain natural electromagnetic energies are concentrated, and designed in such a way as to further concentrate these energies?"

--John Burke and Kaj Halberg, *Seed of Knowledge, Stone of Plenty: Understanding the Lost Technology of the Ancient Megalith-Builders*

Patty Nakamura sat primly on the settee, nervously rearranging her umbrella, picking imaginary lint from her gloved fingers, and methodically taking a book from the stack next to her, opening it and then adding it back to the pile in a slightly different order. She repeated the sequence and seemed to read the titles while murmuring under her breath. From the lounge sofa, a freckle-faced student watched her bemusedly from under the bill of his ball cap.

Bernadette recognized The Creep as she floated down the elaborate staircase toward the main floor. She'd been on patrol for a couple of days, watching for him. Yesterday, the ice storm had closed the library for a day, and Bernadette took the time to leisurely look over the displays. The History of Science collection was planning a special display of the Galileo, a rare book with Galileo's handwriting in the margins. While floating in front of one of the changing television monitors in the entrance way, reading about the technology in the redesigned learning center on one of the lower floors, Bernie had felt something. She noticed that the monitors emanated some field she could feel in her bones, although she was sure she didn't have bones. She hadn't noticed it before, perhaps because so many students passed through the library with phones and laptops such that things were constantly disturbed, swirling molecules and energy. It made her think again about what she was and why her self-awareness changed when she touched Sarah.

As Bernadette headed toward The Creep, she could feel herself getting riled up. His smug amusement irritated her. But, as she floated past the settee, Patty Nakamura jumped up, knocking her stack of books to the floor. Patty took off in a hurry, and the student manning the security desk looked up, shaking her head as Patty fled out the old oak doors. The student walked over to the settee, picked up the books and loaded them on a cart next to the desk, clucking and smiling at The Creep with shared derision. Bernie stopped and wondered. She actually hadn't looked Patty's direction, but it seemed like Patty jumped up exactly as Bernie floated past. Was it coincidence or did Patty see Bernadette?

The comment from Stanley had given Bernie a lot to ponder, and she was rearranging some of her assumptions about her existence. Previously, she attributed her ability to sneak around to her clever camouflage. Now she realized she was invisible, but apparently not to everyone. Floating through the book was disorienting, but she wasn't sure she could turn the pages in the normal sense and she didn't think it wise to animate a book next to the student who was manning the exit gate, even if she could actually make that happen. After dodging ink molecules and moving in and out for a perspective that could let her read, the book seemed to be a Wild West in space kind of shoot 'em up with trained assassins and lots of weaponry. It didn't seem like something Patty would read. Then it struck her – light theory and specters. The memory came into focus, and Bernadette suddenly knew why Patty gave her that nagging feeling. She'd touched Patty.

It had been several human years ago. She remembered and began to understand that she had accidentally hurt Patty in the process. Patty hadn't always been so odd, although she had been a steady library inhabitant, even then. The woman was brilliant, and Bernadette had sensed it. She'd even shared Patty's interest in light theory, and that's how it happened. Bernadette was looking over Patty's shoulder one day, dancing among the ink molecules and thoughtlessly passed through Patty, still dancing and mixing. It had been a disaster. Patty had fainted and woke up changed. It hadn't been pretty when the police took her away to a local psych ward screaming about ghosts and light and pain.

Now things began to fall into place, and Bernadette began to understand how she had rediscovered herself when she touched Sarah. Bernadette had been in denial, big time. She'd withdrawn into the masonry of the building, inhabiting one of the gargoyles, trying to escape feelings of guilt about Patty. In staying so long among stone molecules, she'd forgotten things but emerged when Sarah asked for help. When Bernadette extracted herself, she kept the construct of a physical being. It was a mind trick. She caught herself for a moment with the question, "Did she have a mind?" But that was a matter for another time.

She refocused, a difficult thing to do here, close to the computer monitors on the desk. Bernadette had begun to associate electromagnetic fields with her short attention span. Electromagnetic fields made it difficult for her to concentrate and hold a thought. She floated toward the ceiling to escape the EMFs, concentrating on the encounter with Patty. Yes, that was why Bernadette had tricked herself into believing she was just a clever human. The more real she made the fantasy, the clearer the distinction between herself and others, and the less chance she could accidentally merge with another person. The problem was, she'd begun to believe it so completely that it hadn't occurred to her that Sarah wouldn't see her and would walk through her.

Wait, something was different. Sarah hadn't fainted, there was no pain, no screaming. She hadn't started wearing gloves and carrying umbrellas. What was different between the encounters with Patty and Sarah? Bernadette floated up to the old dusty deck level above that was closed to the public. Among the old bank ledgers and dissertations, she could concentrate. Sarah had asked for help and Patty had not, so could Bernadette be a being that was part thought? She'd been "dancing" when she passed through Patty, reveling in the molecules' movement, and she'd been focused, maybe more molecularly organized, when Sarah walked through her. Sarah was younger, and she seemed a bit more grounded and practical than Patty. There were a multitude of variables, including the fact that Patty had been next to her laptop and Sarah had been 50 feet away from the nearest monitor during their encounter. It was maddening.

Perhaps she could fix what she had broken? Maybe, just maybe, she could use her connection with Sarah to repair Patty? Bernadette couldn't fathom where her sense of responsibility came from, but she knew she felt responsible and obliged to make amends. Sarah was going to be key, and she'd have to be very, very careful to make sure that the effort didn't hurt Sarah. Ahh, that might be what the shaman meant and maybe, just maybe, there was someone like her, someone linked to Stanley. The thought thrilled her. She wasn't sure why she hadn't perceived the presence, but she now had an idea to work with and she floated downward, just as the elevator alarm sounded.

She'd been so focused on Patty that she'd forgotten TC. He had that smug look on his face and was on his laptop. She looked over his shoulder, staying back to avoid the EMFs, but realized he was manipulating a program. He tapped the keyboard, and instantly the elevator alarms stopped. Interesting. This time he was manipulating the newer elevators in the '58 addition. It was curious because they were in a busy area of the library, and she was sure he'd never be able to use that ability to harass a coed. Why mess with these elevators? Why trap people only to let them go again? It occurred to her that she could touch The Creep, but, frankly, the idea scared her. She suspected some of her moral sense may have come from touching Sarah. The thought of being infiltrated with nefarious thoughts seemed creepy, even though she might gain an understanding of his purpose. Heck, she was invisible. That ought to be enough to ferret out why he was doing it and determine what she was going to do about it.

Calmly, The Creep got up from his seat, loaded his laptop into his backpack and sauntered away. She knew he'd be back, and she knew that she'd be on him like stink on a pile of manure. Bernadette felt an intense resolve, following him all the way to the exit. After living in a gargoyle and owning the masonry molecules for so many years, the tie to this building was innate and possessive. As she passed the monitor at the gate, however, her attention was turned toward the basement. The coffee pot in Chaucer Variorum was just beginning to brew, and Bernie found the aromatics irresistible as the EMFs from the monitor dissolved her focus. She floated down the staircase, picturing sugar and java molecules wafting in the dust motes as the afternoon sunlight flooded through the old casement windows in the basement offices.

Sarah caught herself thinking about the previous morning, awakening to see Adam on the air mattress. They had all slept past noon. Lubna and Stanley talked about moving in together since Lubna's roommate had left at the end of the last semester and she needed to split the rent with someone. Practically, it made sense, but Lubna was concerned about her parents' perceptions and knew it would take some diplomacy. She was waiting to hear about interviews for medical school admittance, hoping good news in that quarter would be a nice preamble for a talk about roommates. During an interlude in that discussion, Sarah asked, "So, Stanley, do you mind my asking more about your spirit guide and how you came to know you have one? Tell me something about how you communicate or do you?"

"I don't initiate communication, and my guide isn't with me always. In fact, the guide seems kind of place-bound. I see it when I am back home in Sulphur. I don't really see it here on campus. It came to me when I was hiking around the park; it seems tied to the waterfalls and springs there. And it doesn't always come around when I'm in the park. If it hadn't been that I had just lost my dog and if my grandfather hadn't recognized that I had seen something, if he hadn't already had a similar experience, I might have freaked. You might say my grandfather is the guide and the spirit just lives its life as an acquaintance or a friend. Honestly, after more than a decade of interacting, quite a bit in my teen years when it was easy to walk over to the park after school, I've come to believe it is another species, a kind of light- or energy-based being with its own agenda and other pursuits. It's not like this Blanche hangs around me like some movie character whispering in my ear. It's not like that. It's more like I have a friend that's home sometimes when I go visit and sometimes not, so to speak."

"But you call it Blanche; do you think it's tied to your dog in some way?" Sarah queried.

"I think there is a tie. I've thought about it a lot and have a theory, but it's my spin, and it may not be anything but spin," he warned.

"Look, you're the only "expert" I know, and I'd appreciate some help. I know that I sense something and it's disorienting. I need some kind of operating theory, even if it's wrong. I need somewhere to start. I don't always understand Physics, but if I have some theory to hang it on, then it helps me work out problems. Maybe your spin is like Einstein's theory of relativity, a good working model until quantum evidence makes other theorists tweak it," Sarah's problem solving skills were evident in her reply.

"OK, I do think Blanche, the spirit, has some link to Blanche, my dog. I get feelings that pass through me in the park sometimes, and they feel like my dog is with me. Other times, the feelings are like a friend, independent of dog affection. I think that dogs and these beings sense one another. I think dogs are open to these beings because I think that dogs have the ability to sense them in a way most humans can't, and they aren't freaked by these beings at all. To a dog, they're just part of the landscape."

"But if your dog is gone, why do you think that this being, Blanche, gives you dog feelings?" Adam interjected.

"Well, it's either my construct for interacting or the being somehow absorbed or co-opted part of Blanche. I don't mean like *Invasion of the Body Snatchers,* more like a mixing of energies. If this being is composed of light or energy like I think it is, then it might be able to pass through living things and retain some piece or thought wave, or I'm not sure. I'm not a Physics major, but there have been times when an idea entered my mind in the park that I felt sure originated with Blanche, the dog, and sometimes Blanche, the spirit. Somehow I pick it up, and, usually when that happens, I feel a little nauseated, a little confused temporarily.

"I think that's an intersection. I think these beings intersect with dogs commonly but not so often with humans. I know, it sounds like I've been watching too many 1950s science fiction movies, but that's my spin. That's how I organize my thoughts when I try to understand Blanche. It parallels some of the ideas my grandfather shared before he died. He'd been thinking about it for a lot longer, some 50 years, and he told me my spin seemed to fit his experiences. I'd like to add that this is not information I would share with just anybody. I've made that mistake. I told a friend once, who told his minister, and it got around town. Kids were actually accusing me of needing to be exorcised. It got bad, and I finally just decided to say that I'd made it up as a joke. My grandfather knew different, but he helped me spread that rumor. He said you can't be a shaman for everyone, you can only be a shaman for those who share your perspective. He said it was like different ministers, some people go to a church because they are comfortable with that pastor and others go to a different church for the same reason. Each minister brings their own spin to their congregation, and that's why different religions exist."

"That's an interesting perspective, one I like," said Lubna. "It fits with the religions that have pantheons of gods and goddesses. Maybe the people who originated some of that mythology could perceive these beings, just like you do."

"Have you read any Neil Gaiman? He wrote a book called *American Gods*. In it, his characters are super beings that run around among us," said Adam.

"Yeah, I read it, but that doesn't fit my construct, and I've never seen any physical embodiment of Blanche, except light and shadow. That's what I saw behind Sarah, a kind of flickering of light and shadow that affects your aura," Stanley said.

"I think I can operate in the construct you've described. At least it will anchor me if I ever have that feeling again. Do you think these beings are nice or not nice? Benevolent or malevolent? Or is that even a relevant question?" Sarah queried. "What's a dog feeling, exactly?"

"Well, I think that might be like asking if an armadillo is benevolent or malevolent. I think they are just a different species sharing our world, and some people see them and some never run into one. And a dog feeling is the feeling you have when you spent years growing up with a dog from the time you were a baby. I don't think I can put it into words," Stanley stammered. "Blanche is a part of me."

"That sounds like love," Lubna commented sympathetically. "I saw a PBS show recently about dogs, and there's lots of evidence that suggests we have co-evolved with them. Who knows if some of us share a genetic predisposition to communicate better with dogs or other species of all kinds? What with epigenetics, who knows what genetic triggers might occur if you "intersect" with this species?"

"I'm more interested in what type of energy you're dealing with. You know the Earth is one big magnet, and atmospheric disturbances are triggered by sun spots and gamma rays as well as radiant energy and visible light," Adam stated, his meteorological viewpoint evident in his question, just as Lubna's biological bent showed in her line of thinking. "My professor even talked about an atmospheric phenomena called a sprite. They're created in the upper atmosphere in thunderstorms and sometimes look like jellyfish or angels. They even have pictures of them on the Internet. They're an energy discharge associated with lightning that can be observed. It makes me think that there may be lots of different types of "invisible" energy phenomena or at least invisible to some people. Maybe that kind of activity could give birth to this kind of life form?"

"That's kind of beyond my specialization. I'm into what light does to art, but I'm not sure I'd be able to give you any meaningful answers about electromagnetism, except to say that I have just always felt like EMFs should be something I shy away from, and I think it is related to Blanche in some way. It's also sacred to me because it's sacred to my grandfather, or maybe because it just feels that way. I always try to show respect or you could call it courtesy, I guess. It feels natural to do that, like when you interact with a wild deer and you don't want to scare it off. You stay calm, quiet and try not to startle. That's how I approach Blanche," Stanley explained. "Sometimes I *see* Blanche, and sometimes I feel a connection. Sometimes there's nothing."

"In Ayurvedic medicine and acupuncture, there is an assumption that we all have chi or some call it a bio field. It's the energy frequency we all emanate. We use electrical impulses to move muscles and communicate between cells. This is just an idea, but I wonder if you resonate with Blanche? I wonder if your frequency is harmonic? If so, that might explain why you can perceive her, or perhaps you have the ability to tune your own frequency to others? I've often thought that people who are called healers might have that ability. They tune in to someone's frequency and increase its resonance," theorized Lubna.

As Adam chimed in, asking more questions about energy fields and surmising how electromagnetic organisms might exist, Sarah's thoughts turned to her dad. Her eyes watered a bit and she looked down, thinking about him. If there was some real way to contact him, to say she hadn't meant it, to tell him how much she loved him ... that thought moved her to ask, "Stanley, do you feel like you can communicate with Blanche? If you want to say something or tell Blanche something, what do you do? How do you know if you have communicated?"

"I don't know for sure, exactly. Sometimes I get a feeling of good will, of maybe what a religiously oriented person would call divine ecstasy or just a sense of peace? Sometimes I wonder if anything but my imagination was involved. But this is where spin comes in. However I feel, it's going to be interpreted by my reference points, by my perceptions of what I am seeing and feeling. That's not objective. I'm using my sensory perceptions and filtering them through my personal suppositions about spirituality, nature and all that. I can't say what someone else might feel or should feel," cautioned Stanley.

"But why do you think Blanche is another species? Why not an angel?" Sarah questioned.

143

"Well ...," Stanley hesitated. "Maybe because I was brought up in the Native American tradition or because I first related to Blanche through my dog? I can't be sure of anything except that this is my journey. I'd like to be confident, but I don't know what an angel is and I don't know what Blanche is. Another being, another species feels right to me but might not feel right to someone else."

"Maybe angels are one construct for interacting? And maybe it is easier for some people to use that construct than to try and tie it to physical phenomena they have no way to measure or prove? Look at Galileo. He was arrested for theorizing that the Earth orbited the sun. There are lots of people these days killing others in the name of religion. If you call it an angel, you can go to a drugstore and buy an angel and hang it from your rearview mirror. If you call it a species, where's your reference point and how do you prove it?" Lubna philosophized. "Germ theory was scoffed at until microscopes made it possible to see bacteria. Adam, is there instrumentation that could prove Blanche exists?"

"I don't know. There are lots of instruments these days that measure energy we don't normally see. Could be something that might register a field? I read a book a year ago about a researcher who measured electromagnetic fields in the Earth at Stonehenge and other mound sites around the world. He suggested there were geologic formations that emitted unusual electromagnetic fields. Maybe Blanche lives in the park because the rock formations that create the springs create an environment that's favorable?" Adam postulated. "I could go back and see what kind of instruments he mentions. There might be some kind of geologic formation underneath the library, too. Could be that somebody in the Geology Department has already taken readings under campus. Or maybe the old metal decks generate an electromagnetic field of some kind. There's a lot of metal there, and it's arranged in a pattern that might incidentally create some kind of electromagnetic field."

"Before I go out and buy us all a bunch of t-shirts that say 'Gone Sasquatching,' I think we might want to rethink this. I don't want to go around the library carrying some crazy looking apparatus like Igor in *Ghostbusters*. I think some of the programs on television about looking for other species or ghosts are goofy. I'm not interested in getting labeled as a mental health outpatient or a Patty Nakamura. Couldn't we keep a lower profile on this?" Sarah worried.

"Agreed. The experience I had with some extreme religious types when I was in high school was bad, really bad. I shared Blanche with the three of you because I trust you all to look at this analytically, and I thought it might help Sarah decipher her encounter. I don't care if you believe me, and I'm not trying to start a religion or be anybody's spiritual leader. I'd be interested to know if some kind of instrumentation, besides me, could sense Blanche. But I don't need to prove it to anybody. In a way, you might say I'm comfortable with the ambiguity after all these years," Stanley said. "Let's chill for a while and see if Sarah wants to do any investigation after she's had some time to think about all this."

"OK, but a new species would be an awesome discovery," Lubna speculated.

"Yeah," smiled Adam. "Way cool. This would be more than a new species; it would be an entirely new life form. You know, in the book I read, the author speculated that there are people who are more sensitive to these kinds of fields and that's how they knew where to put Stonehenge."

"I've read a lot about acupuncture, and I've often wondered how someone came up with the meridians and the theory of chi. I wonder if someone back then was just born with the ability to see such things and they wrote it all down? You know, kind of like Stanley and his grandfather's ability to see auras," Lubna speculated.

"Could we dial down the *X Files* scripting, please?" Sarah whined. "I need some normalcy. I need to do some homework and think about my upcoming midterms. I don't want to go off track and end up becoming a perpetual student like some old hippie who had a drug experience." Although, internally, she found some of the possibilities exciting. The thrill for her, though, was magnified by the possibility that she could communicate with her dad. Her angel? Or her spin, that's what Stanley would call it. She was open to another life form, but she still clung to the possibility that Blanche could be a spirit. Funny, she thought, she wasn't questioning that Blanche existed, but, rather, what *she* was.

As they picked up their backpacks and sloshed their way to school, Lubna and Adam continued their speculation on who to contact about electromagnetic detection instrumentation, and Stanley and Sarah walked behind, both somewhat mute. The sun was really bright, and melting ice was falling from power lines and trees. They had to pay attention because some spots were wicked slick. Sarah welcomed the cold air and the need to concentrate on where to place her feet. The physical world demanded their attention; eventually even Lubna and Adam dropped their conversation about detection instrumentation and focused on the walk back to campus. Fresh clothes, a hot shower and her electric toothbrush beckoned.

Chapter 10

> *"The behavior of energy waves is important for biomedicine because vibrational frequencies can alter the physical and chemical properties of an atom as surely as physical signals like histamine and estrogen."*

--Bruce H. Lipton, *The Biology of Belief*

Sarah opened the dorm room door and was surprised to see the TV on and Jennifer asleep in her bed. The smell of tequila wafted toward her as she walked toward the bathroom and she stumbled on an empty bottle, catching herself on the small refrigerator and "Ouch ... shit!" erupted from her lips as she hopped on her sore leg. She couldn't help it. As she looked toward Jennifer, she realized that her face was smeared with mascara that had run down her cheeks. She didn't budge, even though Sarah's expletive had not been whispered. Sarah paused and took a hard look at Jennifer. There was something a bit colorless about her complexion, and Sarah stopped short, waiting for her to breathe. She waited, and thought she saw movement but wasn't sure. A sense of fear rushed over her, and Sarah felt compelled to grab Jennifer and shake her.

As she touched her hand, she was surprised at how cool it felt. She began calling Jennifer's name loudly, shaking her by the shoulder. No response. She shook her again and noticed a bluish tinge to her lips that Sarah had previously thought was mascara. Again, no response so Sarah pulled out her phone and dialed 911. She ran down the hall, hopping a bit and banged heavily on the

RA's door. As the RA, Millie, opened the door, Sarah heard 911 pickup, and she looked at Millie and spoke into the phone simultaneously. Her voice had a note of fear, as she told the dispatcher that her roommate was unconscious and couldn't be waked. Millie stepped into the hall and ran toward their room with Sarah following on her heels, asking the dispatcher to please send someone.

"Jennifer, Jennifer, wake up, wake up, honey," Millie implored. "Sarah, help me sit her up." As they each took a shoulder and tried to raise Jennifer to a sitting position, her rag doll body fell forward.

"I think we need to be sure that her airway is clear," Sarah said, worried that her head falling forward on her chest would make it difficult. They laid her back on the bed, "I saw her take a breath!" Relief spread over both of them like a shaft of warm sunlight, but Jennifer was still unconscious. They were both hyper-focused on Jennifer's breathing, and Sarah realized her breaths were irregular and rare. Tears sprang to Sarah's eyes as Millie's eyes saw the empty bottle of tequila and a lime slice on the floor. Sarah's eyes followed hers, and Sarah took in the mess more fully. It wasn't the only empty bottle – the thought that Jennifer might have consumed two bottles of tequila alone made her heart skip. "I just got back from spending the night at a friend's. It was too hard to get back in the ice storm so I slept on her sofa. I texted Jennifer late last night after work, and she answered. That was about 1 a.m. I don't know how long she's been like this."

"We're here now, and she's still breathing. The EMTs should be here in just a couple of minutes. You did the right thing. Help is on the way," Millie said reassuringly. "Was Jennifer doing OK? Did she have some reason to be depressed?" Millie rubbed Jennifer's cold hands as she asked the questions. Sarah began to cry harder. She felt that she had let Jennifer down. She'd been preoccupied with Adam and Physics and work. They had talked two days ago, and Jennifer had seemed really pumped. She'd made a lot of progress on her group project and was spending the night with Zach again. Sarah hadn't liked it because she just felt that Zach wasn't into Jennifer as much as he was into convenient sex. Something must have gone wrong. Sarah knew that Jennifer had a fake ID that let her buy liquor, but she really wasn't a regular drinker. She'd binged one night last semester when they celebrated the beginning of the fall break. They'd both had some margaritas. Sarah noticed that Jennifer didn't stop when she did and ended up sick on the bathroom floor the next morning.

"She had an on and off relationship with a guy. They broke up a few weeks ago and Jennifer was pretty upset, but they got back together just recently, and she seemed really upbeat the last time we talked. I thought Zach was kind of using her, but I don't think he's a bad person. She just seemed more into him than he seemed to be into her," Sarah sobbed. "I don't know if that has anything to do with why she'd drink like this. I should have come back last night. It was just so slick, and I fell walking over to my friend's apartment. We all just decided to stay there until the ice melted."

"It was wicked last night. I went up and down the hallways checking on people, and you weren't the only one stranded. I even knocked on your door. I asked if you were both in, and Jennifer yelled back that you had texted and were staying with friends. She didn't come to the door but sounded normal then. I moved on down the hall, checking other rooms, and sent out a text blast to everybody," Millie explained.

"What time was that?" Sarah asked.

"It was pretty late, so I know she was conscious as late as 4 a.m.," Millie answered and looked up as the EMTs arrived in the doorway. As they moved into the dorm room, Millie and Sarah backed away, giving them access to Jennifer. Millie picked up the empty bottle of tequila and held it up to the EMTs. Sarah walked over to the window and reached down, retrieving the other bottle, displaying it as well. She stayed in the corner, trying to keep out of their way, as they examined Jennifer and tried to rouse her. Their matter-of-fact demeanor calmed Sarah as she watched them work on Jennifer. Millie recited the information they had pieced together about how long Jennifer might have been unconscious, explaining that she probably drank whatever was in the bottles after 4:00 last night. A small sound emerged from Jennifer as they loaded her onto the gurney and her hand fluttered.

"That's a good sign," said the EMT sympathetically, as he looked over at Sarah's tear-stained face.

"Millie, can you give me a ride to the hospital? Should I call Jennifer's parents or should you do it? Is there some protocol?" Sarah asked, picking up Jennifer's phone and trying to sound sensible when she felt something very different. She was panicking, now that the first adrenaline flush was easing off, and she was looking to give herself a task that would make her feel useful and stop her mind from racing toward bad outcomes.

"Actually, there is a protocol. Give me about 15 minutes to do what I am supposed to do. I will come get you, and we'll go over to the hospital together. We've done all we can do right now for Jennifer. Hand me Jennifer's phone and I'll make the contact with her parents. We're trained for this."

"Do I have time to take a shower and change clothes? I think we might be at the hospital for a while, and I want to look more together when Jennifer's parents get here," Sarah said.

"Sure. We'll probably be in the waiting room for some time before we get an update on Jennifer, so I think we can take some time getting there. You did a good job Sarah. You acted quickly. Thanks for keeping it together and getting me. I know Jennifer's parents will be grateful," Millie said, hugging her solidly. The hug brought more tears to her eyes, but she appreciated Millie's kind words. Today had been a rough ride.

After a long talk with Abby, which had continued through the ride to the hospital, Sarah's mom called and they spent an hour on the phone in the waiting room. Her mom asked everyday questions about Physics and told Sarah about her own classes at the community college. It was a gabfest, and Sarah sensed that her mom just needed to hear her voice, confirming that Sarah was OK. Sarah certainly needed to hear her. It kept her mind from circling back to the days when they had spent lots of time at the hospital when her dad was sick. They talked until Jennifer's parents arrived in the waiting room, and Sarah hung up, wanting to explain things to them.

Millie was a trooper. A counselor from the university had arrived in the waiting room, and they both tag-teamed the parents, consoling them and praising Sarah's role in getting Jennifer help as quickly as possible. It helped. Sarah still felt a twinge of guilt about not being there to prevent the incident. Luckily, the doctor came out not long after Sarah narrated her version of events and pulled Jennifer's parents aside. Sarah didn't really know them well but watched them as they got the news. Jennifer was coming around. They weren't sure yet if there might be some brain damage, but she would live. Her mother and father cried, and Sarah could feel tears flowing down her own cheeks. She reached behind her for a seat and was surprised that her legs gave way, and she allowed herself to sob, unchecked.

Sarah and Millie hugged Jennifer's parents. Millie explained that they needed to get back and that the counselor, Ben, would be with them the rest of the afternoon. Sarah invited Jennifer's parents to stay in the room. Spend the night, whatever they needed. As Sarah and Millie drove back to the dorm, Millie asked if she could help clean up.

"So I can get rid of the bottles and make things neat?" Sarah asked.

"I need to take a couple of pictures with my phone, but I think it would be nice if Jennifer's parents didn't see the mess. I can always show them the pictures, but that can happen later if they ask about it."

"I don't need any help. I can get it cleaned up in 30 minutes. I'll change the sheets for her parents, in case one of them wants to rest while the other is in Jennifer's hospital room. It will make me feel useful."

"If they need both beds, feel free to bunk with me and give them some space. I'll come by with some food in a couple of hours. They'll need something to eat and so will you. Ben will text me as information becomes available. The university has emergency funds to help families in crisis. That includes you, Sarah. Something like this can be pretty hard. If you need to talk to someone, there's counselors I can call. Do you have a friend who I can contact? Maybe having someone hang with you would take the edge off."

Surprising herself, Sarah told Millie about Adam. He was close by, in the dorm across the plaza, she rationalized. Maybe Adam was becoming one of her anchors? He was here, unlike Abby, and she was comfortable with him. Besides, the thought of talking about alternative life forms would divert her, and there were just three people that she could talk to about that. She figured he would take this in stride and have something to say that would divert her. She was right. Adam was there before she had finished cleaning up the room, and he helped her make Jennifer's bed with fresh sheets.

"I don't really know Jennifer. When you texted, I realized that I hadn't heard you talk much about her. In fact, I've never met her. I guess you two don't hang out much together?" Adam surmised. "Do you know what happened?"

"She has a boyfriend, Zach. He broke it off awhile back, but they got back together. I never see Jennifer much when they are on, because she pretty much lives with Zach. But since she was here last night alone, drinking, I assume they broke up again and she was really bummed. Or maybe she just was stuck here with the storm and overindulged? I don't think it's likely that she'd get that drunk unless she was upset or something.

"Is she a binge drinker?" Adam asked.

"I've seen her drink, and she had a fake ID so she could buy alcohol. The way she talked, she and Zach drank together, but I didn't really hang with them," Sarah explained.

"She might have, but you couldn't have come back. Maybe she was already pretty zonked. What is Zach like?" Adam asked.

"OK, I guess. He just seemed less interested in Jennifer when she got more interested in him," Sarah said. Her mind kept coming back to last night. She'd assumed Jennifer was fine, but she hadn't asked her in her text. If she could sense an alternative life form, you'd think she'd pick up on a roommate in crisis. Sometimes she felt so slow, like thinking of something witty ten minutes after a conversation. As she grew silent, blaming herself for missing some sign in Jennifer that she was struggling, Adam watched her.

"When I got back to the dorm, I got on the Internet and started looking up that book I read on Stonehenge and electromagnetic geologic formations. Seems like the author believes some people naturally can sense unusual electromagnetism, and he thinks that's why Stonehenge was built in that particular location. It sounds kind of like the ability Stanley has, an ability to sense energies. Do you think that's just a predisposition like musical talent?"

Sarah thought for a moment, pulling herself away from self-recrimination. "I haven't taken the field's course yet in Engineering, but I might be able to answer more accurately, if I had. That course focuses on electromagnetism. I do remember seeing a Nature program that talked about how birds navigate on long migrations. They're able to sense the Earth's magnetic fields. It doesn't really seem farfetched that humans, some humans, would have a sensitivity to that," she replied.

"Yeah, Lubna seemed to think lots of humans might have that capability, but that it has to be triggered epigenetically. Lots of people might have the ability, she said, but environmental factors would jumpstart it, so to speak," he replied. "If that's true, it could be that modern life makes it harder to take advantage of that particular talent. These days, there are so many sources of energy and so many types of energy waves from man-made sources, radio waves, microwaves, sonar, VHF, even the Wi-Fi in this building that carries the Internet signal. Meteorology uses microwave radiometers to measure the temperature, so there are lots of ways to measure various energy fields. Seems like there would be a ton of interference. Stan has mentioned several times how he works to keep EMFs at a minimum around him. If that underlies his shaman-sense, then I can see how it could confuse the message."

As Adam speculated, Sarah felt her anxiety dwindle and her problem-solving skills emerge. She pulled out her laptop.

"I'm going to start making a list of energy fields that surround us," Sarah stated. She Googled energy fields and got a listing of chakras, auras and the like. But she wasn't really interested in the fields that emanate from living organisms, at least not yet. She was more focused on non-living types of fields that might cause convergence or interference with the fields that living organisms might generate. She refined her search and went to Wikipedia to start to fill it in. Adam pulled out his phone and started to search as well.

"Let's do this competitively. You put together a list, and I'll put together a list; then we'll compare. The winner gets 30 minutes of kissing and hugging," he grinned.

"Wait a minute, so if I win, I get your kissing and hugging, and if you win, you get my kissing and hugging? Hmm … sounds like a win-win to me," Sarah said, warmed by the thought and certainly diverted. "But I don't see why I shouldn't just let you win," she said coyly. "Let's add another incentive. How about loser pays for ice cream?"

"How about loser takes off his or her clothes?" Adam said, hedging for something more.

"Intriguing but not a bet I'm ready for right now. Too much input today about relationships gone wrong," Sarah said diplomatically.

"Hey, can't blame a guy for responding to his *Call of the Wild*. I'm a victim of my testosterone," Adam grinned, as he turned his head in his classic *X Files* adventure grin, complete with raised eyebrow.

"I think you need to spend less time in front of the mirror posing," Sarah laughed, extending her arms and sliding toward Adam who was seated on the side of the bed. She slid comfortably into a cuddle, saying, "You make some good points. This is nice," as she kissed his neck. "I'm figuring this will be motivating. How about some motivation for me?" She lifted her face toward his, and Adam responded with sincerity. For several minutes, Sarah forgot about Jennifer driven by the comfort of affection.

A knock at the door halted their motivational endeavor, and Sarah slid away and sat up as she said, "Come in."

Millie replied, "I've got pizza, salad and news," as the door swung open. She had three large pizzas and was followed by the counselor, Ben, who Sarah had met at the hospital. He was holding a couple of sacks. "We're here in advance of Jennifer's parents. They're coming to get a few of Jennifer's things and to have some time to talk with Ben. They asked if you could spend some time talking to them about Jennifer's state of mind. Good news is that her blood alcohol level is going down although she isn't totally conscious yet. I think that her parents want to get some clothes and take her home tomorrow. They should be here in about 15 minutes.

Sarah felt a wave of relief and at the same time concern. "I want to help, but I feel bad about telling Jennifer's parents how little I know. What do I tell them about not seeing her? I'm not sure they know much about how she was pretty much living at Zach's apartment. I feel really uncomfortable. I want to help, but I don't want to rat her out. They have a lot on their plate as it is."

"I've spoken with her parents, and they are realistic about her relationship with Zach. What you have said will not be a revelation to them. But if you don't feel that you can add anything useful, it's OK to say that," explained Ben. "I believe their first concern is whether Jennifer should return to school."

"Wouldn't you and Millie be the best people to ask about that? I mean, don't you have experience with this kind of situation and training, too?" Adam interceded protectively.

"That's true and that's why we're here. But every situation is unique. And it takes a village. We can provide support, but Sarah is, well, an imbedded observer. Sarah may see behaviors that signal trouble," Ben stated. As Ben explained further, Sarah's mind raced along, courting high anxiety. What if she was expected to see something important and missed it?'

Millie interceded, "Sarah, what are you thinking?" Clearly Millie had picked up on Sarah's lack of attention and anxiety-laced facial expression. "Sarah, if you aren't up to it, you can say so, honey. That's perfectly OK."

"I'm afraid, Millie. I'm afraid I'll miss something, and it will be bad. I'm afraid of being responsible for Jennifer and having it all go wrong. Even if you say it won't be my fault, I'll feel that way inside." Sarah cried. A knock at the door prevented Millie from answering, and she got up and welcomed Jennifer's mother into the room. She left to get a couple of chairs from her suite, and Sarah introduced Adam as a friend who was helping her cope.

"Mrs. Avery, we were just discussing your question about whether Jennifer should return to school, but I think it would be a good idea if we all ate first, before the pizza gets cold," Ben said, opening a box and passing around paper plates. He passed out soft drinks and water, and the comfort of comfort food eased tensions. Adam asked where the pizza came from and started a discussion about the best pizza in town. Millie and Ben both had favorites, and a discussion about deep dish and thin crust got them through the first few minutes. Sarah ate. The comfort food helped, and she looked at Jennifer's mother with considerable sympathy. Mrs. Avery looked like she'd been "rode hard and put up wet."

Sarah swallowed and said, "I don't think Jennifer was trying to kill herself. I think she was just trying to get drunk. She was upset when she and Zach broke up a few weeks ago but never said anything that would make me think she was suicidal. She has more gumption than that. She was mad and felt used a bit, but that's all. I know she was happy to get back with him, but I thought she was more realistic after the first breakup. I honestly feel like she just overdid it and didn't realize that she could make herself that sick. I think she should stay in school. She'll feel like a failure if she goes home. I would, anyway."

Jennifer's mother's eyes filled with tears, she jumped up and sat on the bed and hugged Sarah, saying, "I think the same thing, and I appreciate you saying it. Believe me, I feel guilty myself. Seemed like Jennifer was less and less interested in talking to me about Zach and her personal life. We used to share a lot more, and I thought she had just outgrown me. Today, I felt that I had somehow let her down and just wasn't as perceptive as I should have been."

"It's pretty normal to feel guilty in this kind of situation," said Ben. "And we still aren't clear on exactly what happened. I suggest we focus on some productive actions now and see what Jennifer has to say when she is able."

"Yes, I need to get some clothes for her and toiletries. And I need to get back to the hospital soon. The doctor said she would probably not wake up for several more hours. She is still intubated, but the EEG looked normal. I want to be there when she wakes up. Can I take a box of pizza? Jennifer is pretty partial to pepperoni, and I think smelling pizza might get her moving faster. Her dad needs to eat, too. He decided to sit with her, since I would know better what clothes and things she would need," said her mother. The next few minutes Sarah busied herself with helping pack a suitcase, finding Jennifer's phone, packing up her laptop and books. Adam carried a basket of laundry down to the car, and they loaded the food and other necessities. Sarah reassured Jennifer's mother that she would help, and Millie and Ben gave her a packet of materials, and hugs were exchanged. She seemed buoyed and uttered many thank yous. Sarah watched her pull away, feeling better herself and waving her phone in the air.

"Text me," she yelled. Mrs. Avery held her thumb up and turned to back away. Sarah felt a wave of relief as she waved. Immediately, her thoughts turned to Physics and Calculus, and how the last two days seemed like a week. She felt behind although she knew classes had been cancelled because of the ice storm. Concentrating would be difficult since her mind kept obsessing on Jennifer. But trying seemed like a good idea.

"Adam, mind if we study? I'm feeling behind, like I've been somewhere else on a vacation to hell. I think concentrating on some of my Physics homework would help me feel a bit more normal. It probably seems silly, but I'd like to go to the library coffee shop and get a mocha, and sit there and work," said Sarah. "Physics seems easier when I study there. Guess I've gotten used to it."

"I hear you and am with you. Let me go get my backpack, and I'll meet you in the lobby in about 15 minutes. I'll even spring for the mocha," Adam replied, as he turned and took his leave from Millie and Ben. As Sarah, Millie and Ben walked back to the dorm, Ben handed Sarah his card.

"Sarah, my number is here; feel free to text or call anytime. I think your idea to study is a good one. But if something comes up and you want to talk about anything, I'm available. I need to drive back to the hospital and see if the Averys need anything," Ben stated, as he turned back to the parking lot.

"I've got some reports to write about the situation myself," said Millie. "I'll check on you this evening, Sarah, and see if you need anything."

"Thanks, Millie. I'm sure I'll be fine. Adam is a big help, and I do better if I have something to focus on. Physics usually gets my attention," Sarah said, with a hint of sarcasm.

"OK. I'll keep you posted if I hear anything," Millie said, turning toward her door at the end of the hall.

Sarah and Adam walked briskly north into the wind, both responding to the cold breeze and the need to move. Adam seemed to sense Sarah's need for silence. The walk reminded her of their initial kiss and how Adam's company right now, in the midst of a crisis, meant more to her than the physical attraction she normally felt in his presence. Just walking together, matching their pace, felt companionable and comforting. She looked at Adam and confirmed that her feelings were laced with sexual attraction, but there was something even better. She began to feel that she could count on Adam and that she could rely on him to value her problem-solving skills. She knew, at this moment, she valued his common sense and compassion. She hoped he felt the same. It mattered to her right now, more than her fantasies.

As they entered the south doors of the library, Sarah automatically looked up and silently sent a greeting upward. The warmth of the building rushed blood to her face, as they climbed the stairs of the entranceway and passed the security gate. Sarah nodded to Michelyn, who was staffing the exit desk, and kept moving briskly through the old addition heading toward the coffee shop. Adam didn't slow either, and they both seemed eager to hit the books. Oh, she knew he'd be back in her sexual fantasies, but right now his solid, rational presence gave her energy and intention. They were here to apply themselves and make a difference in the world somewhere, sometime. Right now, that meant conquering Physics and savoring a mocha, maybe a white chocolate mocha – yeah, white chocolate sounded just right.

Bernadette sensed Sarah's energy was forward directed, so she stayed a few feet behind. Actually, Bernadette didn't see Sarah, exactly. Rather, she perceived her energy frequency, and the aura gave Sarah's form definition. Now that Bernadette had given up the delusion she was human, some of the trappings of her hallucinatory perceptions had fallen away, and she realized that frequencies attracted her. Sarah's frequency was invigorating, while other frequencies seemed to diminish her. As Sarah entered the stairwell headed down to the lower level and the coffee shop, Bernadette began to lose focus. She stopped, unable to proceed with cohesion. The newly renovated lower level was inundated with large screens and study rooms with active boards and computers. It hummed, electromagnetically speaking, and Bernadette began to lose her focus. Momentarily forgetting why she was there, she began to mix with the strong coffee aromatics and simply floated upward in the stairwell, dancing among the molecules of coffee and wondering why she was in the stairwell of the new addition.

She'd been destabilized by the discordant electromagnetism of the lower level and only began to vibrate again with a consistent frequency as she hit the fifth floor. She refocused and floated into the fifth floor lobby, the entrance to the special collections. It had been years since she had been here; she wasn't sure why. It was quiet and closed in the early evening. She floated through the walls into the reading room, hovering over the display cases. Some of the items were old, very old, and still retained the frequency of previous owners. Items long-used by an individual acquire their frequency sometimes, and long after, centuries even, that item vibrates sympathetically, resonating with that particular energy, or so it seemed to Bernadette.

A resident of that quantum sphere herself, Bernadette floated over the books, resonating with some and not with others. A few felt like the computer monitors and seemed to conflict with her personal frequency. These she backed away from quickly. She passed through walls into the vault and sensed the change in humidity and various security lasers protecting the contents from more corporeal invasions. She browsed the books, resonating. She wasn't mixing with the molecules, although that would have been interesting considering the vellum bindings and old inks. She was simply sensing frequencies and humming along when she encountered a synchronicity.

Eventually she felt a need to return to the older part of the library. There she felt stronger, more like she did when she merged with Sarah. Perhaps she was just vibrationally aligned with the old masonry? After all, she'd spent some serious hang time on the parapet, molded to a figure there. The building had its own frequency, which didn't quite match the newer addition but which made Bernadette feel safe. She headed that way, floating down the elevator shaft in the newer section and passing into the elevator carriage as it headed upward.

Instantly, she froze. TC was riding the elevator alone. Bernadette, hovering over his head, watched as he pulled the emergency stop, keyed open the operation panel and silenced the alarm. What was it with this guy and elevators? She'd found him in every elevator in the building, and generally he was up to no good. As she watched, he pulled out his laptop and called up a program. He then pulled out a cord and plugged it into the USB port in the panel. As she looked closer, the laptop began to interfere, and Bernie drifted off, forgetting the encounter completely. She languished, confused, and headed toward a distant frequency that drew her out of the elevator shaft and toward the older sections of the library. As she moved toward the old decks, she felt stronger but couldn't recall exactly what she'd been doing and why she had a lingering feeling of disquiet. Oh, well, she headed toward the library school offices and her old hangout. Sugar crystals, stale coffee and the old restroom drew her. There she rested, trying to recapture her elusive thoughts, disrupted by the computer's EMF. Unfortunately, Bernie's mind couldn't reassemble the interaction, and TC escaped her completely, apparently satisfied as he reengaged the elevator.

The elevator door opened to reveal the fifth floor lobby. TC remained in the carriage behind the elevator panel and reached into his pocket. He pulled out a selfie stick, attached his phone and moved it very carefully into the space of the open door. As he panned the lobby, he took pictures, careful to include the position of security cameras and the construction changes that were underway. He remained carefully behind the panel, put away his tools, closed the elevator door, pulled down on the brim of his ball cap, positioned himself underneath the elevator camera, and reached up to remove a cover he had made of black construction paper and tape that covered the camera in the corner. As the elevator carried him to the lower level, he exited, allowing the camera to catch only his back. He immediately walked to the 1950s addition and entered the men's restroom. He removed the ball cap, which came off with a brunette wig. From the back, he looked like a man with long dark hair but actually had a shaved head. Next he removed his jacket, turned it inside out and exited the bathroom stall, unrecognizable. From there, he exited the building at the west entrance, looking solidly at the security cameras. Sauntering smugly away on the sidewalk, he moved toward the parking garage.

Sarah looked up at Adam as he focused on his laptop screen and sipped the last of her white chocolate mocha. He was concentrating, and she was taking a break, having finished the problems at the back of the chapter. She needed to read the next chapter and had that set of problems to do but signaled to Adam and got up to walk to the restroom. There was a line in the lower level restroom, and she needed to get her blood moving so she walked up the stairs and headed toward the old part of the library. She liked the 1930s bathroom in the old basement and figured a walk there and back would invigorate her and help her focus on the next chapter. She estimated she had about another hour's worth of Physics. As she approached the old staircase, her remembrance of a glitter-filled winter afternoon with Abby in the kitchen making Christmas cards entered her mind and a slight dizziness. She breathed deeply and felt more settled as she headed down the staircase. She hummed to herself and felt relaxed, in tune with the world momentarily. Her phone vibrated, and suddenly the feeling dissipated. There was a text from Jennifer's mother. Jennifer was conscious and talking.

Relief surged through Sarah as she typed "Hooray!" and stopped to forward the message to Adam and others in a group mailing. Then she put her phone back in her pocket and skipped the last two steps, filled with energy and gratitude. A tune came to her lips again, and humming to herself in the toilet seemed just right. She wasn't really following a song, just humming and basking in her sense of relief.

Maybe it was the overwhelming feeling of relief and happiness, but as she sat on the toilet, she experienced the odd sensation of looking down on herself. This time, it was disorienting but didn't scare her. She continued humming, having flashes of glitter and the kitchen at home interspersed with the sensation of seeing herself. This time, she consciously tried to think about what Stanley had said about Blanche. She had finished her business but stayed seated on the toilet, humming quietly and hoping she might communicate. If this was another life form, Sarah guessed she had seen her use the toilet. Just then, Sarah realized she'd used a female pronoun. Wondering if that was significant, she closed her eyes but still saw herself from above. Oddly, she noted that the part in her hair was crooked in the back and she should probably make some effort to comb her hair when she got up.

"Hello," Sarah said out loud in a subdued voice. A moment passed and then she felt a rush, like she had when she was pulled on a raft behind their boat at the lake. She could feel the inertia of herself, just like when the raft tried to pull away from her fingers. It was that same thrill of moving forward suddenly, and Sarah unconsciously grabbed the toilet paper dispenser.

"Hello … Bernadette," Sarah stumbled. Why Bernadette? She couldn't explain and had no idea where the name came from, except that it emerged without any effort on her part. Just then her phone dinged with a text reply, and the sensation faded somewhat. Another text dinged, and Sarah found herself feeling rather ordinary and ready to abandon the toilet stall. She pulled out her phone, texted a response to a "Hallelujah" that she had received from Abby and a response to Adam, indicating she would be back in a couple of minutes. Then she remembered Stanley's aversion to EMFs and turned her phone off.

The moment the phone light blinked off, she felt the rush again and found herself humming under her breath, expectantly waiting for something, but what? Glittery thoughts emerged, and she opened the stall door and walked toward the sink and mirrors. Perhaps she imagined it, but it seemed like the lighting wavered over the stall she had exited. It's not like she saw something tangible, but she sensed something, and that sensation intensified as she hummed under her breath. She focused on the mirror, watching the stall behind her and perceived, or maybe just imagined, a sparkling, wavering something that seemed to have a shape and hold together more substantially when she hummed steadily. It flickered, and Sarah forgot that she was washing her hands and stood motionless at the sink with the water running. Her senses were heightened, and she became aware of the smell of stale coffee that always hung around the old building. For some reason, she really wanted a cookie, the kind that has too much frosting and sprinkles – a kind of cookie that Sarah generally disliked because they were too sweet.

The door to the bathroom opened, and Sarah turned, surprised, to see Patty Nakamura walk in.

"Hello, Dr. Nakamura," Sarah said. "How are you today?"

Patty Nakamura seemed to hesitate and look toward the stalls. Sarah gazed into the mirror in front of her, but the wavering was gone. She turned off the water and grabbed a paper towel.

"Dr. Nakamura, I'm glad we ran into each other. I don't know if you remember me, but you helped me get out of a stuck elevator on deck four. I wanted to thank you again and ask you about something you said back then," Sarah continued. "You mentioned that you felt you were being followed in the decks. Do you still have that feeling?" Patty Nakamura looked nervously around the bathroom and stepped back.

"Why?" she asked suspiciously, her eyes scanning the room as though she expected to see something.

"I always have a feeling in this part of the library that there's something here, something friendly – a kind of guardian angel, so to speak. I feel awkward saying it and wouldn't have mentioned it to you now except that I think you might have a similar feeling." The words came out of Sarah's mouth, and she knew they weren't her words. She felt a bit like a puppet in the hands of a ventriloquist. Her mouth was moving, but her brain wasn't. That certainly got Patty Nakamura's attention as she suddenly looked hard at Sarah, like a dog at the dinner table focused on getting a leftover.

"What makes you say guardian angel, what makes you think it's friendly?" she asked. "Have you ever seen anything?"

Sarah waited for an inspiration, but apparently the puppetry was over, because she stood there silently, until she felt compelled to say, "You might think I'm crazy, and I'd hate to foster that impression. But just now when I was in the toilet stall, I felt I saw something wavering or a little sparkling out of the corner of my eye. It might just be the beginning of a migraine, but it seemed different, and I felt a wave of … comfort," Sarah stumbled, now resorting to her own machinations, she found herself trying to explain. In for a penny, in for a pound, she told herself. Maybe admitting to something that sounded crazy to a crazy person was a good place to start. She knew she hadn't started the conversation, but she did want to continue it. This woman wasn't stupid, and Sarah could sense Patty was intrigued, though guarded, as if it was a road she'd been down before and got lost.

"You're sure it's not voices in your head?" Patty queried, looking to snag Sarah in sanitarium talk.

"I know I sound like a character in a movie headed for the local mental health facility. I understand if you'd rather not pursue the conversation. I'm just saying that I seem to sense something when I am in this part of the building and I thought it might be related to what you mentioned that day," Sarah said, now feeling like she should back off.

"That day, it was the crawler," Patty stated matter-of-factly. "I saw him a couple of times after that. He always takes his shoes off so he can sneak up to women and look up their skirts."

"I know who you're talking about! I reported him to security. He wears his pants really high on his waist and has dark-rimmed glasses. Is that the guy you're talking about?" Sarah said, somewhat excitedly.

"I haven't seen him lately. Are you going to wash your hands again? You know you have to hold them under the water 30 seconds, fully lathered, to kill the germs," Patty eyed the paper towel like a thing contaminated.

"Huh, I guess I was distracted by the flickering light. I'll wash them again, now that it seems to be gone," Sarah said, attempting to accommodate Patty's OCD and extend the discussion. She lathered up again, elaborately, and held her hands under the cold water. She could see Patty counting silently, so she kept them there until Patty seemed satisfied. Then she carefully pulled a paper towel from the dispenser and used it to turn the handle of the faucet. Patty nodded, unconsciously approving her hygiene technique. Sarah could relate, as she sometimes felt similar concerns when it seemed like every student on campus had the flu. During flu season, she'd try to get through doors without touching the handles.

"That light can hurt. Keep your distance and stay away from computer screens. Computer screens confuse it," Patty stated, as she carefully removed her gloves and entered the bathroom stall using her foot. Sarah could hear her tear off toilet paper and use it to slide the lock closed. Sarah couldn't help but look slyly at the base of the stall and realized that Patty had climbed onto the stool to squat as her feet disappeared one after the other. Sarah hoped her preoccupation with germs never got that extreme, but there were days, there were bathrooms, that might warrant such efforts.

"I'm sorry – you said *it*?" Sarah commented awkwardly, turning toward the occupied stall. "I hate to talk to you while you're in the john, but what is *it*?"

The flush of the toilet paused the conversation, and the door swung open, Patty, standing with a wad of toilet paper in her hand, looked piercingly at Sarah. "Well, it's not an *us*, is it?"

"I have a friend who thinks it's another life form. He's communicated with another *it*," Sarah said, hoping her general reference, without mentioning Stanley, did not breach a confidence.

Patty began washing her hands intently. Sarah shifted her position, feeling the need to return upstairs but unwilling to lose a chance to hear something more that might verify what she had perceived. "The hospital psych ward isn't exactly the Mardi Gras. You might not enjoy that party," Patty murmured under her breath as she soaped up a second time.

A student entered the bathroom, and Sarah felt unable to continue. "Maybe we can talk again? I work in the library about 20 hours a week and am at the circulation desk on Thursday evenings. My name is Sarah Felton ... thanks." Patty looked in the mirror at Sarah and nodded slowly.

Sarah climbed the stairs heading back to the coffee shop in the new addition of the building. Glitter and gratitude, somehow these ideas tumbled in her head and, again, she noticed the shimmering at the edge of her vision. It felt good, like standing in the ocean being washed with peaceful waves on a calm, sunny day. She passed the big directional display screen and noticed a perceptible diminishment of the sensation. It returned again as she turned the corner and slipped away as she descended the newer stairwell toward the coffee shop. She hesitated to lose the contact, but saw Adam look up as she came through the stairwell doorway. "See you later, alligator, after a while, crocodile," slipped through her mind, leaving Sarah to wonder if it was her phrasing or Bernadette's.

Chapter 11

"We can't all be heroes, because somebody has to sit on the curb and applaud when they go by."

--Will Rogers

Bernadette was delighted. She felt her contact with Sarah had gone well and that she was on her way to repairing the damage done to Patty. She longed to touch Patty and immerse herself in Patty's brain's electrical activity. However, Bernadette felt that patience was important. Her feelings of responsibility had been magnified by her intersection with Sarah. That girl had a lot of guilt and anxiety, but Bernadette was comforted by that and by Sarah's courage. She seemed able to handle Bernadette's presence without losing her own frequency. In fact, Bernadette sensed that she and Sarah had coherent frequencies and that Patty's frequency wasn't always consistent. There must have been a destructive interference between her frequency and Patty's that flat-lined, momentarily, Patty's vibrational frequency, causing her to pass out during their first intersection. Bernadette wasn't sure that it would ever be safe to try and touch Patty again. It would be better if she tried to repair the damage by using Sarah to establish a relationship that could show Patty she wasn't alone; she wasn't crazy.

In the meantime, Bernie floated up the staircase and moved out into the main atrium. As she did, she sensed TC, heading toward the main doors. On one level, something about him seemed different; on another level, his frequency was the same angry signature she had come to know and distrust. Good riddance, she thought, unable to remember her previous observation of his elevator escapade. She still had that dancing mosquito feeling, something she couldn't quite recapture, but her elation over the intersection with Sarah overwhelmed those feelings, and she floated past the display cases gingerly touching books and finding some that resonated pleasantly.

She accidentally bumped into a pillar in the 1950s addition, avoiding a rushing student, and backed off immediately, sensing that the building itself vibrated at an uncomfortable frequency. It wasn't discordant, just not as invigorating as the older addition. She moved up the old staircase and felt herself vibrate with restored vigor as she passed through the old metal stacks. They hummed with her frequency, and she realized, suddenly, that it explained her affinity for the older building. Maybe it wasn't the stale coffee and sugar cookies, but rather the structure. Or maybe it was a combination of all the vibrations, coffee, people, and books? Everything has a frequency.

Why now? Why was it so obvious to her now? She guessed it was her intersection with Sarah. Sarah was an Engineering major and knew about waves and particles, frequencies, quantum mechanics – clearly Bernadette was "thinking" like Sarah on some level. She found her favorite spot on the old elevator and understood now that the elevator motor hummed with a harmonic vibration that comforted her. She danced around the attic, reveling in the harmony, elated by the hum. Time became irrelevant, and dust motes swirled as Bernadette pirouetted around the steel girders and the massive air handlers, riding waves like a surfing ballerina. Eventually, she curled up, giving herself up to the feeling of riding the rhythmic wave like flotsam caught in an ocean current and relaxed.

Adam rose from the table as Sarah approached, saying "Watch my stuff?"

"Sure," Sarah replied. As Adam headed toward the lavatory, she was excited about telling him that she'd had an encounter. But as she settled down in front of her notebook of scribbled Physics equations, she couldn't help but recall Patty's ominous remark, *you might not enjoy that party*. As she paused, she also recalled Stanley's description of being the target of religious fanatics who wanted him exorcised. The thought quelled her excitement. This was big, and she knew Adam would think it was exciting – it would be his *X Files* response. But she wondered how she could really prove what she'd experienced? After all, it sounded like the description of a migraine. Sarah's natural predisposition to run below the radar surfaced, and she decided to wait and talk with Stanley first. After all, Stanley could relate.

"Sarah, you were gone for quite a while. Are you feeling OK?" Adam asked, as he sat down.

"Yeah. I took a short walk around the building, and then I ran into the Oracle in the bathroom of the old building. The bathrooms here were pretty crowded, and that one is never busy," she replied.

"So did Patty have anything to say?" Adam queried.

"Well, you know, she's the Oracle, so she had some cryptic warning about Mardi Gras. But she did say that she had seen the crawler, or that's what she called him," Sarah replied. "Remember the weird dude that I told you about who takes his shoes off and crawls around the book aisles trying to look up people's skirts? And I got a text from Jennifer's mother. Jennifer's awake!" Sarah exclaimed, remembering that she had turned her phone off. She pulled it out of her pocket and restarted it.

"Yeah, I got the text. That's great. It's been some kind of day. Jennifer and the Oracle. You're a lightning rod. I'm thinking I'll never be bored around you," Adam said.

"Thanks, Adam. Thanks for hanging with me today. I really like that you not only hung around for the drama, but that you are here now studying with me. I also like that you're open to possibilities. Would you be up for a walk? I'm ready to get happy about Jennifer's recovery. I may even skip," Sarah said, as she finally gave up the anxiety and, grinning, felt a wave of joy and relief.

Adam tilted his head, lifted his eyebrow and smiled. He began gathering his books and pushing them into his backpack.

"Let's walk back to the dorms, dump our books and head for the golf course. That place is ripe with profound happenings."

"That's fine, just so we don't have any more happenings today. I'm kind of full up," Sarah laughed.

"Understood," Adam replied, and they headed out. She and Adam barely made it through the doors before she found herself skipping and twirling in the early evening air.

"Race you to the seed sower statue," Adam yelled, taking off at a lope.

"Hey!" said Sarah, as she took off, books bouncing on her back. She pushed herself hard but didn't have a chance at beating Adam. It didn't matter, she ran as hard as she could all the way. She hadn't felt like this for years. Life felt close and treasured. They spent two hours walking and dancing through the golf course. Laying in the grass, pointing his sky app at the constellations, Adam called out names after she failed to guess.

They lay on the manicured fairway of the 12th hole. The sky was crisp, the stars close and Sarah focused on Orion and internally thanked her dad. It was his favorite constellation. She was grateful and felt the need to say so. She hoped somewhere, somehow, he heard her gratitude and forgave. As she closed her eyes, the stars seemed more than brilliant, more than close. Something glittered in the corner of her eye, and she wasn't sure if it was the starlight reflected in a tear or the energy of the universe flickering just beyond her reach, an infinite life form.

Thursday arrived and Lubna, on their regular evening shift, stood at the circulation desk counter perusing a book she had pulled from the book drop. Sarah looked up and signaled Lubna.

"Can I take a break?"

"Sure, it looks quiet right now. Can you bring me a latte?" said Lubna, as she dug in her pockets for some money.

"Yeah, I'll swing by there. A white mocha sounds pretty good right now," Sarah said, anticipating the sweet, warm stimulant.

The library was busy. Sarah needed to go to the bathroom and now made her way to the old basement. She was hoping to intersect with Bernadette, although she still felt unsure of anything but the name that recurred in her mind as she walked into the old addition. Bernadette, Bernadette. The name washed over her consciousness like the waves on a beach, and Sarah began silently humming. As she passed the new book display, she stumbled. It felt like she had been slapped by a rogue wave, and it was difficult to recover. The sensation emanated from a young man seated there with long dark hair, a ball cap pulled low over his eyes and an incongruous splash of freckles across his nose and cheeks.

As the semester had proceeded, more and more students got serious or desperate, depending on how regularly they had attended to assignments. Lots of groups had begun to form, and all the spare group study rooms were full. Many students slept on couches. This guy looked odd, but he was alert and typing steadily on his computer. She suspected she was feeling Bernadette's thoughts about him because she had no other explanation as to why she would have noticed him at all. Funny, though, as she turned away and headed down the stairs, she thought his hair looked like a cheap wig. Lots of unusual dressing styles on campus, but wigs were a bit uncommon.

Sarah pushed open the heavy door to the bathroom. She could feel a wave that felt like more than the warm air pressure emanating from the closed room. Yes, it was warm and enveloping, but as she sat on the toilet with her eyes closed, a thought popped into her head. Funny, it's not like she felt Bernadette talking to her, she just had thoughts, electrical activity in her brain, and it seemed like *her* thought, even though there was a very elusive, ventriloquist quality to the thought. *Patty, we need Patty.* Sarah grew a bit tense by the thought. Although she felt better about Patty after their bathroom encounter, she still had qualms about being seen with someone who was so different. She didn't mind Patty, it was more her aversion to being seen as a kind of Patty; someone weird, someone to be made fun of, someone who stands out in a crowd. It just went against Sarah's predisposition to stay under the radar.

However, Sarah felt intensely alive, strong, vibrating like a string on a cello and curious as to where this would go. She smiled to herself, she apparently had some *X Files* adventure-seeking in her, too. She heard the door open, and as she emerged, Patty stood in the bathroom doorway.

"Why are you calling me?" Patty said, without preamble.

"What do you mean? I don't even have your phone number," Sarah asserted in her grounded, real-world response.

"Right. Do you really think that an electromagnetic entity needs a cell phone to make a call?" Patty said with a distinct air of sarcasm.

"OK ...," Sarah hesitated. "Let's assume that I emanated a field that you felt, and it acted as a call." Sarah kept trying to ground her perceptions in some theory that she could understand. Traversing into another matterless dimension required some kind of sea anchor. Could she just be getting crazy, or was this something more important than sanity?

"You resonate with Bernadette. She makes you stronger. You're highly entangled, and you've lived together before in past lives. She's harder for me to deal with because we both have to significantly modulate our frequencies to come together. She's been explaining this to me all day today. She's spent a lot of time working with me, and I'm reintegrated. That means I'm not batshit crazy, at least for the time being," Patty smiled subtly, then crossed her eyes.

"Just kidding," she grinned again.

"It's nice to be back," said Patty, as her eyes filled with tears. "I know you'll understand, though, because Bernadette's entangled with both of us. Frankly, I don't really have to say this, because I know you feel the love. But Bernadette thinks you need real-world references until you get comfortable. Aren't you going to wash your hands?" Apparently, Patty's OCD was not Bernadette's doing.

As Sarah stepped over to the sink, true to Bernie's rationale, she said, "Why are we meeting in this bathroom?"

"It's the building, the nature of the steel construction and the underlying geologic formation. This is the room in the building that most resonates with Bernadette. When she is here, her frequency is locked in and strong. It's easier for her to communicate. There's a lot of interference in the rest of the building, more so with all the computer screens these days. Bernie can get around the building, but unless she is moving in tandem with someone whose wavelength is the same, she can become disorganized," explained Patty. It was a bit disorienting to Sarah as she listened to Patty. She did feel a kind of affection for Patty, a warmth that wasn't there before. But she hadn't yet totally shaken her memory of Patty's behavior at the circulation desk, and she still hesitated. Boy, was Adam going to be pumped about the underlying geology. It had been his idea, and it looked like he was right.

"There's something about to go down," Patty interrupted Sarah's thoughts.

"What do you mean?" Sarah asked.

"I don't know what I mean, exactly. It's Bernie's idea, not mine. Can't you feel it? It feels like an itch, a twitch in your eyelid or a visual distortion like the beginning of a migraine. Then an idea coalesces, and you say something to yourself that surprises you. Believe me, I've had a lot of really extraordinary thoughts over the last few years, and surprising myself is a bit hard to do," Patty panned.

"I hear you. But how do you know, how do you feel absolutely sure about the feeling and not just assume it's a hormonal change or something you ate?" Sarah said.

"You don't. That's why intersecting with these individuals isn't for everyone," said Patty. "People have been burned at the stake for a lot less."

Sarah's anxiety was immediately tweaked, and it was hard for her to stuff the feeling and move forward with the next question. But somehow a wave of comfort flooded her consciousness and she said, "So what's coming down, and when and where?"

"Timing is a bit dicey. Bernadette's perceptions of time are not like ours, another little problem with intersecting. Also, she may not know for sure herself. She's here and experiences waves, fluctuations, frequencies of all kinds, in ways we can't. I'm sure it's about the library. I'm sure it is a possible development, but who knows?"

"When I headed down here, I got a funny sensation that seemed to come from a guy sitting on a sofa in the new book area. It felt negative. Do you think that has anything to do with this?" Sarah asked.

"Probably," Patty stated drolly. "I'm beginning to think that you work here because Bernadette needed you, and I'm here for something else she thinks is important." The mention of work pulled Sarah out of the warm feeling of riding an ocean wave.

"I need to get back to the circ desk," Sarah said, as she pulled out her phone to check the time. Patty reached suddenly for her hand; too late, the feeling of warmth and rhythm stopped as her phone came to life.

"Phones are disruptive," said Patty, as she looked a bit confused, automatically turned to the sink and began washing her hands.

"If you need Bernadette, the third stall has the best frequency," she stated casually and focused seriously on washing and rinsing.

"I need to get back, I'm sorry. We can talk more soon," Sarah said, as she turned to rush up the stairs. She'd been gone too long and needed to get back to let Lubna take a break. She hurried up the stairs and glanced at the sofa where The Creep was sitting, feeling again the disquiet that came from his direction. Sarah made the turn and almost ran into Stanley.

"Stanley, I need to get back to the circ desk but have something to tell you. Can you come back with me so that I can let Lubna go to the bathroom?" Sarah asked.

"I was looking for you. I just came from the coffee shop. Lubna asked me to check on you, but I thought you might be in the old addition for some reason," Stanley answered. "What's up? You look bright, kind of lit up."

"I had an encounter again," Sarah said, as they turned back toward the circulation desk. "The Oracle was there, too." Stanley padded softly next to her as they headed in the door to the back office. Lubna was slammed. There was a line of students asking

174

for reserve materials, and, for the next few minutes, Sarah and Stanley called students to the other computer terminals and provided services until the line disappeared and things quieted.

"I'm so sorry, Lubna. I didn't think I was gone that long. I had an encounter with Dr. Nakamura and ...," Sarah said, looking chagrined.

"So what happened to my mocha?" Lubna laughed.

"I never made it to the coffee shop. I decided to go to the old addition bathroom and ran into The Oracle there. It was a pretty unusual encounter," Sarah trailed off.

"Well, maybe Stanley can interpret. I'm going to the bathroom and the coffee shop. I need to get off my feet for a few minutes. Do you want me to bring you something?" Lubna said. Sarah fished the money Lubna had given her out of her pocket and added her own.

"Thanks for understanding. I do need to talk to Stanley, and I think what I have to say might require security and another white chocolate mocha," Sarah stated. Lubna smiled and headed out the back door.

"So, Sarah, what do you think requires security?" Stanley asked. "Is it something you observed or something Patty saw?"

"Both. Kinda. I hate to sound goofy, so let me just summarize things chronologically. I left to go to the bathroom and had the urge to go to the old addition bathroom in the basement. As I passed the new book area, I got a really bad vibe from a guy sitting there wearing a ball cap and what I think was a black wig. I got to the bathroom and was "contacted" by Bernadette, my Blanche," Sarah said, involuntarily lowering her voice at the mention of Bernadette and Blanche.

She continued the story, telling Stanley about Patty, the crawler and the "reception" in the old bathroom, occasionally interrupted by a student asking a question. The narration continued and Stanley listened, silently watching students move in and out of the entrance atrium, rocking silently on his feet. Sarah could tell he was listening intently and found herself following his glance, looking across the atrium toward the bank of computers and tables that were packed with students intent on midterm

175

study. Her voiced trailed away, as she caught sight of TC weaving his way toward the men's bathroom, passing between tables. She silently pointed to TC just as he entered, and Stanley nodded, quickly spotting him.

"That's the bad vibe guy. Patty was pretty solid about saying that it was a feeling Bernadette pushed my direction. Patty said that the old addition has a frequency that resonates with Bernadette and that Bernadette is strongest in the old bathroom in the basement because of the reduced interference. I know this is a lot to take in, and I don't have anything substantive to pin on this guy. I just thought you should know about it, and, frankly, you are the only person who would listen and not think I'm nuts," Sarah said, emphasizing the last syllable.

"It's worth watching this guy," Stanley said, staying focused on the bathroom door and briefly glancing at the computer screen to enter a password combination and type. "I'll just get him on a videotape so it will be easier to go through older security tapes and see if we can spot him doing anything suspicious. They both watched the bathroom for a good 15 minutes, but he never left. Sarah intermittently helped students who arrived at the desk, and, when Lubna returned, Stanley left the front desk service area and calmly entered the men's bathroom. He came back with a quizzical look. Shook his head no when Sarah asked if TC was in the bathroom and headed back to the security office area. Stanley was gone for an hour.

In the meanwhile, Sarah and Lubna sorted books, emptied bins and helped students who stopped at the desk. Lubna asked Sarah for details, and Sarah provided an abbreviated version of her story. The second telling increased Sarah's anxiety about sounding crazy because she listened to herself and realized that, without the background of Stanley's story about Blanche and Lubna's appreciation of Stanley's compassion and shaman-sense, her story would be *Patty-Nakamura-crazy*.

Sarah's natural predisposition toward high anxiety kicked in, and her mind wandered through various scenarios in which her mom was called because she was at the student infirmary being held for observation or other somewhat extreme outcomes, none of which were good. She was grateful for the regular interruptions of students needing help. It kept her from – what did they say? – "Neurotics imagine castles in the air, psychotics move in." Always doubting, Sarah wondered if she had gone too far and "moved in" to a place that didn't actually exist. It seemed unlikely that she and Patty both could harbor the same delusion, but even that logic was overwhelmed by fear. She could count on her mom and her sister believing she believed it, but wasn't sure even they wouldn't wonder behind her back and worry about her if she told them about Bernadette.

It was getting late, and Stanley would begin his last round soon. Lubna took a bathroom break. When she returned, Sarah asked her if she could take a break and walk over to the old addition basement.

"I'd like to go with you," said Stanley, as Lubna was about to reply. Stanley had returned to the desk area with something worth hearing. "Sarah, Bernadette's vibes are on to something. If you and Lubna are able to stay late after we close, I have something to show you on the video cameras. I'd like your opinion before I talk to Luke about it tomorrow." Sarah could feel some of the tension ease between her shoulders. Maybe she didn't seem so crazy, but the anxiety resurfaced as she tried to imagine how she would tell Luke why she noticed the guy with the wig.

"It's quiet, take your time," said Lubna.

"Thanks, gorgeous," Stanley said, smiling at Lubna and gently yanking her long braid. "We might be awhile. There's something on the video that seems to tie this dude to the elevator problems we had in the old addition. I'm going to see if Sarah can channel any ideas from Bernadette."

"Who's Bernadette?" Lubna questioned.

Stanley turned to Sarah and raised an eyebrow.

"She's my Blanche, or that's what I think right now. I'm just saying I'm open to the possibilities. Could be my imagination, could be errant brain activity associated with a migraine, could be a natural detective instinct … just saying, just saying," Sarah

177

hedged, watching Lubna's expression with an underlying mental anguish or *fear of crazy*.

"Nothing wrong with being open to possibilities," Lubna responded gently, sensing Sarah's apprehension. "You're in charge, and you're a solid, analytical person. Worry less. You remind me of myself when I was getting used to Lawton. It felt like a different dimension, but it turned out I could handle it. I just needed practice."

"I guess we're going to go practice a little," Sarah quipped. "Adam said he might come by to walk me back to the dorms. If he comes by, can you let him know I'll be back in a few minutes?" Lubna nodded.

"Sarah should be back in about 20 minutes. We're going to the old addition, and, once I start my rounds, I'll send her back to help you close up," said Stanley. "I'm turning off my phone, but I'll have the radio." Lubna turned to help a student who had walked up to the desk asking for chemistry reserves. As they walked toward the old addition, Sarah commented,

"Thanks for believing me Stanley. I'm kind of doubting myself and wondering if I'm just sorta copycat believing after you told us about Blanche."

"Sarah, you forget, I saw Bernadette the first time we talked in the sort room. I don't have to believe you. I just have to believe my shaman-sense. I would say eyes, but it's not that kind of seeing, exactly. I could say paranormal perception, but that's a little too Hollywood. Too many movies, too many special effects associated with that label. Makes us seem too much like ghost hunters."

"Word! My uncle makes derogatory comments about going Sasquatching, so I get it. In fact, I'm worried about how we tell Luke without saying something about electromagnetic beings? I'm not comfortable telling him that Patty Nakamura and I got together and came up with this. He'd freak. And we'd get nowhere trying to get him to investigate The Creep," Sarah replied. "Patty's got a long history of odd behavior in the library, and I think he'd lump me into a category; a category that might cost me this job. I'm not sure I'd blame him. If I'd had this experience without hearing your story first, I might be freaked. I'm close to being freaked as it is."

"I hear you. Things can go downhill fast when you start talking about concepts outside most people's experience. Fear is a dangerous thing. I'll be honest, I wouldn't have told you about Blanche if I hadn't seen Bernadette and figured you were in for some unusual experiences. It helped that you didn't freak in the elevator, too. You need to be grounded to handle this kind of input and still keep your footing. But what you might not realize is that Bernadette will actually make you stronger. She's resonating with you, strengthening your frequency. That helps," Stanley counseled. They headed down the old east staircase, and Sarah glanced at the painting hanging in the stairwell, mentally noting the cluster of angels rising to the heavens. It made her wonder if that was the label people gave such beings in the Middle Ages. As they turned the corner, she was surprised to see Patty Nakamura sitting primly at one of the tables in the basement study area, eating a sugar cookie. She watched them descend the staircase.

"It's about time. I've been waiting here for over an hour, and it's past my bedtime. Bernadette says there's not much time before The Creep does something. I'm supposed to get you to do something soon," she said, licking the corner of her mouth to retrieve some sugar crystals and green icing. Oddly, she seemed unperturbed by Stanley's presence, although she had been paranoid about others earlier in the bathroom.

"Did she say what The Creep was going to do?" Sarah queried.

"You know it's not like that," Patty looked at them both, exasperated. "It's a *feeling*: a vibration of urgency, danger, pending loss. Bernadette doesn't know what exactly is going to happen, but it has to do with the elevators. I keep feeling a need to ride them up and down and up and down. I'm getting tired of pushing buttons and changing altitude. I need to go home and go to bed," she said, sliding on her gloves and eyeing a remaining cookie in the plastic container on the table. She paused momentarily, removed one glove, reached for the cookie and carefully wrapped it in a handkerchief in her purse. She put her glove back on and gathered her umbrella. "Feels like I'm standing in a tidal pool down here, and the tide is rising. The waves are really strong. You've got the ball, and it's in play. Good luck." With that, she abruptly turned on her heel and headed up the staircase, humming softly under her breath.

Stanley pursed his lips and said, "Can you expand on that in any way?"

"I don't know, but Patty said the third stall in the bathroom was best. Maybe if I go in there?" Sarah surmised, wondering what tune Patty had been singing as it now seemed to be bouncing around in her brain like a bad commercial jingle.

Stanley opened the restroom door and called out, "Security. Anyone in here?" There was no response, and Sarah entered, checking underneath the stalls to be sure. Stanley stood in the doorway to turn away anyone who wandered downstairs, however unlikely it was this late in the evening. Sarah entered the stall, turned to face the door and wondered if she should sit down? Before that thought passed, Sarah again recalled Christmas in the kitchen with her sister, surrounded by glitter and homemade Christmas cards. She felt herself relax and began humming with a steady rhythm. Being trapped in the elevator was her first thought, then a persistent picture of the elevators in the new addition popped into her head. She saw the elevator panel in her mind, and the button panel was lit for the fifth floor, then a picture of the third set of elevators with all the buttons lit up popped into her mind; each time, she felt she was looking at the button panels. Then she began rocking forward and back until she felt propelled to leave the stall and the bathroom. Almost, almost she could feel a small push – or at least she imagined it.

"Elevators, elevators, elevators. Patty was right – whatever's bothering Bernadette, elevators figure into it," said Sarah to Stanley, as they headed back up the stairs. "But I don't think she knows why exactly."

"OK, we need to get back to the circulation desk, and I need to start my final round. If you don't mind, I'd like you to review some camera shots in the security office before you leave tonight after we've locked everything down. I'm going to send a message to Luke and tell him we're going to stay about an hour late, after we lock the doors. I'm going to put together a report for him," Stanley explained.

"What can you say, exactly, without mentioning Bernadette or Patty?" Sarah worried.

"I've got something tangible that I found from some camera shots. I need you to take a look and confirm that the shots I've identified are the guy you saw with the wig," Stanley said.

"OK, sure. I have class pretty early, but I can skip it if I need to. I don't have any tests scheduled, and I'm caught up in Calculus," said Sarah.

"Thanks," said Stanley, as they walked in the back door of the circulation area. Sarah approached the desk and saw Adam leaning on the desk in the atrium, talking to Lubna. Stragglers were leaving, and it was pretty quiet. Stanley slid over the low disability counter, and Adam turned to join him.

"See you later, Sarah," Adam said, with his standard *X Files* eyebrow lift and grin. Sarah couldn't help but laugh inwardly as she looked over to catch Lubna's eye and saw a suppressed smile hovering around Lubna's lips. The guys headed upstairs.

"This is turning into a real *X Files* adventure. I'm thinking it's worthy of a television script. Too bad that series is over," Lubna giggled.

"Hey, I'm thinking *Sleepy Hollow*-worthy," Sarah laughed.

"Well, Adam certainly has the look. Let's clear the book drops and get everything checked in before they get back," said Lubna. "I don't want to leave work for the morning crew. Luke shouldn't think we just sat around talking up the mystery."

"Sure," said Sarah, as she grabbed the cart of books that Lubna had just loaded and rolled it over to a computer terminal. The last hour, they checked in all the books that had been turned in and busied themselves in the sort room until Stanley and Adam turned off the last of the lights.

"Come on back to the security office. I've isolated some video segments that I want Sarah to review. I had an idea, and I have another one now that Sarah has gotten some additional information from Patty and Bernadette," explained Stanley.

"Stan, should Adam be here? He isn't an employee. Nothing against you, Adam, but security is security," Lubna said, worriedly.

"No worries, Lubna. I understand. But I am an employee. In fact, this is my first night of training," Adam said, smiling. "I decided you guys were having too much fun. I put in an application right after that first night I walked on rounds with Stanley. I didn't mention it, because I figured that I was too late to get a job this semester. But Luke called me yesterday. One of the guards got mono, and he needed someone who could start right away. Stanley put in a good word for me, and Luke called and told me to come in tonight and go through closing procedures with Stanley. I'll be working nights when you guys aren't scheduled, but I'm on the crew." He turned to Sarah and smiled.

Sarah grinned back as she sat next to Adam. It was crowded in the small office, but they pulled in another chair. Stanley sat in front of the keyboard and called up the video camera in the new book area. "Sarah told me tonight about a bad vibe she got from a guy in the new book area. I pulled up the footage from that area and found this."

A picture of TC came up on the screen; he was sitting on the north sofa with his ball cap, typing rapidly on his laptop. From the camera's angle, he seemed pretty innocuous. "Is this the guy, Sarah?" Stanley asked.

"Yeah, that's him," she replied. Stanley entered some commands and saved a segment of the video in a specially labeled folder. As he did so, he explained some of what he was doing to Adam.

"Now, here's a clip from the camera in the computer area, outside the men's restroom across from the circulation desk. Here's the guy walking into the bathroom. Remember, we stood there watching, waiting for him to come out tonight, and he never did. When I checked the bathroom, he wasn't there. So after that happened, I went back through the tape and looked again."

Stanley fast-forwarded through some of the footage and stopped when a young man with a shaved head exited and froze the screen on his image. "What do you think, Sarah?"

"He seems taller than the guy with the ball cap, and he has on a different jacket, but there's something about him. The goatee looks a little off, like he didn't take time to put it on straight. Do you think it's the same guy?"

"You are right, he's definitely taller. This guy has on cowboy boots with heels. But look at the backpack. It's the same backpack the guy with the ball cap was carrying, and nobody else entered the bathroom with that same backpack during the 30 minutes that preceded this segment," explained Stanley. He captured the video shot, split the screen and placed a screen shot of both characters side-by-side. Lubna was the first to remark.

"Look at the freckles, there's a definite pattern. It is the same person. But why would anyone go to such pains to change his appearance in a library?" Lubna asked. Sarah's mind immediately thought of the hours of practice she'd spent with her dad at the park, tossing the Frisbee. Her dad always said, you have to practice if you want to get better. He always gave her pointers and interjected positive comments when she threw a good one.

"Practice. He's practicing for some reason. He wants to be really good at changing his appearance in an ordinary bathroom. How long did it take him?" Sarah queried. Stanley reran the segment at normal speed.

"One minute. Tops," concluded Adam. "That's fast. He must have been practicing for a while. He's got it down, and he's thought about it quite a bit. The change in height really makes him seem like a different person, and the heels change his stance and gait. That alone would make you tend to overlook him if you were checking the surveillance cameras. He must know we have them. He must have a reason, and it's probably not very nice."

"But how does this relate to the elevators?" Sarah asked. "We know they are important. Bernadette and Patty were very clear about that." Sarah looked over at Adam, who had raised an eyebrow. "I'll tell you about that on our walk back to the dorms."

She was pleased to see that Stanley hadn't said anything to Adam about Bernadette.

"Good question, and I thought about that," said Stanley. "Remember when the coed was caught in the elevator in the old addition? I wanted to see if I could find him in that area about the same time that all occurred. Since I filed the report, I remember the date and time." Stanley sat for a few minutes at the keyboard, typing in search fields. He chose the camera in the lounge area outside the Great Reading Room. It was close to the deck elevator. He set the replay to fast-forward. They all focused on the screen, watching the characters dancing quickly in and out of the camera's range.

"Stop, back up," said Lubna. "That's him. The camera missed his face because he was putting on his cap when he walked through the frame, but look at the backpack as he goes down the stairs." Stanley slowed the segment to normal speed and froze it as The Creep descended the staircase, which placed his backpack in full view. Stanley enlarged the picture.

"It looks like him, but what does that really prove?" said Sarah, the consistent skeptic.

"I have to agree. He's just there. So far, we just have a guy who likes to wear costumes and happens to be in the vicinity when elevators malfunction. I think he's up to no good, but this doesn't really prove it," said Adam, with a frown of concern.

"Yeah, there are lots of people on campus who like unusual clothes," said Lubna, smiling and eyeing Stanley's favorite bowling shirt. "Maybe it is just coincidence? Maybe this guy is a theatre major? I don't think that's the explanation, but I'm not sure we have much to go on here. It's creepy, but …"

"Could be you're right," replied Stanley. "That's why I wanted all of you to look at this. We can't tell Luke why this guy caught our attention, exactly. Anybody have a good suggestion?"

"I'm a little confused. Why did this guy catch your attention? I think he's up to no good. I think this is beyond just creepy. But what made you watch this guy's costume change?" asked Adam.

"It was me; well, me and Bernadette," said Sarah. "I was going to tell you as we walked back to the dorms tonight."

"It's getting really late. Let's think about this overnight. That will give Sarah a chance to explain more to Adam, and we'll all have some time to think about it. Frankly, if we stay here much longer, we're going to look suspicious ourselves," said Lubna.

"Good point. I'll text Luke in the morning and tell him that I think we have someone doing suspicious things which might explain the elevator problems," said Stanley. "I'll tell him that's why we were slow to close tonight. I'll be vague about why we checked the video and saw him change."

"Why don't you just tell Luke that I saw him tonight and thought he looked like someone I thought I saw hanging around the elevator that day I was trapped?" asked Sarah. "It's not true, exactly, but he could have been there, since he was around the other day the elevator malfunctioned."

"Why don't you ask Luke if you can try to correlate all the elevator problems with this guy being in the building? Statistically, if we can find that he has been here when the elevators have been reported to have problems, then that makes a difference. It's correlations that make a weather modeling more accurate in predicting future events," said Adam. "Do you record every time the elevators have problems?"

"Yeah, it's in the log," said Stanley, getting up from the terminal. They all headed for the locker room and the exit. "I'll see what Luke says tomorrow. I'll text him and see if I can come in and talk to him after lunch and show him the quick change that we isolated on the videos. It's creepy enough to get him thinking."

Sarah yawned and grabbed Adam's arm. "Come on, I'll tell you about Bernadette as we walk back." As they gathered their backpacks, Stanley stopped at the alarm panel and gave Adam a summary of how to engage the motion detectors and confirm all the cameras were in operation. They exited as the temporary alarm sounded, warning them of the 60-second window they had to leave before the intrusion alarm fully engaged. Lubna hugged Stanley around the waist, and they turned north. Sarah and Adam headed south, their long legs matching in stride as they aimed for the dorms. Both could cover considerable ground quickly, and, before Sarah began her narrative, they had passed the Physics Building.

"OK, I'm counting on your *openness to possibilities*," Sarah said, taking a deep breath, pulling in the moist air that promised spring. A light fog could be seen thickening the air around the street lights, and Sarah almost chuckled at the aptness of the setting for a tale that had such incorporeal characters. "Bernadette, she's like Blanche, she's one of the other life forms that we talked about that night at Lubna's apartment. I communicated with her ... in the bathroom tonight," Sarah explained, as she giggled nervously.

"Are you yanking my chain? I'm really serious about new life forms. I'd feel kind of crummy if this was just a joke to you, and Stanley made up a story to keep us entertained around the campfire. I'm working on that list of energy fields, and I asked one of my professors today about instrumentation," Adam said, with a tinge of irritation.

"Hey, I'm just nervous about telling you, and I thought it was funny that this happened in a bathroom. Also, I guess that I'm worried still that I'll be pegged as crazy as Patty Nakamura. I like spending time with you, and I guess I'm saying that I want you to be part of this, whatever it is. I think I could look hard all over this campus and not find someone I'd be comfortable talking to about this; someone who I could trust not to roll their eyes when I wasn't looking and to be analytical without judging. It's not like this is easy. It's a big leap for me, and I have to ask myself if this is some kind of hallucinatory groupthink. Is it really happening or am I just copycatting Stanley's story; jumping to a sound in the dark because I heard a ghost story?" Sarah replied, with a similar level of irritation and an additional dose of anxiety.

Adam stopped in midstride and turned to Sarah, holding her arm. "Slow down. I think I heard something in there about how you like to be with me," he said, suddenly grinning.

Sarah's eyes rolled and she replied, "Really, REALLY. That's what you got out of this? We're talking about new life forms and communicating with energy-based beings, and that's what you focused on?"

"Well, a guy's got his priorities. Bernadette may be incorporeal, but I'm still a guy standing in front of the mirror every day, posing like Wonder Woman. I'm … matter," Adam quipped.

"Don't you mean I matter?" Sarah questioned.

"I was hoping," Adam answered, with his characteristic eyebrow lift and turn of the head. Pausing, Sarah looked into Adam's eyes and said quietly,

"You matter … to me. And you don't need to power pose to get my attention," Sarah said, hugging Adam tightly. "In fact, I'm counting on you. I'm counting on you going on this adventure with me, questioning, analyzing, but not giving up on the possibilities just because we might get labeled wacky …. In fact, you're cuter when you're thinking."

"OK, shoot," Adam said, as he walked over to a nearby bench and sat down, pulling Sarah over to sit as well. "I'm ready to get irresistibly cute." After a fairly detailed explanation, punctuated with Adam's questions about the bathroom stall location and comments about Patty's sudden sanity, Sarah ran down. The fog had thickened, and the night was softly quiet, rhythmically beating with the drip of accumulated moisture falling from the nearby street lamp. They were wrapped in texture. The space between things was filled by the visible fog, and Sarah wondered if this really mimicked the quantum universe, where dark matter filled the vacuum of space and entanglements abolished distance.

"I wonder if Bernadette benefits from triangulating with you and Patty somehow? Maybe it's easier for her to have more than one person connected or frequency matching? I'm kinda guessing here, but I must be thinking so much, I figure I'm ingeniously attractive right now," Adam said, breaking the silence, and stood up. "Cute as I can be, but really tired," he said, yawning. Sarah could feel a copy yawn coming and felt the relaxation that comes from unburdening to a trusted friend and finding your worries were overblown.

"Thanks for not freaking and for being so cute," Sarah yawned, muting her truly sincere gratitude.

"Yeah, I'm hoping to capitalize on that at some point, but right now, I'm interested in lying down and watching some eyelid movies. Looks like they're going to be really interesting tonight," Adam said. During the walk back they talked about the fog and quantum mechanics, and how sound waves were affected by the moisture. Walking through the fog muffled and yet made closer the sound of occasional traffic and the distant warning horn of a train traveling through town.

Bernadette felt the couple on the bench and responded to the rhythm of Sarah's storytelling, a distant entanglement, like a vibration felt from a motor. It comforted her. Now that she was in tune, she also felt Patty, dreaming and restless on the other side of town. She could now distinguish these rhythms from the background noise of so many frequencies. Tuned in, like an antenna capturing a radio station. She had senses that helped her focus, which had long gone unused. Maybe it was the energy of youth, but she had awakened those atrophied senses. The practice, the effort she had put forth to touch Sarah and the accidental reintegration of Patty, made Bernadette resonate. Maybe it was just feeling good about Patty. Bernadette had intended to avoid "touching" Patty, but an odd occurrence had changed that.

Patty had been in the bathroom stall. Bernadette hovered over her, trying to determine how she might best help the odd woman, when the automatic toilet flushed unexpectedly. The swirling water created an almost imperceptible magnetic field, and Bernadette, overhead, somehow aligned and vibrated in tune with Patty. Both were surprised, but this time it was a peaceful strengthening of both, and Bernadette could sense that electrical pulses from Patty's troubled mind began to regularize and pulse less erratically. After several minutes, Patty was humming, and Bernadette was busily examining Patty's thoughts, which eventually focused and pulsed in a comforting rhythm. A toilet. Who knew?

Of course, it wasn't just the toilet. It was the configuration of the steel girders that supported the building, in conjunction with the underlying geologic formation and the combination of Bernadette's frequency, which was at its most intense in this particular spot. These factors, combined with Patty's erratic frequency, her most recent diet choices and the abrupt flush of the toilet caused by Patty's OCD-enhanced approach to squatting on the toilet seat, created a vibrational fluke that resulted in a harmony. Once the waveforms united, Bernadette encouraged Patty to hum a sustaining frequency and so began their symbiotic relationship, a relationship untroubled by a cell phone, as Patty didn't carry such a germ-ridden device.

Bernadette now remembered she could range outside the library, since the geologic formation underneath the library that enhanced her ran diagonally across campus and made it possible for her to move into other buildings with a similar girder structure and sustain herself – at least that had been the case for decades. The proliferation of electromagnetic fields on campus, however, disrupted Bernadette, and she had, more recently, spent years forgetting herself and wandering campus confused into believing her own delusion. Sarah's job at the library had an integrating effect because her frequency was so compatible with Bernie's and because Sarah, unconsciously, wanted a connection.

The tide now had synchronized, and Bernadette felt strong. If she could avoid errant EMFs, she should be able to stay integrated. Her sense of time would always be difficult to integrate with human time perceptions, but her enriched entanglements with Patty and Sarah gave her reference points. Their circadian rhythms changed the intensity of their frequencies, and she could sense those changes and use them to alert herself that time was moving in one direction for them.

Bernadette spent the next several hours mapping her range. She had a close encounter with a cell phone as she moved between the Zoology Building and the library. She actually forgot herself, but the moment passed as the coed hurried down the sidewalk. There were fluctuations in the underground formation and the water table that also weakened her, but she knew that some of those areas could be traveled if she was in close proximity to Patty or Sarah. She sensed greater vibrational intensity with them and a better ability to withstand discordant frequencies.

Bernie floated through the reading room, adorned with carved angels and halogen lighting. The combination acted like a stimulant, and Bernie radiated with health as she experienced it. She was in a good mood as she floated down the staircase, her senses more acute than they had been in decades. She spied Patty, shaking the rain from her umbrella in the entry way, and welcomed her. She felt a slight sensation of guilt as she realized her influence had caused Patty to obsess about sugar cookies. Bernie sensed some molecules of sugar hovering around the latch on Patty's purse and eagerly awaited the moment when Patty would pull them out and take a bite. Anticipation of that moment overwhelmed her watchfulness for TC, who she had been looking for since late morning. As luck would have it, TC came in the entrance in the new addition, as Bernie and Patty settled in downstairs at a table in the old addition. TC walked past the circulation desk while Stanley and Luke sat in front of a monitor in the back office.

"Hey, Stan, so what can you tell me about the videos you isolated last night?" asked Luke.

"I think they may be related to the elevator problems and might be even more serious. I'll pull them up and point out the patron who we think may be responsible," said Stanley, typing in a password and selecting the files he had stored, while Luke expanded on the Thunder basketball game in which Oklahoma City had beaten Chicago. Always the sports enthusiast, Luke recounted numerous shots.

"OK, here's the guy we've identified entering the bathroom in the computer area. As I said, Sarah noticed something about him, call it a bad vibe, when she saw him in the new book lounge. He happened by not long after I spoke with her, and she was able to point him out. Here's the interesting part," said Stanley, as he fast-forwarded and the characters rushed across the screen. "This is a 15-minute sequence, and you can't

190

see him exiting the bathroom. I actually watched the bathroom from behind the desk and thought it was peculiar. So I checked out the bathroom and found it empty," he explained. "That's why I pulled the camera footage, to see if I just missed him or if something else was going on."

"That's pretty observant of you," said Luke, skeptically.

"Well, it was really a combination of Sarah's noticing something funny about him and my concern that he was trying to hide in the bathroom. You know we've had students trying to spend the night in the building, and I thought he might be locking himself in a stall and waiting out closing rounds," explained Stanley.

"Makes sense. I'm glad you were being careful of that. I hate getting here in the morning and having the Dean's office call me about motion detectors going off, and campus police and my boss following up on the alarms. She's really bummed when she has to come in at three in the morning." He grimaced and then grinned. "That's why they pay her the big bucks, though."

Stanley's eyes remained focused on the screen, and he split it, placing TC's wig outfit on one side and his cowboy boot ensemble on the other side.

"Here. It's the same guy going in and the same guy coming out, but he's a regular transformer, because you'd never guess it's the same guy," Stanley said. "We figured it out by looking at the backpack and a close up of his freckles. He's even wearing cowboy boots to change his height. Since we think we got a shot of him around the time Sarah got caught in the elevator, Adam and I were going to look through the security videos of the most recent elevator problems to see if he's in the vicinity when those occurred. Do you think it's worth looking?"

"Well, it's not illegal to dress alternatively. But why do it here? I guess it passes the creep factor test. I'll contact the IT staff and see if there's a facial recognition or some other kind of pattern recognition program that we can use. We don't have one right now, but there might be a license on campus for one that can do some sorting for us. In the meantime, I think you and Adam can spend a couple of hours on it. When you review the logs and compile a list of the elevator problem times, send that to me in an email. If you and Adam can't get through the list in a day or two, I'll get the other security guards to look, too," Luke said. "I think we need to figure this out. It seems like the elevator problems are escalating, but I need to check. I think the last few times we've had problems, it's been at night and I haven't been around. I'll send an email to all the guards and ask them to send a text to all of us whenever the elevators misfire. If all of us are looking for this guy when that happens, we'll be able to figure out quickly if he's linked to the situation. I wonder what he's up to? I'm going to check the video when Rachel found the elevator panel in the decks hanging off the wall. That would really point to something suspicious," concluded Luke.

Sarah slept late and was awakened when Jennifer opened the door carrying a basket of clean laundry. Scooting into a seated position and stretching, Sarah said, "Hey, glad to see you. I thought you'd be coming back on Sunday."

"I thought I'd get here and get settled back in. I figured you would be in class. You usually don't miss Calculus," Jennifer said. "I was going to surprise you when you got back from class, but since you're here, I've got something for you. It's in the car. I'll be right back." Jennifer parked the laundry basket on her bed and left. Sarah thought Jennifer looked good and wondered to herself just how she was handling things. It was nice, Sarah thought, having her back. She'd just been gone a few days, but the room had felt lifeless when she'd come in last night. Maybe it was Bernadette, maybe it was spring, but Sarah wanted life around her. She wanted to be in touch with living things and friends, especially Jennifer, for whom she now felt protective. She'd been pretty diverted by Bernadette and Patty and Adam. Spring, hormones, the library mystery, and Adam's calm acceptance and sensitivity to Bernadette as a life form, rather than judging Sarah as a nut, made him particularly attractive. He intruded on her thoughts even now, and she involuntarily blushed as those thoughts warmed her. Jennifer opened the door holding a bouquet of tulips.

Sarah looked deeply into Jennifer's eyes and began to cry. The tears came in a flood, and Sarah reached out as Jennifer placed the flowers on Sarah's study desk and sat on the bed. They hugged long and hard, and Sarah sobbed repeatedly, surprising herself at the release of tension and concern that she'd stuffed in the back of her consciousness.

Jennifer cried, too, saying repeatedly, "I'm so sorry I caused all this trouble and worried you. I am so sorry. I am so sorry. I wasn't trying to do myself in. I had no idea that it could make me that sick. I was really just drinking and watching movies after the card game ended. For some reason, I couldn't sleep, and I just thought I would finish the bottle to see if I could do it. I saw someone kill a bottle on YouTube and just did it. I wasn't thinking about hurting myself. I guess I was already so drunk that I just wasn't thinking at all."

"It's OK. I just am so glad you are here. I know we haven't been very close, but the thought of you not being here," Sarah sobbed again, interrupting herself, and tears flowed down Jennifer's cheeks as she watched Sarah weeping.

"My mom cried a lot, too. She particularly mentioned you saving my life and how hard it is for the people around you when something like this happens. Sarah, I never meant to burden you like this. I'm so sorry." They hugged again, and Sarah looked over at the tulips.

"I love the flowers. They are beautiful. But just seeing you makes me wickedly happy. You are the flower today for me," Sarah murmured, looking downward.

"Hey, since you missed Calculus, maybe we could spend some time together today? Are you going to your other classes?" Jennifer asked. "I was hoping we could become closer. I think that I may have been missing out on someone who is really worth knowing."

"I think I have been missing out, too," Sarah said. "How about lunch together and a game of Frisbee this afternoon? I'd like you to meet Adam, and I'd like to be outside this afternoon. I've got spring fever, bad."

"Adam? I'm intrigued. What if I call Zach, and we play together? Would that be OK?" Jennifer replied.

"Sure. Adam's always open to possibilities. I'm sure he'd welcome some more Frisbee players," said Sarah.

"I hope he doesn't expect much. I'm not very good. I'm not even sure that Zach plays, but I'll text him. We could pick up some snacks at the cafeteria and have a little picnic," Jennifer suggested.

"That's a great idea. There's a park over by the golf course. We can take a blanket," Sarah said, jumping up and heading toward the bathroom. She glanced out the window at the fading fog and the beginning of blue skies. "It's going to be great." And it was, because they were all determined and so was Mother Nature.

Luke sat in front of the security monitor reviewing the elevator incident in which the police had been called because the panel in the deck elevator had been removed. He checked the deck camera and then the landing lounge with its overstuffed chairs and sofas. In the corner chair sat a young man who might be the guy. He had reddish hair, but the ball cap looked the same. He watched the policeman stop and ask the guy to leave the area. When the young man picked up his backpack, Luke paused the video and enlarged it, focusing on the backpack. It was the same! He backed up the video and watched the entire sequence; this time he noticed the smug smile that Bernadette had observed. There was a fuzzy glitch in the video, and Luke made a note to have the camera checked. Unbeknownst to Luke, it was the moment when Bernadette walked across the room. The transformer definitely seemed to be taking pleasure in seeing the arrival of Luke and then the police. It was like he was waiting for them to show up. Luke picked up the phone and dialed the campus police. He asked for Sergeant Yost.

He'd worked with Yost on several security issues before, and he felt comfortable talking to her about this rather awkward series of events. Later, Luke eblasted all the security staff and sent a still of the transformer as a baseball fan and as a cowboy. He wanted them all on alert for this guy. He would just be a person-of-interest, but if anything went wrong with the elevators, they'd know who to look for.

Chapter 12

"Time is nature's way to keep everything from happening at once."

-- Ray Cummings, *The Girl in the Golden Atom*

Sarah entered the library for her afternoon shift that Monday. She looked up as she passed under the gothic façade and repeated her regular ritual, speaking under her breath to the faces riding the library turrets and wondering to herself if one of them personified Bernadette. It was probably silly to anthropomorphize an alternate life form, but it was almost impossible not to. She wanted to see a face when she pictured Bernadette. Even Stanley, shaman-anchored, somehow attached Blanche, his dog, to the being he communicated with.

Sarah passed through the entry way, moving past the new book area and toward the newer addition of the library. Her eyes adjusted from the sunlight to the more subdued building lights as she passed the display cases that detailed the upcoming reopening of the History of Science collections on the fifth floor. Facsimiles of several centuries-old texts were laid out in the cases, and she stopped briefly, enthralled. It always amazed her when scientists, observing new phenomena, came up with original theories. She wondered if she would interpret her encounter with Bernadette so openly and analytically if Stanley hadn't shared his experience first? Would she just have continued to assume she was having a hormonal episode or doubt her sanity? Anxiety tickled her thoughts as she turned from the display and headed for the

196

circulation desk. But she began to hum under her breath and relaxed as images of a glitter-colored kitchen table replaced her anxiety with feelings of cozy warmth. She felt Bernadette's influence and welcomed the pleasant thoughts.

She signed in on the computer and headed toward the front desk, expecting to see Michelyn in the sort room. Surprised, she saw Lubna instead, wearing a shimmering turquoise sari. Lots of students were sick with the flu or spring fever, so Lubna must be subbing. Her long black braid was threaded with white chrysanthemums, and she looked stunning. A big grin suffused Lubna's face, as she said,

"I got in! I just received the letter this morning. I'm celebrating getting into medical school!"

"Hooray! I knew you would," said Sarah, hugging her enthusiastically and jumping in circles.

"They just had to take someone so into the healing arts – someone who wants so much to help people and who feels it in her blood. I love the flowers in your hair, too," Sarah observed.

"Stanley gave them to me. He says I should always wear white flowers in my hair because of my name. It means a white-flowered tree," Lubna explained.

"Your black hair really sets them off," said Sarah, genuinely approving. "How are your parents reacting?"

"They're over the moon," Lubna laughed. "Now that we know I'll be in Oklahoma City at the Health Sciences Center, Stanley is going to look for jobs in the city when he finishes his MFA. When he gets something, we'll tell my parents. I'm hoping to do that in the summer and start looking for places to live after Stanley figures out where he'll be working."

"Gosh, I'm really happy for you but feeling kinda bad that you two will be leaving in the summer. I'm going to miss you big time," Sarah said, subdued.

"We're just going to have to stay friends. We'll just be 30 minutes up the highway. Besides, Stanley and Adam are adventure buddies, and, frankly, Stan isn't about to give up on working with you to see if Bernadette and Blanche can be 'introduced.' I think you're stuck with us," Lubna said.

"That's a good feeling. I'm not sure I'm ready to tell anybody else about Bernadette. At first, I felt that way because I thought people would think I'm crazy, but I'm beginning to have an attachment to her, and now I'm feeling a little like the kids in *ET*. Maybe people would feel threatened and try to hurt her. Do you think that's paranoid?" Sarah asked, giving in to her anxieties.

"I think that is just being careful. When you read the blogs and tweets out there, you realize there are a lot of people with negative vibes. I suspect Bernadette is pretty wise to the world, but it's hard to know for sure. I know Stanley feels protective of Blanche, and he appreciates just how easily people can turn on you because you are different. I know that I'll not be mentioning Bernadette or Blanche in medical school," Lubna grinned. "But I'm going to be thinking about energy-based creatures and energy fields as I go through medical school. I think it's an untapped opportunity to relate Ayurvedic medicine and Western medical research. Who knows, maybe we'll find ourselves working together on some new instrumentation that taps that potential? You can be the engineer, and I can be the innovative physician," Lubna fantasized.

"You know, that may not be as farfetched as it sounds," Sarah answered, buoyed by the idea that she and Lubna would remain friends and perhaps even become working colleagues. "I may be able to get some help from Bernadette in some way. Who knows?" Students began streaming into the front doors as class change occurred. Their conversation was cut short by patrons. Sarah stepped up to the desk, "May I help you?"

That night, Adam found himself on rounds for the first time as a guard. Sarah had walked him to work and gone down to the coffee shop to start on her Physics assignment. She needed the caffeine boost to focus for hours nonstop. Although Adam had several nights of experience with Stan, Sarah noticed he seemed nervous being on his own. Another guard was scheduled to come in at 10 p.m. and close, so this was a short shift, and Sarah figured it would be a good time to catch up. Seemed like she struggled to stay caught up in this course and Calculus but congratulated herself on finding a place and a ritual that helped her get through the problems. Highly focused, Sarah was surprised to see Adam walk toward her.

"Back already? Feels like you just left," Sarah observed.

"It's been two hours, and I'm taking my break," Adam replied.

"Wow. Now that I think of it, I need a bathroom break. Wanna walk me over to the old addition?"

"Checking on Bernadette?" Adam asked.

"Maybe. I'm not afraid that I'm crazy anymore, so it feels like I'm visiting a friend," Sarah replied.

"Sure. Let me get a cup of coffee, and I'll walk you back. I need to check one of the camera's in the reading room lounge. It's working but gets a little fuzzy every few minutes," Adam explained. "I was just going to see if there was something in the room affecting it before I left Luke a note." Adam climbed the staircase to check the cameras, and Sarah walked down to hit the basement bathroom, unconsciously humming as she pushed the heavy wooden door and made her way to the third stall. The third stall was locked, and Sarah moved to the next stall, sitting down and surreptitiously looking for feet. Seeing none, she assumed it was Patty, an idea reinforced by a mental picture popping into her mind – a picture she suspected was Bernadette-induced.

As the coeds left, both Sarah and Patty emerged, nodding silently to each other while looking at the mirror. Patty began her elaborate hand washing, and Sarah felt compelled to linger over the sink longer than her regular ablutions, just to relieve a wave of anxiety that seemed to emanate from Patty. Sarah held her hands under the running water, enjoying the falling cascade in a way she hadn't noticed before, catching the play of water and light as her hands moved under the flow.

"Did you see him? Bernadette's been pacing back and forth upstairs for an hour, trying to get your attention," said Patty.

"Really. I didn't feel it at all. I guess I'm not in the flow," Sarah replied.

"Where have you been the last hour?" asked Patty.

"In the coffee shop. It's a good place for me to work on Physics questions," Sarah explained.

"No wonder. That place is so wifi'd and computer screened, it's an EMF overdose waiting to happen," Patty explained. "Bernadette loses herself when she even gets close to that area. She avoids it entirely."

Sarah wanted to ask how Patty knew this, but the need to ask seemed to evaporate, and she somehow knew it to be true before the question emerged from her lips.

"Do you feel it? Bernadette is intense right now. She's been pushing me to go up to the reading room. I thought it would be better if I waited for you, but I didn't realize that you would be out of reach for so long," Patty explained.

"But I'm not even scheduled to work right now. How would Bernadette push me to be here to help …," Sarah asked, but stopped in midsentence as she thought about quantum entanglements and the irrelevance of distance. "OK, dumb question."

"Yeah, distance is no object, but EMF interference, it's kind of like a cone of silence. You are pretty much unreachable in the coffee shop immersed in all the technology on that floor," Patty replied to Sarah's unasked question. Now that was a bit spooky, and Sarah paused until the sparkly feeling reemerged, and she felt the comfort of a Christmas kitchen.

Bernie could feel the merging of the energy waves among the three of them, growing the strength of the frequency and giving her additional stability. The old basement wifi interference was relatively low, but it felt good to be stronger, more reliable. She sensed the negative vibrations of TC radiate through the metal structure. They weren't strong but had a frequency pattern that was dissonant. She could feel the origin of the wave move above her, and she needed to communicate to these two children that their help was needed. Something was about to happen.

Patty and Sarah looked at one another and simultaneously said, "Uh oh."

"I guess we both felt that," Patty observed dryly.

"Yeah, it felt like a push. Like my muscles twitched in response to some signal, like you would feel if you got a static electric shock," Sarah observed.

"Something's afoot," Patty stated, turning quickly and heading out the door. They both trotted up the stairs and then stood on the landing, unsure exactly what to do next. Sarah heard the ringing of the emergency stop bell on the elevators by the new book area and realized someone must be stuck in the elevator. Before she walked over to the elevators to investigate, Adam came down the staircase.

"Sarah, glad you're here, I need to call in an elevator problem in the decks, and I'm headed to the office," Adam said.

"I guess you have two elevator problems, because it looks like these elevators are also messed up. Adam, this is Patty Nakamura," Sarah said.

"Good to meet you. Sarah, I'm getting a bad feeling about this," said Adam, as Lubna's voice could be heard over the radio clipped to his belt. Sarah and Adam's eyes met as she overheard Lubna report elevator problems in the new addition.

"What are the odds all three sets of elevators go down at the same time?" Sarah asked, as the hairs on the back of her neck stood up. "Do you want me to stay near this entrance and look for 'our friend'?"

"Good idea, I'm going back to the office and alert Lubna to keep an eye out, while I call the physical plant emergency service crew. We have to have some elevators working for wheelchair students, and I need to see if anyone is caught in the elevators," Adam said, with a tone of worry in his voice. Sarah could tell his normal *X Files* excitement was overwhelmed by the concern for people stuck in the elevators and the need to get them out as quickly as possible. After all, it was Adam's first week on the job, and this was no coincidence.

"Bernadette is helping us, I can feel it. I'll check these elevators and watch this exit while Patty goes up to the deck elevators and pushes some buttons like she did to get me out. You and Lubna can cover the other entrance and check those elevators." Adam gave Sarah a look of intense gratitude and took off jogging quickly toward the newer addition.

"This is an old business," Patty replied cryptically, and headed up the stairs. Sarah wasn't sure what Patty meant but found herself looking toward the new book lounge sofas where she had seen The Transformer before. However, she saw only a young woman texting, so she headed toward the 1958 elevators and pushed the call buttons. "Hello, is anyone in there?" Sarah yelled into the crack between the elevator doors.

"Help, it's dark in here, and the elevator won't move," she heard someone yelling above the ringing of the emergency stop alarm. It sounded like the elevator was frozen on the floor above her.

"Push in the emergency stop to turn off the alarm. I can hear you better that way," said Sarah, raising her voice to be heard above the old fashioned dinging sound. It reminded Sarah of the bell in her elementary school that rang at the end of recess. "The elevator repair people have been called. We should be able to get you out soon."

"Please hurry. It's pretty creepy in here," replied the elevator occupant, who seemed to be female.

"We're working on it. Hang in there," Sarah said, trying to be encouraging. Some students studying across the corridor looked up curiously as she stood by the elevator, but she turned her attention to a group of students coming into the building and a couple headed toward the exit. The Transformer wasn't there, and she worried that he could be anywhere in this large building doing just about anything. It could take more than 30 minutes for all the people trapped in the six different elevators to be freed. If he did this, then it was a really effective way to keep security tied up. As her worry increased, she saw Stanley trot into the building. He'd obviously been running and slowed as he saw her.

"Stanley, I'm really glad to see you. We've got a really creepy situation here. All the elevators are down. Adam is over in the new addition," Sarah explained.

"Yeah, Lubna texted me. I was on my way over to pick her up. We were going to spend the afternoon celebrating. So I picked up the pace," he said, between deep breaths. Suddenly, the elevator door opened, and a coed stepped out.

"Thanks for getting me out," she said.

"… Sure," Sarah stuttered. She turned to Stanley with her eyes wide and lifted her shoulders in a universal expression of surprise.

"That's interesting," Stanley observed, as the coed walked away. Just then, Stanley's phone dinged. "It's Lubna; the new addition elevators are working now, too. What do you want to bet the decks have started working as well?"

"Looks like you're right. Here's Patty now. She was checking them," Sarah said, as Patty came down the steps to the landing.

"Did the elevators just start working spontaneously?" Sarah queried Patty.

"It would seem so. Both the east and west elevators started moving at the same time, because once the west elevator opened, I ran down to the other end of the decks and heard the east elevator moving," said Patty.

"Hmm … looks like a coordinated effort of some sort. Has anybody seen The Transformer anywhere?" Stanley asked.

"I'm hanging here to see if we can spot him leaving," Sarah said.

"He's acquiring experience. It's an old business," Patty said again, in a manner that made Sarah realize their moniker of The Oracle might have stuck because Patty retained an odd predisposition to phrase things obliquely.

"What do you mean, 'an old business'? You said that earlier. Do you mean it's been happening for a long time or what?" Sarah queried.

"It just popped into my head, so I figured it was Bernadette-generated. I can't explain it exactly, but I get a mental picture of old things, historical thoughts, when I think of the elevators," Patty said, as she shrugged. Obviously, Patty was comfortable with stray thoughts that didn't seem to make sense in the current moment. Sarah tried to relate and wondered if Bernadette would resonate with her and create the same mental picture if she tried herself to 'feel it'? She focused for a moment but felt out of touch. Maybe Bernadette was busy?

The Creep pushed in the door of the men's restroom in the old basement. He'd traveled from the fifth floor in the new addition all the way to the old basement restroom, checking his watch, timing how long the trip between the floors took. He pushed into a stall and began a rapid change of clothes and shoes. Bernadette floated through the doorway and hovered in the bathroom, feeling particularly strong in her favorite area of the library. She radiated a wave of energy toward The Creep but stayed disentangled in a waveform that did not intersect. The Creep finished a quick change, looked at his watch and headed up the steps, pulling a ball cap brim low over his eyes and immediately turning toward the door and heading for the exit.

Sarah, Patty and Stanley were discussing the elevator situation and would have missed him entirely except that Bernadette issued a burst of energy and Patty's attention was immediately turned. She caught a very brief look at the back of The Creep as his backpack descended the steps and the wooden door opened. Sarah and Stanley's attention followed Patty's, and Sarah felt like she had missed something important as Bernadette's sense of concern flowed toward her. They recognized the backpack.

"As the world turns," said Patty, a typically cryptic utterance that seemed to come from nowhere.

"What do you mean?" Sarah asked, sensing the muttering was important but not sure why.

"I don't know. It just came to me," Patty muttered. "I have a feeling like the one I got on the decks when I felt like I was being followed. I don't really know how that relates to what I just said, but I assume Bernadette does."

"Sounds like a feeling I sometimes get with Blanche … those feelings usually turn out to be important, but I don't always figure it out soon enough," said Stanley. "I'm going to check on Lubna. She's getting off in a few minutes, and I've got plans to take her to the springs to celebrate."

"I'm coming with you. I'm going to check with Adam and get my books," said Sarah. "Patty, do you have any more feelings that might help us figure out the elevator situation and why The

Transformer seems to be around doing his thing when the elevators flip out?"

"Not really, but I'm going to browse the book stacks. If I'm drawn to some titles, it might give me a clue. Books speak to books ...," Patty muttered, as she wandered away without concluding their conversation, much like she was drawn by an invisible hand. As Sarah watched her go with some anxiety, she could hear Patty humming under her breath. Sarah's anxiety seemed to dissipate spontaneously. She turned toward the circulation offices, humming softly to herself as she walked with Stanley. He turned toward her, noting that she and Patty hummed the same melody, and he made a note to try and remember it. It was familiar, but he couldn't quite recall the song's name.

"I think we saw The Transformer leave the building just a few minutes ago," Sarah said, when she saw Adam at the desk with Lubna.

"We should check the south exit cameras to be sure," said Stanley. "I wish we could be sure that he was tied to all this. If we hadn't caught him changing in the bathrooms and gotten suspicious, we wouldn't even be looking for him. There could be a number of other people in the building who have always been here when the elevators screw up. We just might be focused on the wrong person or persons."

"I'm going to check the video and see if I can sort of track The Transformer, maybe get an idea of where he was when the elevators messed up. I might be able to track him backward from the exit and see if he looks like he is doing anything at that time or if he's just an innocent oddball," said Adam. "I called Luke, and he wants the service people to check out the elevators and see if there's any way they can explain how they all malfunctioned at the same time."

Sarah stood by, humming quietly to herself, and then said, "Whatever is up, the elevators got our attention. Did you notice how we all were focused on helping people in the elevators? If you wanted to do anything creepy, that would be the time to do it."

"Good point," said Lubna. "If we weren't already alerted to The Transformer, then we'd have all been totally riveted on the elevators. If he isn't just an innocent oddball, then we have that advantage. We're on to him, even if we don't know what he's up to."

"Patty's got a feeling about it, but you know how enigmatic she can be. She's out browsing the stacks, looking for clues in books," said Sarah. Rachel and Fotis arrived to relieve Adam and Lubna. As they came on and Adam turned over the radio, both he and Lubna explained the elevator problem. Rachel remembered finding the books in disarray and the deck elevator panel removed from weeks ago. Fotis had helped Luke then as well, so they were both properly concerned.

"Look, Rachel, I'm going to review the video and set aside some clips if I can backtrack The Transformer's movements in the building. I've got about an hour before I need to get to the Weather Center. I've texted Luke so he's aware. He's concerned about the dedication day after tomorrow in the History of Science collections. He said there will be a lot of donors and a number of them will need elevators. He wants to make sure nothing happens while they're here."

"I'll help," said Sarah. "I need to get my books. See you in a few minutes."

Sarah returned to the security office to find Adam poring over video.

"That's him," she said, recognizing the ball cap and backpack."

"Looks like he came up from the staircase," said Adam, changing the screen display to cameras situated in the old basement by the fire exit. "Look, here he is making his way to the old restroom, but he's in his other persona, with the black wig. He must have made a change in the old bathroom before he left."

"The time there is 2:42. The time of his exit is 2:45. He made that change really quickly, two minutes max. I still think this is all practice. He is practicing to change fast and get out of the building undetected. But why?" Sarah asked out loud.

"The people caught in the elevators were in there less than ten minutes," Adam observed. "Let's back up all the videos and fast-forward through them to see if we can find The Transformer." They found him sitting in the reading room lounge, apparently studying on his laptop about the time the elevators malfunctioned. Other than a sly smile, he looked uninvolved. They could see Patty walk past, headed for the deck elevators, but The Transformer just typed something for the next minute or two, closed his laptop, packed it up somewhat hurriedly, and quickly took the staircase.

"Luke's going to look at this and think Patty looks guiltier than this guy. I'm not sure we should mention that Patty helped us. It'll be hard to explain why, and he has a long history of her being bat-shit crazy. I don't want him to question her. I'd feel responsible," said Sarah. "After all, she's involved because of me, sort of. He believes she is crazy, and he'll think I'm crazy, too. I feel there's something with this guy, but I can't see how I'd explain that feeling without mentioning Bernadette," said Sarah, anxiously.

"Don't worry," said Adam, after he looked hard at Sarah and realized the extent of her concern. "We'd all like to be heroes and solve this, whatever it is. But Stan and Lubna and I are all on your team. We're not going to sacrifice you and Patty in an effort to be the Sherlock Holmes of library security guards. Let's see if Patty can give us a hint, and we can talk about it tomorrow night. You will all be here on your usual shift, and I'll come in like I usually do to walk you back to the dorms. I'll get here a couple of hours early and we can discuss it."

"I'm not sure I'll see Patty before then," Sarah said. "I'll come early and head toward the bathroom. If Bernadette is going to help, I guess she'll be there?" Sarah imagined she felt something and hoped it was a confirmation from Bernadette that she would be there to help. But Sarah's predisposition to anxiety made her doubt that.

"Adam, I'd like to tell you just how much it means to me that we're sitting here talking about Bernadette and Patty, and you are acting like this is all normal stuff. It's hard to put into words, but I've always had a fear, based on an experience, that I might be kind of crazy and that I'd lose people I cared about because of it," Sarah said, very quietly.

Adam turned to Sarah, sensing the seriousness of her admission. "Do you mean you think you might go postal or be converted by some religiously extreme cult and blow yourself up? That kind of crazy?"

"No. I just mean that sometimes I get scared and angry, and I say things that I regret. It seems that I do that more with the people I care most about," Sarah observed ruefully.

Before Adam could interject, she went on, her voice wavering "Just so you know, when my dad was pretty sick, I said something really awful, and I loved my dad. I loved him a lot. He was really sick and on a lot of medications. I didn't really understand how that was affecting his behavior, but he came into the living room and began yelling at me. He screamed at me to get off the computer and quit gaming."

Sarah looked up, squared her shoulders and took a deep breath. "I don't remember everything he said, but I remember what I said. I told him I wished he was dead and ran out of the room." Sarah said, a soft sob escaping as she inhaled deeply, blushing as she recalled the incident. "I was really ashamed, because he was dying and because I never really said I was sorry for saying it. I'm still ashamed, and I'll never be able to take it back." As she said it, she looked up at the ceiling, trying to keep a tear from dropping out of her flooded eyes.

"Sarah, I know you'll remember that forever, but I wonder how many times in your life you said something good, something loving to your dad? I remember a big fight I had with my dad. Funny, it was about gaming, too. It was one of the times I biked over to see my uncle afterward. I was blowing off steam with my uncle, telling him how much I hated my dad because he didn't get it. My dad was big into hiking and sports, and I was pretty nerdy. He didn't understand why I liked gaming and thought I was a grade - A couch potato. My uncle said that it was normal to have conflict with your parents. He said it was how Mother Nature kicked you out of the nest, so to speak. Then he reminded me how many times he'd seen my dad patiently playing ball with me and trying to find a sport that I was good at, even trying to play Zelda. My uncle told me about how my dad worried about me and spent hours with him talking about me. I have to admit, I listened but really didn't hear everything he said because I acted like a jerk. I guess what I am saying is that it is hard to be flawed; hard to admit you're a jerk. I look back on that sometimes and feel embarrassed. I had some choice names for my dad that day, but my dad is paying my tuition and has worked his whole life to get me here. I'm grateful, but I haven't always shown gratitude," Adam said, looking back at the screen, composing himself.

"Well, at least your dad is here, and you have a chance to let him know how you feel," Sarah said, consoling Adam and abusing herself at the same time.

"Yeah, but my uncle isn't. I wish that hadn't been our last conversation. I'm not proud of it. It's painful to think that my uncle's opinion of me was colored by that conversation. His good opinion meant everything."

"I'm sure you had a lot of conversations with your uncle that made him glad you were his nephew. If I shouldn't measure myself by one conversation, you shouldn't, either," Sarah said. "Let's go by the dorms and pick up a couple of Frisbees, and play a game in their honor. We can't bring them back, but we can be glad they were in our lives." Sarah wiped a tear from her face and jumped up, trying to dispel the somber tone. "At least I know that my dad would take me to the park when I was trying to work something out. He said standing in the grass tossing the Frisbee was good for inspiration. Maybe we'll have an idea about The Transformer?"

"Good idea," said Adam, welcoming the change in tone. "I'm thinking that the loser buys pizza?"

"Then you'll need to bring money," said Sarah, glad to be grinning. Their walk back to the dorms focused on pizza toppings and a debate about what The Transformer might be up to. The late afternoon was warm, and the park was full of dog walkers and kids. After tossing the Frisbee back and forth, they lay in the spring grass, careful to find a spot unmarked with dog droppings, away from the walking trail. Sarah spread her jacket under their heads, and they basked in the welcome sun. The air was still cool in the shade, but bees hovered in the nearby vetch and evening primrose. The smell of freshly cut grass drifted from a mowed lawn across the street. Adam turned to Sarah, propping himself on his elbow.

"I assume you have sufficient booty for my tastes in pizza," Adam queried, pointedly assuming the attitude of a Frisbee victor, beating his chest with his free hand and holding his arm up with two fingers pointed skyward.

"To the victor go the spoils, captain," Sarah replied, feeling the warmth of the sun warm her thoughts as she noted the curve of Adam's cheek. Without hesitation, her arm encircled his neck and she pulled Adam into a kiss. His enthusiasm was unmistakable. As he lay on her, he pulled away, staring down. Her arms fell over her head, and Sarah could think of nothing but Adam, how he smelled and how the sunlight encircled his head, making his hair sparkle like a halo. Sounds of children on the slide and mothers gossiping on the bench, yards away, seemed distant. A bee buzzed close to her right ear, but the languid warmth that pervaded her made that seem unfocused and unimportant. Adam looked at her, and she noticed for the first time that his eyes were a mix of brown with a subtle green edge on the outside border of his iris. His expressive eyebrows were a shade darker than the sun-touched hair, and one raised in his usual display of curiosity and excitement. He breathed deeply, and she mimicked the deep inhalation, pressing closer and relaxing with no awkward thinking, no anxiety about bad breath or mental calculations about how she appeared. She couldn't take her eyes off Adam's face.

"You're beautiful. You look like spring," Sarah said softly, reaching up and running her hand through Adam's hair. She could feel him begin to shake in quiet mirth.

"Whaaat?" Adam replied. Sarah began to laugh herself, enjoying the feel of them both shaking. Unwilling to let him roll away, she grabbed him on both sides.

"That's a first," Adam gasped. "I've never been called a season, and I've never been told I was beautiful."

"Do you mind? I've never called anyone a season before, and I think you may be the only guy I've ever called beautiful, at least out loud," Sarah said, still too languid to feel embarrassment.

"I don't mind, matey. I just wish I'd said it first," Adam whispered, bringing his lips to her ear and softly biting the lobe. Sarah giggled, tickled.

"I love the feel of you laughing underneath me. I love thinking about making you laugh that way, somewhere else. Somewhere where there aren't quite so many babies in strollers and so many bugs," he said a bit drolly, as he flicked a determined beetle from Sarah's shoulder and then moved his hand to her hair, brushing a stray strand off her forehead along with a ladybug that had run aground.

"I'm with you, captain. I kind of feel like we are under attack by alternate life forms right now," Sarah said, waving her hand over Adam's hair as a bee buzzed closely, intent on the soft pink evening primrose blooming next to their heads. As she turned her head to follow the bee landing a few inches away, they both watched it gather pollen and nectar, moving from blossom to blossom.

"Somehow, though, I'm not willing to give ground. Retreat isn't appealing right now. But I guess the bees don't actually make honey until they get back to the hive," Sarah said.

Adam kissed her neck as she turned, "I'm just mapping terrain right now," he said, kissing her on the shoulder and cheek, moving to her lips. "Retreat with a plan, that's starting to sound like victory." He jerked suddenly as a gnat flew into his eye, and he appeared to wink conspiratorially as his eye watered; he grabbed his eyelash, failing to evict the ill-fated flier.

"Wait, I can get it," Sarah said, reaching for his eye and carefully squeezing the gnat in her fingers, slowly pulling it away, trying not to remove any lashes as she extracted it.

"Thanks," Adam said, as he rolled away, blinking repeatedly, staring up at the blue sky dotted with small puffs of white gossamer.

"I'd enjoy mapping your topography," she said, grinning. "But I couldn't guarantee we'd be free of alternate life forms...."

"Bernadette would be a welcome alternative," Adam quipped.

"Maybe I'll switch my major to Cartography," Sarah inhaled deeply and got to her feet.

"Well, then you'll need practice," Adam responded, grinning.

The pizza that night was perfect. Sarah's senses remained heightened, and Adam remained beautiful. After much kissing on their favorite bench, they made plans for Adam to walk Sarah back after her shift the next night. As Sarah walked up the stairs toward her dorm room, she was surprised that she ever thought Adam looked awkward, as he had seemed to when they first met. Now, his loping gait seemed to fit his frame and his mannerisms, especially the lift of his eyebrow, his *X Files* response, and his openness to the possibility of Bernadette felt good. She recalled him saying, "That's just commercial crap. I'm not into it. I am open to the adventure, in being somewhere and doing something I have never done before. It doesn't have to make sense. I'm suspending disbelief." As she drifted off to sleep, Adam seemed as perfect as the pizza.

Chapter 13

"Mathematics is the language in which God has written the universe."

--Galileo Galilei

Sarah woke early and lay in bed remembering the spring afternoon with Adam. It was worth savoring, and she wondered if this feeling was love or a bad case of spring fever. She recalled Zach and Jennifer's uneven relationship. She wondered, if she was in love and told Adam, would he react like Zach and lose interest? Did desire disappear when certitude entered the picture? She loved her sister and her mother a lot and knowing that – well, they had her back, made her value them even more. Adam's acceptance of Bernadette as a possibility made her value him as much. That was something, something important in her reckoning, and she didn't want to lose that.

Sarah rolled over and looked at Jennifer. Jennifer was beautiful and intelligent, albeit naïve about alcohol. If Zach had lost interest in her, had it been because they didn't have enough in common or because Zach was only interested in the chase, or maybe Jennifer just wasn't a good lover? If she and Adam took their relationship to the next level, would she be a good lover? The thought was unsettling and stimulating as the same time as Sarah thought about Adam's hair bathed in the sunlight and how he felt on top of her. She savored the thought of intimacy, but anxiety intruded. What if she was a bad lover or what if she didn't like sex with Adam? He knew about Bernadette and seemed accepting, but what if he tired of her? Would he remain a friend, a friend she could trust with the idea of Bernadette?

Sensual thoughts intruded as she lay in her cozy nest but dropped away as anxiety about being inadequate intruded. Sarah, in an attempt to expel the negative thoughts, rolled out of bed and padded to the bathroom. She had three classes this morning, and it was getting close to finals. She needed to get moving. She couldn't afford to skip any of these classes. In Calculus, she still had a chance to avoid the final. She had two more quizzes to bring her grade up just a few points to ensure she wouldn't have to take that last exam. The warm shower muddled her thoughts further as she tried to recall calculus formulas but lost her concentration repeatedly, thinking of Adam. Spring fever or love? Her entire day was a comedy of events, as she tried to concentrate but found thoughts of Adam interrupting her every effort. By the end of the day, she'd made little progress in academics but had luxuriated in countless sensual daydreams.

So much for college, she thought, if this continues. She made a decision to go straight to the library after dinner and set up in the coffee shop with a double espresso. Maybe caffeine could overcome Mother Nature for a couple of hours before she started her work shift.

Bernadette felt the intensity of youthful energy as her entanglement with Sarah vibrated throughout the day. It was a bit like holding the end of a can connected to another can by a vibrating string. You could "hear" if you really focused. If not, you could sometimes feel, but not clearly understand, what was happening on the other end. She actively tried to listen for Patty and Sarah, so she often focused on their "cans." Sometimes, she could feel the strings of other entanglements vibrate. Then again, the library itself was a can of sorts. It was a collector of entanglements, ideas, associations. Some very old, some close, some distant, some dimensionally independent. The books themselves were organized attempts at demonstrating entanglements, so they reached beyond the touch of the authors and reached back to those who had touched them.

It was this concentration of energy entanglements that both drew Bernadette to the library and sometimes negated her own frequency, thereby dampening her life force until another synchronous waveform reignited her, as Sarah had. As she pondered these purposeful and errant waveforms, she felt an unsettling vibration, an itch. She had an unwanted tendency to try and match waveforms in frequency and intensity – a sync. However, this itch was not a frequency she cared for. It was The Creep, and he was wired, strung tight. Bernadette floated down to the main floor, following the trail, and saw The Creep sit down in the new book area and open his laptop.

Bernadette sensed intention and urgency, and the intention wasn't nice. How she knew that, even she couldn't explain. There was a quality to the energy she felt radiating from The Creep, a kind of pushy waveform that was unaccommodating and unlikely to merge with other energies in the building. Life was a dance of energies constantly entangling and merging, but The Creep's energy was unaccommodating, forcefully pushing out without heeding or interest in other energies. It was destructive, and other waveforms touching it retreated in intensity. It made a wake like a boat, washing over weaker energies, forcing them to change to save themselves or be synched in a destructive rhythm.

Bernadette sent out a warning waveform to Patty and Sarah. Patty was on campus several buildings away and found herself thinking about the library. Bernadette could feel Sarah, who was surrounded by EMFs emanating from all the computer screen displays in the technology area, but couldn't touch her. Sarah was in the zone, focusing on physics problems and hyped on caffeine, determined to finish the problem set before her evening shift began. Unfortunately, Patty was hungry, and real world thoughts of food overwhelmed Bernadette's push, so Patty headed home for dinner with a growling stomach and a nagging feeling that she'd left something undone. Patty was used to odd thoughts, so she failed to grasp this as more important than her normal jumble of stray intuitions. Bernadette was frustrated but not desperate, as The Creep seemed to have settled in, munching on a sandwich he'd pulled from his overstuffed backpack.

Sarah looked up at the clock and realized it was almost time to start her evening shift. After several attempts to banish spring and Adam from her thoughts, anxiety about grades and school took over. She'd finished her problem set and sat back with a sense of accomplishment. Even now, that sensation was overcome again with thoughts of Adam, and she feared the last few weeks of school were going to be the hardest she'd encountered, even harder than having a job. Who knew? Maybe, just maybe, she wasn't so different from Jennifer. Was she besotted? It didn't do her any good to ask that question now, she needed to get upstairs. She was looking forward to seeing Lubna, and work would give her something to do, something to focus on.

As she headed out of the coffee shop, she felt something else and decided to make a pit stop in the old bathroom before she checked in. She took the basement route and had a premonition as she pushed open the bathroom door. But was it a premonition or was it her imagination? That was the problem with communicating like this. What was it Stanley said? He didn't exactly talk to Blanche and sometimes wondered himself if a feeling was just his imagination. Well, Sarah thought, with an unexpected sense of appreciation, she had Patty. Patty, the woman she initially devalued as crazy. Patty now represented a second witness to the phenomenon of Bernadette, and Sarah's scientific bent reinforced that appreciation. It was like repeating an experiment and getting the same result.

"Hi, Sarah," said a voice emanating from the third stall and, momentarily, Sarah thought Bernadette had somehow found a voice. It was Patty. Sarah caught herself wondering if that idea of the voice being Bernadette's had overlaid her senses for a moment and tangled with Patty's reality? Could Bernadette's intention be tied to Patty's utterance? It was so confusing that she focused hard on Patty to get grounded.

"Did you see him when you came down?" Patty asked.

"See who? I just came through the basement by the Chaucer Variorum office. I didn't see anybody in particular. Are you talking about The Transformer?" Sarah replied.

"Yeah, he's in the new book area, and Bernadette is buzzing about him, or at least I think that's what she's so intense about. That's what popped into my head anyway," Patty answered. Sarah found the same thought in her head and felt a push of urgency – undefined, but definitely there.

"I feel it, too," Sarah said haltingly, as she tried to examine the sensation. Or I think I do. Confusion swirled in her mind about what she felt and what she might be imagining because Patty had suggested it.

"I've got to check in for work at the circulation office. I'm thinking that Bernadette wants us here and thinks something is going to happen. I'll have to be at the front desk, but maybe you could be a free agent?" Sarah queried, taking in Patty's current garb, which included gloves, currently on the sink edge as she OCD'd her way through an interminably long hand washing. She quelled a small anxiety that formed in her mind, wondering exactly what she had gotten into; Patty, Stanley, Bernadette. It was an odd crew, but a sense of loyalty to this group was forming in her heart, and she was resolved to see it through.

"This beats NCIS. Besides, I'm a fixture in the library, and most people probably look at me as a harmless wacko. And it's possible that's what I am," Patty observed cynically. "I'll find a spot by The Transformer and watch. If I see something or Bernadette communicates something, I'll just have to come get you," Patty explained. "I don't have a phone; too many germs."

"OK. I'll leave my phone on, but I'll lay it on the computer table. That should keep it from interfering with Bernadette. Stanley is the guard tonight, and he can come looking for you if we see something happening from the other end. In the meantime, I need to get upstairs," Sarah said, as she pushed the door to the third stall to take care of business before she checked in. As she sat down, a vision of the solar system entered her mind, unbidden. It was vivid but brief, and Sarah thought it might be something Bernadette wanted her to see. She immediately

217

wondered if that's where Bernadette came from. Maybe she was a life form from another planet? But that thought felt wrong, and Sarah puzzled over the image as she washed her hands.

"Planets, suns and orbits," Patty said, spontaneously.

"You, too? I guess we're getting the message loud and clear, but I'm not sure what the message means? Do you know?" Sarah asked.

"Clueless," Patty replied, as she eyed Sarah's hand-washing technique and handed her a paper towel with her now-gloved hand. "I'll keep holding the idea in my head. I think that makes it possible for Bernadette to nudge the concept toward an explanation. Or not." A jaded perspective seemed to color Patty's observations. "I do get a little tired of never feeling sure while I'm feeling sure, if you know what I mean."

"Yeah, I know exactly what you mean," replied Sarah, as images of planets swirled in her thoughts, mixed with the need to get to work on time. "Later."

"For sure," replied Patty, with a hesitant chuckle. Sarah giggled as she turned to leave. That was a surprise in Patty's personality. She had a dry wit that Sarah was just beginning to appreciate. As Sarah hit the main floor landing, she stole a sideways glance at the ball-capped, bewigged Transformer. He was keeping his head down but looked relaxed and busy with his computer. She felt something Bernadetteish as she walked past, and an image of the solar system popped into her head again. It did little to ease her mind, because she still hadn't formed a clear idea of why that image was important. As she clocked in, she saw Stanley and Lubna talking in the sorting area between book shelves.

"Hey, Sarah, how's it going?" Lubna asked. "You look a bit perplexed. Talked to Bernadette lately?"

"Actually, I think so. I just came from the basement bathroom. Patty was down there, and we both seem to be getting a message from Bernadette that's hard to understand. She is intense about The Transformer, who's in the building in the new book area, but Patty and I are both stumped about what she thinks he is going to do," Sarah replied. "How was your trip to the springs? Any conversations with Blanche that might help?"

"Had some thoughts while we were down there," said Stanley. "I've got a new phrase for living. Work the problem, don't worry the problem. I found myself repeating that in my head as we hiked the park looking for a connection with Blanche. It just popped into my head. Pretty cool, huh."

Sarah stood still, took a deep breath and tried to recall if she had said that phrase to Lubna or Stanley before. It was something she frequently said to herself, a reminder of her dad that she used as a personal mantra, but she couldn't remember saying it out loud. She could have, although it was something she sort of held on to as a private thing between her and her dad.

"It was one of my dad's favorite sayings. Are you sure you didn't hear me say it sometime?" Sarah replied slowly. "Maybe you had it in your subconscious from something I said and it just connected while you were hiking around getting more blood to your brain?"

Stanley furrowed his brow, trying to recall. "I think I would have remembered it. It resonated so strongly with me I wrote it down and even talked with Lubna about getting a tattoo with that phrase woven into it. I'm sure it was tied to Blanche. I'm not saying that you couldn't have said it to one of us, but I had a really strong feeling that Blanche put it in my head. Maybe I had it in my subconscious, and it popped out when Blanche and I intersected, but I really don't remember you actually saying it. I know that Blanche and I did communicate because it felt like times in the past when we made a connection. Besides, I had other things in my head at the time. I'm not going to spin it, but it just doesn't feel like the right interpretation to me. What do you think, Lubby?" Stanley asked, closing with an affectionate nickname for Lubna.

"You know, I believe you both are communicating with alternate life forms, but I'm not prepared to make any assessments. I'm not hearing or feeling what you are. Apparently, I don't have the genetic predisposition you two seem to possess. I felt good at the park but didn't feel like I intersected with anybody but Stan," said Lubna, grinning. "I sure wanted to, and I could tell that Stan was impacted. I can draw some inferential conclusions, but I'd feel more confident if Adam and I could put together some equipment that could measure electromagnetic field changes or other energy changes. Let's just say that I'd be the guy with the Igor equipment if we "went Sasquatching." The artistic side of me is convinced, but the scientific side wants to prove it. If you are asking me if I remember hearing you say 'work the problem, don't worry the problem,' then I'd have to say no." Lubna shrugged and walked toward the desk to help a student who had walked up.

"I'm going to do a round and make sure The Transformer is still in the new book area. When I get back, maybe we can all try to unravel Bernadette's message," Stanley said, walking toward the door.

Sarah went to the desk and began unloading the book drop while Lubna helped the student with reserve materials. Sarah's mind was swirling with planets. Maybe Bernadette was an extraterrestrial and was trying to tell her where she had originated? She didn't think that was the message because she didn't understand why the feeling was so intensely tied to The Transformer – unless he was an extraterrestrial, too? This was getting really weird. She was going to have to get back with Patty. Maybe she'd figure it out. One thing was sure, Bernadette wanted to get their attention and the idea kept popping back into Sarah's consciousness. Several students stopped to return books, and Sarah spoke briefly with a coed who she recognized from Calculus class.

"Sarah, the south entrance needs an empty book cart. Can you take them one and bring back the loaded cart they've got?" Lubna asked, after answering a phone call from the south exit security desk.

"Sure, I'm on my way," Sarah replied, grabbing an empty cart and wheeling it past the display cases toward the south entrance. A couple of the cases had early telescopes in them with materials from the History of Science Collections on the fifth floor advertising the dedication of the newly renovated area the next morning. Galileo Galilei was going to be the subject of a special lecturer at the dedication. Luke had eblasted all the employees to recruit some students for extra shifts tomorrow. They were expecting lots of guests. Sarah couldn't work the hours because she had classes that morning, but she thought Adam was going to take a shift.

She picked up the loaded cart at the south desk and slowly pushed it past the new book area, surreptitiously glancing at The Transformer and noticing he had settled in, reading the student newspaper. As she turned the corner, quietly humming to herself, she saw a book in the display case showing the Copernican solar system. Sarah felt something at the back of her neck, like she had been touched by someone who had static electricity. She felt herself shiver slightly. She was far from any person and wondered if the cart had developed a static electric charge as it moved over the carpet. In the next moment, it occurred to her that Bernadette might be the electric charge and stopped for a moment as planets swirled in her head. She made the connection; The Transformer was planning something, something to do with the dedication. She felt sure this guess was right but parked the cart next to a pole and headed back toward the old staircase to see if she could find Patty.

Patty was nowhere in sight so Sarah headed back to the circulation area, pushing the loaded cart. The Transformer was actually napping on the sofa in the new book area, and Sarah shrugged as she passed the display cases. She'd share her thoughts about the dedication, but her mind kept returning to Stanley's mention of her dad's mantra. She began to wonder if her dad was trying to tell her something. She felt a bit better about the guilt she had carried for the last few years and knew that sharing with Adam had helped her place that in perspective. Maybe, just maybe it was her dad's forgiveness energized through Blanche? Or maybe it was a wish and she had imagined a link to her dad.

As she pushed the cart into the sort room, she hurried to the desk. There was a line of students so Sarah manned the free terminal and said, "Who's next, please?"

The next few hours were really busy. Papers were coming due in a lot of classes, and the library was slammed. In another hour, the night students hit the doors and they were swamped. Lubna and Sarah hadn't gotten a break for about three hours. Stanley had circled back and took time to help pull reserve materials. But he'd had to go on his next round before they'd had a chance to talk seriously about Sarah's thoughts about the dedication. Several students had come to the next terminal and unloaded, complaining about the wait. A faculty member also showed up to check on his reserve materials. When Lubna handed him the packet, he was upset about some pages missing. Lubna explained that they tried to check the packets every time they were turned in, but sometimes they didn't have time and she suspected a student had copied the packet and left some of the pages lying on a copy machine. It took her a few minutes to calm the professor and suggest he send an email version out to all his classes. He was an older professor and seemed uncomfortable with that but acquiesced when Lubna pointed out that it was the only way to be sure every student got the same chance to see the materials.

"Gosh, I can't remember a busier night. I guess it's the full moon and the end of the semester together. I'm beat. It's almost midnight. Looks like we all were worried for nothing," said Lubna.

"You handled that situation well with Professor Abrams," Sarah said.

"Competition for grades in the biological sciences is pretty bad. Lots of students are trying to get admitted to medical school. I remember a class I had my sophomore year when I got an incomplete packet. It almost cost me a letter grade," Lubna recalled. "Most professors use the online system now, but some of the older profs still do it the old way." Stanley returned to the office as Sarah and Lubna began emptying the book bins, which had filled up as they handled the rush of patrons.

"I just walked past the new book area, and it looks like The Transformer has gone home. He wasn't there, and I didn't see Patty," Stanley said, as Adam entered the office.

"Sorry I'm late, the weather tonight is getting pretty dicey. There are possible tornadoes, and the Weather Center was hopping. A front is moving in, and I biked from south campus. The wind is wicked. I barely made it here before the rain started," Adam said breathlessly, his hair whipped into a gravity-defying arrangement that he patted down as he spoke. Sarah glanced toward the front doors and noticed a lightning flash. Just then the weather radio alarm sounded, and Stanley listened as the mechanical voice described the counties affected. It included Canadian County. Since nearby Moore had been hit repeatedly in the last decade, all university personnel were eblasted at the beginning of every tornado season about shelter locations and procedures. The library was a designated shelter.

"Looks like we may have to use the intercom and move everybody to the lower levels if this gets worse," said Stanley. "We've got to do that if it transitions from a watch to a warning."

"The Weather Center forecasters were predicting tornadoes. We should be prepared for it to get worse," added Adam.

"Looks like we might be here a little late. We can't kick people out into the storm if they change this from a watch to a warning. I'm going to run downstairs and get a mocha before the coffee shop closes down. Anybody else want something?" asked Lubna. There were no takers. "I'll be back in a few minutes."

Sarah turned to Stanley and Adam, "I think I might have an idea about The Transformer. I passed the History of Science display and seemed to get a push from Bernadette when I saw a picture of the Copernicus solar system in the case," Sarah started to explain but was interrupted by a student approaching the desk. As she was helping the student, Adam talked about the weather front with Stanley and estimated the worst would be over them in about 20 minutes. He had the Mesonet app on his phone and checked the radar but was deterred by a line of students forming. Both Stanley and Adam manned the other desk computers to help Sarah. A few moments later, Lubna came back and relieved Adam until the line subsided.

"This is definitely a full moon event night. It feels like everybody is hyper," said Lubna, as she turned to Stanley and said, "I thought you said The Transformer left? I saw him down in the coffee shop just a minute ago. He was working on his laptop and having a drink." Sarah overheard the remark as she finished helping a student and turned to Stanley.

"You know, Stan, Patty says that computers and phones confuse Bernadette. I'm wondering if she even knows he's here," Sarah speculated. As she uttered those words, Bernadette floated aimlessly upward, stopping herself on the fifth floor. She'd followed The Creep as he entered the new computerized learning area, intent on keeping an eye on him. But she'd become confused. She began to refocus as she floated upward aimlessly into the fifth floor lobby, but a nearby lightning strike caused a shift in her frequency and she lost herself again, overwhelmed by the energy wave that traveled upward from the ground discharge. The underground geologic formation absorbed the discharge and its magnetic field shifted slightly, unable to fully absorb the energy without a disturbance. Bernadette was overcome.

Before Stan could reply, the alarm sounded on the weather radio behind the desk, and the mechanical voice issued a tornado warning. Stanley walked over to the intercom and began his announcement, calling all the people in the building to move away from windows and calmly proceed to the basement levels of the library. The sirens outside could be heard, mixed with the rising winds. He rang the closing bell three times and repeated the warning.

Stanley turned to Adam and said, "Grab a radio and go to the Great Reading Room and get people moving. I'm going to head up to the fifth floor and walk down, floor by floor, getting people to move to the lower levels. Lubna, wait a minute and repeat the announcement every minute or so," instructed Stanley, as he took off, jumping the handicapped counter and trotting toward the stairwell. Sarah stood at the computer and called up the local weather station. The announcer was describing a rotation just west of the campus. It was unclear if the rotation had touched down or not, but it looked to be headed toward them. Her pulse quickened and anxiety bloomed, but Sarah repeated her dad's familiar mantra and forced herself to analyze what needed to be done.

"Please proceed to the lower levels. We are under a tornado warning, and a rotation has been sighted in the vicinity. Please do not attempt to leave the building at this time, and move away from all windows," Lubna repeated.

"Everyone, please stay calm and move to the lower levels. The radar indicates that the rotation should pass by in the next five minutes," announced Lubna. Some students ran into the building, heads covered with their backpacks, whipped by a cruel wind. Sarah could feel her ears popping as the doors shut with a whoosh. She was afraid, wondering if the glass doors would shatter. She looked over at the stairwell, students huddled on the staircase, and checked the lab across from the main desk. Everyone had cleared that area.

"Lubna, we need to move away from the glass doors, NOW!" yelled Sarah, as the sound of the wind picked up. Sarah grabbed her phone and pushed Lubna. They slid across the handicapped desk and ran toward the stairwell, urging the students to move down the staircase as a low-pitched sound seemed to move overhead. Sarah heard some windows shatter and her ears popped again, as all the students in the stairwell ran down to the next landing, their curiosity abandoned as the danger became clear. Moments later, it was over. The odd low-pitched sound faded away. An eerie quiet was interrupted by a student with a phone who said the rotation was now east of campus, according to his app. Other students began talking, and the sensation of relief and safety welled up from the staircase like a palpable collective sigh, as nervous voices began to comment on what had happened.

Sarah and Lubna stuck their heads out of the stairwell and looked into the lobby. The glass doors were intact, but they could feel the wind moving through the atrium down the stairwell and surmised that a few windows must have broken on some floors.

Lubna called on the radio, "Stanley, where are you? It looks like there are some windows broken".

Stanley's voice came back, crackling, "I'm in the 1952 addition with a wheelchair student in the stairwell on the third floor. The police frequency is kinda busy right now. Looks like some other buildings on campus had damage. Adam doesn't think the tornado touched down, but it may have pulled some roofing off the library. He says there is some rain running into the Great Reading Room and a few broken window panes on the west side. The police have asked us to hold people in the building for the next 30 minutes. Can you get to the intercom and make that announcement?"

Sarah looked into Lubna's eyes, and they both headed across the atrium. Lubna picked up the intercom and began telling people to be patient and wait until they had received the all clear from campus police. As she kept announcing the information, Sarah moved to block a few errant students from leaving.

"Please, the campus police are worried about downed power lines and want to be sure problems are located before people get tied up in traffic. We've been asked to keep everyone inside," Sarah said, feeling like she was herding cats as some students seemed to want to escape to ogle the damage. She was beginning to doubt their willingness to stay inside but was happy to see the flashing blue lights of a campus police car pull in front of the main doors and two uniformed figures stepped inside. Even the pushy students backed off, and she was grateful to be able to turn the herding responsibilities over to them.

"Sarah, grab the employee call sheet. We need to start calling the library emergency preparedness team. I think they are going to have to come in and pull some plastic sheeting over book stacks before the leaks damage anything. I'm not sure how quickly they will be able to get here if the streets are clogged, but I've got to follow the telephone tree," Lubna explained. Sarah was relieved that Lubna knew her purpose and forced herself to remain steady and focused.

"This is Lubna …."

As Sarah punched the number of the next person on the emergency call list, she tried to sense Bernadette but had no luck. Nothing. Her eyes scanned for Patty in the crowd milling in the study area across from the desk. With the officers at the door, most settled down to wait. Lubna and Sarah completed the call list and looked expectantly at the officers, who were regularly talking on their radios, turning their heads to their shoulders as they kept in touch. Eventually, one of the officers walked over to the desk and asked if he could use the intercom. He wanted to tell people they were free to leave but give them some information about which streets were closed. As the officer briefed everyone on the intercom, he warned people to be careful returning to dormitories and homes. Two streets were closed due to downed power lines, but damage overall was modest and the few people with injuries had been transported to local hospitals. Students began to file out, and Sarah watched carefully, looking for The Transformer. At that moment, the elevator alarm sounded.

"Adam, this is Lubna. The elevators in this addition have stopped working. Can you watch for our friend at the south exit?"

"Adam here. Patty and I are at the security desk and the '58 addition elevator alarms are going off, too. We're staying here until the building empties. Patty can't seem to make any contact. I know that tornadoes can generate their own magnetic field. I wonder if that has affected Bernadette?"

"Lubna, this is Stan. We need to get the crews in to mop up the water and cover things with plastic. I'm going to head to the Great Reading Room to check on leaks and come down the staircase to the south exit. I'll be there in about five minutes."

"Stan, we're calling the emergency preparedness team." As Lubna replied, the officers in the atrium snapped to and one ran toward the staircase. The other officer turned to Lubna and asked her to wait. There was a problem, the alarms in the History of Science Collections had been activated. No one should leave the building.

"Stan, the History of Science Collections alarms have been set off. Officer Cagle just told me to hold off on closing." As she spoke with Stan and then passed similar information to Adam, it was announced that due to additional information received, no one could leave the building yet. There would be a brief delay. Sarah's pulse quickened again.

"Lubna," said Stan, "I'm on the police frequency, and they're telling their officers to look for a guy with long, dark hair based on what they saw on the monitor at the station. You know what that means. Don't let The Transformer out the front door. Start examining backpacks and require everyone to stop. That will slow him down. I'm going to explain to the officers that we have a suspect who might look different. I'm headed to the south exit to help Adam."

Sarah stopped the exiting students and raised her voice to explain, "Due to electronics being affected by the storm, we will need to examine all backpacks as you exit. Please open your backpacks and purses so that we can search them as you exit. I need to get the all clear from the police, but that should be just a few minutes. Thank you for your patience," Sarah said, raising her voice so it could be heard across the atrium. "

"Sarah, I don't think we should announce that over the intercom because it will warn The Transformer that something is up."

"I agree," said Sarah, as a line formed by her, and she began the slow process of examining backpacks. Students queued up and waited. "I need to get the all clear from the police, but that should be just a few minutes. Thank you for your patience," Sarah repeated. As she did, she sensed that students were losing patience and eager to leave. As the volume of voices in the atrium increased, the elevator alarm stopped, and moments later the elevator disgorged a load of disoriented students.

"That means we've got about two minutes before we should see our friend," Lubna said.

"We're in contact with the police, and it should be just a few more minutes before they allow everyone to leave. Please listen for announcements about roads to avoid and where to walk if you are going back to the dorms. We should have some information for you very soon," said Sarah, improvising to calm the group that was now clearly getting impatient. Lubna signaled her with a raised thumb, as she helped some students who wanted to check out books at the counter.

Another police car pulled up in front of the door and parked behind the one already there. Sarah sighed deeply, grateful to see another officer who could help search packs before the crowd was freed. She just realized that this late at night, the library probably had the biggest group of people not in the dorms, and it was buzzing with alarms.

"I'm here to make sure no one leaves the building until we have cleared up the problems with the History of Science alarms," said the officer. As she spoke, Sarah saw the curator for the collections rush in breathlessly and head for the elevator. As she watched him, she thought she saw The Transformer, lurking at the back of the crowd at the stairwell, but he ducked into the staircase out of view.

"Officer, I just saw someone I think might be involved. Our security guards have been monitoring a guy who comes in the library regularly, usually at the same time the elevators malfunction, and seems to change clothes. He starts out with a dark wig and then leaves the library with a shaved head and cowboy boots. I know this sounds weird, but please verify it with our guards and Luke, the circulation supervisor," Sarah explained. "I think I just saw him by the stairwell, with the shaved head and cowboy boots."

"Stan, Sarah thinks she just saw The Transformer, but he ducked back into the stairwell. Keep your eyes open. He may be circling back toward your exit," Lubna replied.

Sarah overheard some of the radio transmissions to the officer, and the curator verified that two books were missing from the display cases, books that had been put out for the dedication the next day. Two books normally in the vault were laid out for viewing by VIPs arriving before the ceremonies. She sensed the officer go on alert, and her heart pounded harder. She looked over at Lubna and could sense a fierceness in her. Sarah had the same feeling. She wasn't about to let The Transformer succeed.

"Stan, stay on your toes, there are books missing from the fifth floor," Lubna radioed.

Sarah thought about the fifth floor, and the thought seemed to remind her that Bernadette was missing in action. She wondered if Bernadette reminded her of herself or if Sarah generated the thought on her own? She focused on that thought and found herself humming quietly, below the sound of the general hubbub in the atrium generated by impatient students and faculty. As she did so, Bernadette awakened. She sensed Sarah and found Patty, sitting on the settee at the south entrance. Both women hummed, generating a frequency that renewed Bernadette. Bernadette awoke confused, in search of stale coffee and sugar cookies. She recalled very little but could feel a tenuous connection with Sarah and Patty, and sensed some sugar cookies in Patty's purse as she floated toward the south entrance.

The tornado had done a number on Bernadette, whose own energy field had a magnetic field component. Perhaps that's how Bernadette lost herself the last time? This time, Patty and Sarah, thinking in conjunction and generating their own compatible frequencies, had reintegrated Bernadette, and she wasn't looking at a long hiatus in the masonry of the building as a disintegrated entity, unable to integrate herself. It was good to have friends.

As Bernadette touched Patty, she instantly came into focus and vibrated with the alarm Patty had shared about The Transformer. She knew who she was and sensed the negative energy of The Transformer in the building. Bernadette understood her antipathy now to The Transformer. It was an old entanglement, rivals centuries ago, an inquisition. This time, she wasn't going to lose if she could help it.

She floated toward The Creep, who stood on the landing of the second floor balcony, occasionally leaning forward to get a quick look at the front door, clearly planning some strategy to avoid the police. She followed him, and the desire to kick him in the butt almost overwhelmed her hesitation to "touch" The Creep. She dreaded even an accidental sync with this human. But as she watched him, she saw him walk to the back of the floor and open his backpack. He pulled two books from the backpack, clearly centuries-old books, and shelved them next to some books similar in color to their cream-colored vellum binding. As he put them there, he chuckled under his breath. On the next floor, he entered the men's bathroom. There, he pulled the wig and his ball cap from the backpack and stuffed them both in the wastebasket with his laptop. He tore multiple paper towels from the rack and scrunched them, stuffing them on top of the other items until they were well hidden.

Bernadette fumed but still feared touching him. She vibrated intensely, alerting Sarah and Patty to something, but they couldn't clearly understand what. Both went on alert, and Patty turned to Adam.

"Something is about to happen but not at this exit," she stated, vacillating.

Adam spoke into the radio, "Lubna and Stan, Patty thinks something is about to happen. Do we have all the exits covered?"

"Nobody's on the north exit fire escape," said Stan. "That's got a delay release on it. If someone tried to get out that way, the delay would stop them for at least 30 seconds. Eventually, though, it releases in case anyone is ever trapped in a real fire."

"Stan, I'm closer than you, I'm going to leave the officer here at the south entrance and go check that door," replied Adam.

"Run, Adam!" cried Lubna into the radio. "The north alarm just went off!"

Sarah looked at Lubna as she screamed into the phone and turned to the officer. "Follow me!" Sarah said, as she took off out the front door and ran around the building corner. She sped up as she made the turn. The backside of the building was normally lighted, but the storm had affected some of the electricity on campus and Sarah's eyes were having trouble adjusting to the darkness. She stumbled due to a downed branch but caught herself and slowed only slightly. As she got close enough to see the door, she felt the officer, a bit shorter than herself, catch up to Sarah's long-legged stride and watched Adam lope like a gazelle up the steps on the far end of the sidewalk. Just then, the door opened and The Transformer emerged. He started to take off and realized he was boxed in on both sides.

"Stop," the officer shouted, somewhat breathlessly. "You'll need to return to the building with us. Please surrender your backpack."

"What's wrong, officer? I just need to get home. I need to check on my wife and kids. I'm really worried about them. I just couldn't wait any longer. You know how it is when you have little ones, you want to know they're OK in a situation like this. I've been calling home, but no one is answering. I've got to see how they are," The Transformer lied.

Sarah could feel herself beginning to believe, and she looked to the officer, who hesitated, then said. "I can send a car to your house. Please hand your backpack to this young woman, and let's walk back inside. We'll need to ask you a few questions and get your address. The police can get to your home faster than you can, given the traffic problems we are having." Sarah watched The Transformer and could see his eyes glance both directions. He calmly handed her the backpack and began walking toward the west entrance. Sarah and Adam walked behind the officer and The Transformer. As they turned the corner, The Transformer took off. The officer took off after him, and Adam did, as well, yelling, "I'm following!" as his long legs lengthened their stride. Sarah watched for just a moment, then took off herself, running into the front entrance.

"The guy we were looking for just took off with your officer behind him, and one of our security guards following," said Sarah, breathlessly. "They're headed north." Officer Cagle spoke into his radio to the station, describing the chase and direction. Sarah sensed he was speaking with someone monitoring the security cameras placed around campus and hoped nobody mistook Adam for The Transformer. Lubna and Sarah stood motionless, as they tried to overhear the officer's communications. It was frustrating, because the crowd was getting more restless and the conversations among the students who were all interested in going home were expressing frustration. The noise level was rising.

Stan walked through the crowd, clearly listening to his radio. He stepped up to the officer, and they turned away from the crowd and had a serious conversation. Luke arrived, looking like he'd been awakened minutes ago, with two other library staff and paused to converse with the officer. As that was taking place, Sarah carried the backpack into the office and stood behind the counter with Lubna. Sarah worried about Adam. She was afraid he could get hurt. It was dark out there and chasing someone in the dark with police officers could get dicey.

Moments later, the group moved into the office area, and Luke announced over the intercom, "Please line up at the north or south entrance. We will need to search all backpacks and purses. Please have them open and ready. We will begin allowing you to leave in about five minutes. As you proceed home, please avoid Jenkins Avenue, which is closed between Lindsey and Boyd streets due to some downed trees. There are some problems with power on the east side of town so traffic lights are not working that direction. Some buildings have had roof damage, and there may be debris. Please be careful where you step. Thank you for your patience.

They all gathered around the backpack as Sarah unzipped it. There was a lunch box with a half-eaten sandwich and a jacket, but little else. Sarah pulled out the jacket and found a flash drive in the pocket. Other than that, it looked like the backpack had been cleaned out. No books, no laptop, nothing incriminating but what might be on the flash drive, which had obviously been forgotten.

A couple of minutes later, the curator came downstairs and handed the officer some pictures of the missing volumes as they had been laid out in the display case. He'd taken them for a newsletter story. One was a volume of Galileo's work describing his theories on the solar system, the other was a work by the church, declaring Galileo's work heretical. Lubna, Sarah and Luke perused the photos, and Luke handed copies to Rachel, who had arrived a few moments ago. She took them to the south entrance, and Luke announced that the exits were open. They now knew what they were looking for, and all three stood at the desk while students filed past single file, placing their backpacks on the desk. Luke occasionally asked some students to remove a sweater or jacket as he had seen people attempt to steal books in their pants, and he wasn't going to miss anything. The curator stood by, a worried look on her face.

After an hour of searching and the return of Adam and the officer, the building was clear, but the books were still missing.

Adam and the officer had lost The Transformer in the dark, unlit streets as he snaked through a back alley. They were both deflated. Sarah, really getting tired, took a break with Adam to hear his tale of the chase and walked outside into the evening air to sit by Patty, who had gone through the search line and signaled that she would wait outside on the bench by the fountain under the clock tower. The street lamps on this side of campus were working, but they could see intense darkness as they looked toward the North Oval and the east side of campus.

"We haven't found anything. I get the feeling Bernadette knows something, how about you?" Sarah asked Patty, as she sat on the concrete bench next to her, brushing aside green leaves that had blown from the trees in the high winds.

"For sure," smiled Patty, who began humming. Sarah automatically fell into rhythm, humming as well, and a picture of book stacks popped into her mind. "Book stacks are the perfect place to hide a book in plain sight," Patty concluded.

"I'll bet we can track The Transformer on the security cameras and limit our search to one floor. Let's get Stanley to work with the monitors to see if he can trace him backward from the moment he entered the north stairwell. We can probably figure out what floor he was on when he tried to leave through that fire exit," said Sarah, trying to formulate a plan.

"He's hidden the laptop and the outfit somewhere too," said Adam. As he uttered the words, a bathroom appeared in Sarah's mind.

"Check the bathrooms. I think that Bernadette saw something in a bathroom …," she hesitated, then saw Patty shaking her head affirmatively. "Thanks, Patty," said Sarah, as she grabbed Patty's gloved hand and squeezed.

"It's an old argument. Not easily forgotten," Patty replied, in her cryptic fashion.

"Well, the books are about an old argument between Galileo and the church. Do you think that Bernadette has an entanglement that old?"

"Yes, exactly so. I don't think Bernadette's idea of time is exactly like ours. It may seem like yesterday to her. But if I am going to make any sense tomorrow, I need to get home and get some sleep. It must be nearly four in the morning," said Patty, as she got up.

"Be careful going home. There's lots of debris around to trip on," said Adam, who had tripped during the chase and was still feeling sore.

Sarah and Adam walked back into the library. Luke and Stanley were discussing what floors to search, and Lubna was calling in more staff. The Dean of Libraries had come in and was holding an administrative meeting on the second floor.

Sarah looked at Adam and turned to Luke saying, "You know, we didn't find his outfit or the laptop in the backpack so he must have gotten rid of them somewhere, probably the books, too. Why not check bathrooms? Maybe he hid them in one of the bathrooms and figured he'd come back and get them later."

"Stanley and I can check the security recordings just before the north door alarm was set off and try to backtrack and figure out what floor he came from. We could start there," Adam said.

"Good idea. Stan, you and Adam try to track this guy. Sarah, help Lubna finish calling staff and see who can get here quickly. We're not going to open the library until we find something. We can say that storm damage and safety are a concern. We should be able to close for 24 hours. Maybe we'll get lucky before then. I've got to get a crew working on pulling plastic sheeting and get an assessment of all the damage. Call me on the radio if you find something," concluded Luke, as he turned to talk to some physical plant workers who'd just arrived.

Lubna and Sarah finished the last call on the list and sat stupefied for a few minutes. It was about five in the morning, and they were really beat, too tired to really say anything. Sarah took a deep breath and stood up as Stanley came from the back office.

"We know he entered the stairwell on the second floor. Can you two go up there and check bathrooms? Maybe enlist Bernadette's help? Luke wants me to stay here to direct the staff to the reading room, and Adam is still reviewing the security recordings. Take your phones and call if you find something," said Stanley.

235

"Lubna can take hers, but I need to keep mine off if there's a chance Bernadette can help," Sarah explained.

"Understood. I'll call her number if I need to get in touch with you. Are you two able to keep going for a few more hours?" Stanley asked, observing their slumped shoulders.

"Hey, this is good practice for being on call when I'm a doctor," Lubna mused. Sarah and Lubna left, heading up the stairwell. They entered the men's bathroom and checked the stalls. Sarah felt a static electric prick as she walked past the trashcan and stopped to remove the lid. She didn't see anything but dirty paper towels, but had a hunch that she should dig. She pulled the plastic liner from the container and noticed it was too heavy to contain just paper waste. She dumped it on the floor and a laptop slid onto the tile floor with a clatter, along with the black wig and what looked like a makeup kit. They grinned at one another, and Lubna called Stanley.

"Found something, men's restroom. No books, but a laptop and some other stuff," Lubna announced. Moments later, Luke and a crew of library administrators arrived in the bathroom, eagerly looking at the evidence. Sarah and Lubna were asked to describe how they found the items. A general disappointment about no books being found was discussed, and campus police arrived a few minutes later, forcing Lubna and Sarah to repeat the story of the discovery. After the third telling, Sarah felt a wave of exhaustion. It was almost dawn, and she looked over at Lubna, who had begun to develop dark circles under her eyes.

"Luke, Lubna and I have been here all night. Would you mind if we grabbed a sofa and napped for 30 minutes? I have a Calculus quiz in about two hours," Sarah said.

"Sure, Sarah. I'm sorry. I'd forgotten you both have been here so long. Officer Yost told me you all did a great job getting the library patrons to safety during the tornado. It's been quite a night. Why don't you two grab the couches in the new book area? I'd say go home and sleep, but the police are still gathering evidence and might need to ask some more questions."

"We'll be there," said Lubna, yawning. Now that some of the mystery was solved, Sarah felt the tension of the search evaporate and she mirrored Lubna's yawn, squared. It was like the sandman had buried her, and it was all she could do to hold her eyes open as she and Lubna left the library administrators and the police discussing the laptop and made their way to the main floor and the overstuffed couches in the new book area. They collapsed on the couches. Before they nodded off, Adam and Stanley showed up. Stanley pulled Lubna's head onto his lap and put his feet on the coffee table. His head fell back, and he seemed asleep before Lubna's breathing deepened. Sarah patted the seat next to her, and Adam sat down. He checked his cell phone Mesonet app and told Sarah more tornadoes were predicted for the upcoming evening.

"If I was picked up and carried off to Oz, I think I'd sleep through it," said Sarah, punctuating her comment with a yawn at each end of the sentence. Adam put his arm around her and pulled her into a comfortable spoon.

"I set my phone alarm for an hour. That should give us time to get up and have breakfast at the union before your Calculus class, assuming the police don't need us," Adam said, as his breath brushed the back of Sarah's hair. Funny, Sarah observed, she and Adam were again sleeping together, the result of dramatic weather events. She chuckled slightly, wondering if Adam had some weather mojo. She drifted off, dreaming of a Wizard-of-Oz-style tornado ride that included Adam in the swirling winds, along with flying books, Patty on a bicycle and The Transformer in a monkey suit. And Bernadette, well, Bernadette was the tornado and it was raining keys.

Chapter 14

> *"Lo, all their shifting movement is of old,*
> *From the primeval atoms; for the same*
> *Primordial seeds of things first move of self,*
> *And then those bodies built of unions small*
> *And nearest, as it were, unto the powers*
> *Of the primeval atoms, are stirred up*
> *By impulse of those atoms' unseen blows,*
> *And these thereafter goad the next in size:*
> *Thus motion ascends from the primevals on,*
> *And stage by stage emerges to our sense,*
> *Until those objects also move which we*
> *Can mark in sunbeams, though it not appears*
> *What blows do urge them."*

--Lucretius, *On the Nature of Things*

Sarah dodged a bullet by passing the Calculus quiz, surprising herself. She'd awoken from the sofa and sleepwalked over to the union with Adam, Lubna and Stanley. They'd all coffee'd up and headed out. It was less than two weeks before finals. Adam had a modeling project due; Stanley was still finalizing his computer website designs; and Lubna had an Organic Chemistry exam that she expected to be a beast. Sarah, buzzing from the coffee, breezed through her Calculus quiz. She stumbled her way through the next two classes and met Jennifer for lunch at the cafeteria. She regaled Jennifer with the story of the tornado at the library, and Jennifer shared her experiences watching tree limbs fly by at the Journalism Building. Then she headed back to the library for her Friday afternoon shift.

The library was closed, but Luke had eblasted everyone to come in for their regular shifts. They were all searching the second floor for the missing books, and Michelyn, working in the same area as Sarah, spent the entire three hours talking about the lost dog she'd found in their yard after the storm. Sarah kept thinking about keys but just couldn't come up with a clear picture of what Bernadette might be communicating. She longed to talk to Patty, but the library was closed to patrons so Patty wouldn't be admitted. Sarah took a bathroom break in the old basement and hummed softly to herself in the third stall. Keys kept floating in her consciousness, and she felt hopeless as she rode the elevator to the second floor. The door opened, and she realized that she'd accidentally pushed the button that took her to the third floor so wearily stepped back inside and returned to where Michelyn was texting her roommate about dog food.

Luke stopped Sarah as she was checking out and asked her to stay for another hour. He was calling in all the student workers who had been in the building the night before. The library was going to open Sunday, and they were desperate to find the rare books before then. The conference room was filled with a mixture of administrators, student workers, staff, and police. Sarah grabbed a chair next to Adam and grinned at Lubna and Stanley, who were there as well, although none of them regularly worked that afternoon. They all looked rough and tired. Classes and projects had kept them all up, and Adam whispered to Sarah that the Weather Center had been a hive of activity the whole afternoon.

The meeting was a review of the search that was underway, and the Dean formally thanked the students who had helped during the tornado. Stan, Lubna, Adam and Sarah were mentioned by name, as were the reference desk graduate assistants. It was gratifying, but Sarah's attention kept drifting, and visions of floating keys would pop into her head, as the words of the speech faded in and out.

As they filed out of the room, Sarah said, "Maybe we should look up books about keys and locks, and see if we can search some more? I'm still getting pictures in my head about keys."

"I'm for working the problem," said Stan, "but I need some sleep. I have to present my project in class on Tuesday, and

I am nowhere near done. It's going to be brutal if I don't get some sleep and spend a good ten more hours finishing."

"We've all got to concentrate on classes right now," said Lubna. "Let's give the police and the library staff some time on the problem. I'm not thinking straight anymore, and I have a final on Wednesday. I can't blow Organic Chemistry just because I've received my acceptance letter."

"Yeah, I've got an appointment with my professor to talk about my modeling project. I have some questions about what I need to do before I get it ready to turn in," Adam chimed in.

Sarah thought about the last chapter of physics problems due and had a pang of anxiety about Philosophy, which she'd barely touched the last week.

"Sleep sounds good, and let's assume Bernadette's on guard. Surely she'll be able to do something. I know she's on it, I just can't figure out how," Sarah agreed. They all headed back to their own beds, Adam and Sarah walking toward the dorms.

"I know we both need to concentrate in the next two weeks on school, but I've not forgotten about a topography lesson, matey," Adam said, lifting his eyebrow.

"Aye, aye Captain," said Sarah, hugging him before she turned to enter her dorm. "I'm going to need to cross an ocean of sleep before I can navigate any land mass."

"Right, matey," Adam chuckled.

Sarah barely shed her jeans and crawled into bed, then was asleep almost before her head hit the pillow. She dreamed of sailing a ship, with the wind in her hair and Adam standing next to her, with the sun shimmering in his hair and the ocean waves rolling with flying fish sparkling as they leapt from the water, looking curiously like golden keys.

Professor Matthews, retired from the Classics Department for 20 years, made his way to the library on his usual Monday schedule. He shuffled through the front door after picking up the student newspaper. As he passed the reference desk, he stopped to say hello to the long-time staffer Ralph Gill. They exchanged pleasantries, and Ralph inquired about how the professor fared during the recent storm. The conversation about damage at the library was lively, with Ralph describing leaks, broken windows and the crews of physical plant workers who were still working in the library. Ralph didn't mention the lost books from the History of Science Collection because all library staff had been told to keep that under wraps while they were still searching.

He talked instead about a student who had tampered with the library elevators who was rounded up by the police the night before. The student was taken in, spouting wild accusations about God and science and blasphemy. Apparently, he was delusional and was convinced that Galileo was responsible for the Godless state of the world today. The police actually took him to the state mental hospital because he became hysterical when they confronted him as he entered the building the night before, dressed as a woman. Ralph detailed the hysterical chase through the decks, as the guy threw off his wig and tried to kick off his high-heeled boots.

The Transformer's name was Vincent MacCall, and he wasn't even a local student. He'd been a seminary student at a Jesuit college in Kansas, according to the information on the laptop. The police and security were watching for him. They'd placed a guard in the second floor bathroom, who climbed on the toilet and hung an Out of Order on the stall door. When The Transformer reached into the wastebasket, the guard texted the rest of security. They'd hoped to follow him to the location of the books, but when he realized the laptop was gone, he took off and was caught near the south exit. They were still hoping to convince him to tell where the books had been hidden, but so far they hadn't any luck. Apparently he'd gone off antidepressants, and it would be weeks before his drug regimen was restored and his paranoia controlled. Ralph had never had such a colorful story to tell, and he waxed on for quite a while as Dr. Matthews asked questions

Eventually, Professor Matthews left Ralph at the reference desk and thought twice about riding the elevators. He slowly made his way up the stairs to the third floor, fighting the arthritis in his knees. He stopped at the door to his faculty study, looked both directions and turned away, reaching for a volume of Euripides on the nearby book stacks in which he stored his faculty study key. He removed the key from the volume, and, before he could reshelve it, the whole shelf of books slid sideways and half of them dropped on the floor. He sighed and began to pick up the volumes. As he did so, he noticed two of the books were actually bound in vellum. As he opened the first one, he noticed Galileo Galilei and instantly felt something was wrong. The curator of the History of Science Collections was a friend. He'd spent many hours discussing Latin translations with her. He sensed these volumes would be of interest to her and decided to take them upstairs. It would be a chance to get a cup of coffee, too. They always had a fresh pot of coffee this time of day in the staff workroom and an excuse to get a free cup was irresistible.

Bernadette followed the professor up the staircase, trying to keep from pushing him. He was slow, and she was eager to get the books back in their sanctuary. She'd pushed hard to get the shelf to dislodge and was glad that the volumes hadn't been damaged by the fall. Her efforts to get Patty and Sarah to find them had been too confusing. She couldn't really figure a way to put Euripides in their minds, so she had placed the idea of the key in their thinking when they both came to the bathroom trying to get her to intersect and help. Raining keys was apparently a confusing signal that Sarah and Patty couldn't fathom. They checked the key cabinets in the security area and sat in the basement for hours, discussing what it meant. They'd looked up books on key making and locks. The second floor had been thoroughly searched, but the third floor had gone unexamined, and the library was forced to open.

As Dr. Matthews entered the History of Science Collections, the smell of fresh coffee diverted Bernadette. Although she tried to focus as the professor spoke with the curator, she couldn't help swimming in the coffee molecules surrounding the cup on the curator's desk. She missed the look of surprise on the face of the curator when the professor placed the books on her desk and described his discovery of them on the shelves of classics texts.

Because the theft had been kept out of the news, the curator avoided an explanation and began discussing the inquisition of Galileo with Professor Matthews, the subject of one of the volumes. He'd helped with some translations of other materials in years gone by, and the conversation came easy, as it does with friends who have worked together on projects.

Bernadette could feel herself vibrating intensely as the historians talked about the clash of science and religion during the time of Galileo. There was that feeling of a mosquito, circling nearby as you fall asleep. She knew there was something she should remember, but it was just out of reach. Instead, she floated over to the workroom and rollicked in the coffee and sugar molecules that she loved so well.

Copyright Permissions

Acknowledgements

Barbara and Brooklyn Kowaleski have been inspirational muses. My son, David, and my sister, Dana, encouraged with frank commentary. Karen Schmeckpeper, Donis Casey, Letty Watt, Lu Clark, Donna Martin and Sue Arnn have been generous with counsel. Jan Tindale obligingly contributed her inspirational artwork for the cover design. Dianne Bianchi made it look dazzling. All the friends who listened with patience, please know you are appreciated.

About the Author

P.L. Weaver lives in Oklahoma with her husband Ken, dog, Abby, cats, Myrtle May and Wen Wen and various chickens. *The Habitant* is book 1 in the series.

Made in the USA
Lexington, KY
07 March 2016